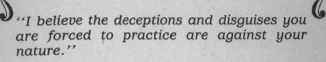

"I believe the deceptions and disguises you are forced to practice are against your nature."

If he only knew, Annalise thought, laughing again, this time to herself, in despair.

"If—nay, when—you come to trust me, please believe that I will do everything in my power to assist you."

To assist her into his bed, Annalise still believed. The man had endearing moments of nobility though, for a cad.

"I have recently come to a better understanding of women's plight," he continued, and she believed him. Now if he just stopped using her home as a house of convenience, if he found a lady from his own class, married, and stayed constant for thirty or forty years, she might change her opinion of him. . . .

B14

Also by Barbara Metzger:

THE LADY IN GREEN

Barbara Metzger

FAWCETT CREST • NEW YORK

A Fawcett Crest Book
Published by Ballantine Books
Copyright © 1993 by Barbara Metzger

All rights reserved under International and Pan-American Copyright Conventions. Published in the United States by Ballantine Books, a division of Random House, Inc., New York, and simultaneously in Canada by Random House of Canada Limited, Toronto.

Library of Congress Catalog Card Number: 92-97265

ISBN 0-449-22080-X

Manufactured in the United States of America

First Edition: May 1993

To all my cousins

Chapter One

*M*iss Annalise Avery's fiancé was keeping a mistress. If anyone had told her that dependable, solid Barnaby Coombes had a paramour somewhere, Annalise would have laughed in his face. Hearing it from Barny's own mouth was not quite as funny.

Miss Avery had not meant to eavesdrop, of course. Her mother raised her better than that. She was so excited to tell Barny the doctor had finally declared her well again after that dreadful fever, that the wedding plans could now proceed, she fair flew down the stairs when she heard his carriage in the drive. Naturally she first had to don a warm dressing gown, and her maid insisted she wrap a dark wool shawl over her shoulders, too. She definitely had to tie the ribbons of a frilly cap firmly under her chin. Her outfit was not quite the thing for receiving morning callers, to say the least, Annalise acknowledged with a smile, but more of her was covered than in her sheer muslins and clinging silks. Besides, it was only her stepfather, Sir Vernon Thompson, Bart., who would see her, and comfortable old Barny. She'd known Barny since she was eleven, when her widowed mother, Caroline Avery, *née* Bradshaw, had returned with her daughter to Worcester ten years earlier. They'd been promised forever, it seemed, but the formal announcement had been postponed by her mother's death; the wedding itself was put off for mourning first Annalise's maternal grandmother, then Grandfather Bradshaw. This final delay for her illness was going to be the last, Annalise vowed, and so she would announce to dear Barny as soon as she made sure the green-tinted spectacles were secure on her nose, lest the bright sunshine damage her weakened eyes after so long in the darkness. She didn't bother trying to pinch color back into her sallow cheeks; there was hardly enough flesh left to pinch. And good-natured Barny wouldn't mind. Annalise knew he was as eager as she to start their life together, so she hurried down the stairs to greet her childhood beau with her happy news.

Barnaby had already been shown into Sir Vernon's library, so Annalise pattered down the hall in her slippers, smiling in anticipation. She hadn't counted on how weak the fever and its aftermath had left her, though. She was forced to lean against the wall outside the library to catch her breath. The door was slightly open.

"You're sure she's out of danger, then?" she heard Barnaby asking, and was warmed by the concern in his voice.

"Yes," Sir Vernon answered, "the sawbones assures me she'll make a total recovery. We can have the first reading of the banns in a week or so. The wedding will take place next month."

"Thank God."

Annalise could hear the clink of glasses being

raised in a toast. Smiling, she pushed away from the wall, ready now to join the men. Her stepfather's voice stopped her just as her hand was raised to knock.

"What, so relieved? Which is it, are your debts so pressing or does your ladybird in London grow restless while you play the pattern-card suitor for your ailing betrothed here in Worcester?"

Annalise's hand fell to her side.

Barnaby grinned and tossed back his brandy. He held his glass out for a refill. "Both, if you must know. Sophy don't like missing Vauxhall and the Argyle Rooms. Says she attends with some of her girlfriends, but I don't trust her."

"Why? Aren't you paying enough to ensure her loyalty?" the baronet asked sarcastically.

"I'm dashed well paying enough to keep her in style, that's for sure. Now that you tell me Leesie ain't about to stick her spoon in the wall, I'll just toddle off to Town and surprise the old girl."

"Ah, yes, your 'business' in the City. Why the devil don't you just install Sophy in Birmingham or somewhere? Save all that travel time and expense."

"I told you, Sophy likes the nightlife in Town. 'Sides, a fellow needs to get away once in awhile, especially after putting his foot in parson's mousetrap."

"I still think you'd find it more convenient having a . . . convenient closer to home."

"Oh, I intend to, Sir Vernon, I intend to. There's a widow in Stourport who'd suit me like a plum. Do you know the one? Mrs. Yarberry. I can imagine Mr. Yarberry dying with a smile on his face. Then there's Marcy over at the Golden Hare. She's got cheeks like peaches, and melons out to . . ."

Annalise trembled in the hall. Not only did Barnaby Coombes have a mistress whom he intended

3

to keep on after their marriage, he also planned on setting up a veritable fruitbasket of a harem! Miss Avery raised a hand to her mouth to muffle a cry.

"Don't suppose you'd care to make me an advance," Barnaby was going on, "with the wedding so soon and the settlements all signed?"

"Not on your life, my lad," Sir Vernon replied. "Dear Annalise could have a relapse, after all. No, you'll just have to wait for the marriage lines to be signed before getting your hands on even a shilling of her dowry."

Barnaby slammed his thrice-emptied glass down on the desk. "I don't see why you're being such a skint. You made me sign back enough of Leesie's portion as settlements to keep you in clover for the rest of your life."

"Ah, but we all have our little vices. You have your Sophys and I have my gaming debts. You've waited this long, while, I might add, my stepdaughter's dowry has grown considerably from the Bradshaw grandparents' inheritances. You can wait a shade longer."

"While you skim off all you can."

"Wedding expenses, dear boy, don't you know. And all those pricey physicians and specialists I called down from London to guarantee the precious girl's recovery. You cannot argue with that. Nor," he added softly, "can the Bradshaw accountants."

"I'd still like to see some of the blunt now," Barnaby muttered, "before I'm leg-shackled and off on a blasted wedding trip. Ireland, faugh! I know— maybe Leesie'll still be too weak to travel. What do you think? If I suggest we wait . . ."

Not only did Miss Avery's betrothed have a mistress and a few in reserve, he was going to support them all on Annalise's money!

When pigs flew, he was!

Seeing red even through her green-tinted glasses,

4

Annalise charged into the room. "You cad!" she shouted. "You slime, you slug."

Barnaby gasped in horror, but Annalise couldn't tell whether his dismay was more for her overhearing his conversation or for her appearance. She did not care either way. "So what if I look like something that crept from a crypt? At least my conscience is clear, and that's more than I can say for you, Barnaby Coombes. You don't have to worry about going to Ireland with me; you don't even have to worry about going down the church aisle with me!"

Sir Vernon rose from behind the desk. He slowly raised his quizzing glass to his eye and surveyed his stepdaughter through the horribly magnified orb. "Fetching ensemble, my dear," he drawled. "I'm delighted to see you back in prime twig. I was just assuring Barny here that you were regaining your health and the wedding can be moved forward again."

"Haven't you heard what I said? I wouldn't marry such a bounder if he was the last man on earth and the future of the entire human race depended on me. He'd find an ape to give carte blanche."

"Leesie—" Barny started to protest, so she turned on him again.

"Don't you call me by your silly baby names, Mr. Coombes. I'm not a child anymore to be taken in by your fervent declarations of love and loyalty. Loyalty, hah!" She poked a bony finger in his thick chest. "I heard all about your Sophy, so don't pretend I'm throwing a distempered freak over nothing, you scurvy cur."

Barny tried to grab her hand. "But Lee—Miss Avery, Sophy means nothing to me, I swear!"

"And I suppose my money means nothing to you, either?" Annalise said with a sneer, snatching her fingers away and wiping them on the skirts of her navy-blue dressing gown.

"Dash it, Leesie, you know I'm not a rich man!"

"No, I don't know anything about you at all, Mr. Coombes. I thought I did. I thought we could build a good marriage based on all the years of friendship and trust, even if we did not share any great passion. You have destroyed—"

"That's it, Leesie, passion," Barnaby exclaimed, clutching her words like a drowning man a lifeline. "I do feel passion for you, more than you'll ever understand. I couldn't show you, of course, gently bred female and all that, don't you know, so I had to find an outlet for my, ah, affection. That's all it ever was, just, ah, protection for your maidenly modesty. That's it, Leesie, I swear!"

"Lust and greed, Barnaby Coombes, nothing else. You make me sick."

"You're sick! That's the ticket! You're over-wrought and upset. A few more days' rest and you'll see my little fall from grace is just the way of the world."

"Not *my* world, it isn't, so you can just take your passing fancies and pass right out of my life."

"But, Leesie—" Barnaby couldn't see Annalise's eyes through the dark lenses, but he didn't need her clenched fists to tell him they were sending daggers his way. "Miss Avery, which is downright ridiculous since I've known you since we were practically in leading strings together. Anyway, Miss Avery, you can't just throw me over like this. Sir Vernon can tell you, we've been promised forever, the notice was in the papers, the settlements have been signed. You can't back off from the engagement now."

"Oh, can't I? Just watch." And she started to fumble with the knot on the ribbon around her neck. The ribbon was holding Barny's betrothal ring safe since she'd lost so much weight that the diamond and ruby band slipped off her finger. Now her fingers were trembling with rage and weakness, making her too clumsy to undo the knot. Frustrated, she jerked the whole ribbon over her head, thereby dislodging her spectacles, which fell to the floor at her feet, and her nightcap. She threw the ring, ribbon and all, at Barnaby, who caught it automatically, his mouth fallen open and his eyes popping out of his skull like a sandy-haired carp.

Miss Avery was as bald as the day she was born.

With the slightest pale down sprouting here and there on her head, Annalise might look like a plucked chicken, but Barnaby Coombes was squawking like one. "G-g-gads, L-l—ma'am, y-your hair!"

Near tears, Annalise cried back, "Yes, my beautiful hair that used to reach below my waist! His fancy specialists"—she jerked her head toward Sir Vernon Thompson—"shaved it off. To save my life force, they said, all the while they bled the strength out of me. It might grow back, they said. But don't worry, Barny, you won't have to look at my ugliness over breakfast for the rest of your life. You should thank me."

Barnaby swallowed and made one last try. He pressed the ring into her hand and said, "Your hair will grow back, Leesie, but no matter. You'll always be b-beautiful to me."

"But not beautiful enough to keep you faithful. Not even Sophy is that beautiful. Here, give her this, and may she get more pleasure from it than I did!" She tossed the ring back, hard.

Barny caught the ribbon, but the ring bounced up and nicked his cheek. "Bitch," he muttered, dabbing at the stream of blood trickling down his neck.

"Good," Annalise said, although actually horri-

7

fied at her own behavior. Quite at the end of her tether, she decided to make a clean breast of things. "And I am glad I don't have to marry you, Barnaby Coombes, because you drink too much. Furthermore, in a few years you'll need a corset and a hairpiece both. And finally, I've seen a sack of potatoes that had a better seat on a horse than you!"

Barnaby's face turned white, then the blood rushed back to give him a mottled, swollen look. "Oh, yeah," he raged, "and just who do you think you'll find to marry a viperish old scarecrow like—"

He was wasting his breath, for Miss Avery's last outburst took more of an effort than she had in her. She quietly collapsed to the floor in a heap of flowing fabric.

Sir Vernon came around the desk and felt for a pulse.

"She ain't croaked, is she?" Barnaby asked.

"No thanks to you. My congratulations on your fine touch with a skittish filly."

Barnaby was pouring himself another shot. "What did you want me to do? Zeus, she must have heard everything we said; there was no use denying any of it." He tossed back the drink, then sank down in a leather chair, looking away from his erstwhile fiancée's shiny pate with a shudder. "Lud, what'll I do now?"

The baronet rose and went to pull the bell for a footman. "I suggest you go visit the fair Sophy for a week or two while my stepdaughter cools down. You might even visit your creditors and tell them not to worry."

"Not worry? Gads, you heard her. She'll never marry me."

"She will if she knows what's good for her. I'll talk her 'round."

Barnaby gave a quick peek at the shaved head

and scrawny neck, wondering if Newgate mightn't be preferable after all. Annalise still hadn't moved. "Sure she ain't going to stick her spoon in the wall?"

"All that lovely Bradshaw money goes to charity if she dies without husband or children." Sir Vernon rang the bell again. "She wouldn't dare."

Chapter Two

Broken hearts mended faster than brain fevers. At least on the outside. On the inside, something in Annalise shriveled and shrank, leaving a cold, hard emptiness where love and dreams and hope used to sing and dance. On the other hand, perhaps she was not so disappointed in her engagement's dissolution after all, for a scant two days later saw her ready to receive her stepfather in her sitting room.

Annalise knew why Sir Vernon had requested this visit, and she knew what her reply was going to be. She just hoped this discussion could be conducted with dignity, unlike the last. She felt she owed the baronet that much, for her mother's memory and for the years of his guardianship, although she now suspected his efforts on her behalf to be less sacrifice than self-serving. Of course he had welcomed an awkward thirteen-year-old into his household when he married Annalise's mother; Annalise was a considerable heiress in her own right even then. And of course he had kept her with him at Thompson Hall after her mother's death rather than have her passed about among the Bradshaw relatives; he kept control of her fortune and got an unpaid chatelaine for his manor house to boot! He might have ignored his stepdaughter, spending most of his time in London, but that had always suited her. Still, Annalise acknowledged, she had never been treated as anything less than a lady until two days ago, when her position was redefined as that of a commodity, an investment, a meal ticket. Well, she *was* a lady, her own papa having been Viscount Avery, albeit he was a disinherited ne'er-do-well. She vowed to receive Sir Vernon with the grace of a duke's granddaughter, not the wrath of a ranting fishwife.

Some vows were harder to keep than others. Sir Vernon entered her sitting room, for the first time ever, she realized, and started prowling about. Instead of taking the seat pulled near the chaise longue where Annalise reclined, wrapped around with blankets and shawls, he raised his quizzing glass and inspected her possessions. If she were a dog, her hackles would be up. When he lifted the jade carving of a horse on the mantel, turning it upside down as if to look for a mark of its value, Annalise coughed delicately. "You wished to see me, sir?"

Thompson swung his glass in her direction. "Ah, yes, my dear." He took slow, careful note of her gaunt and pallid cheeks, the heavy coverings pulled up to her chin, the cap pulled low over her forehead. "Not quite the blushing bride."

Annalise started to correct him, but Sir Vernon held up one long, tapered finger. "No, no, my dear, do not excite yourself. Let us keep this a comfortable little coze, shall we?"

She nodded, for that was her intention, too, and

indicated the chair and decanter and glass placed nearby for his convenience. "Please help yourself, sir."

His thin lips twitched into a semblance of a smile as he poured, but he remained standing, so Annalise had to crick her neck uncomfortably to see his face. Finally he deigned to take the seat, flicking a bit of lint off the velvet cushion first. "You have led quite a sheltered life, haven't you?"

Annalise wondered if that was a question. He knew very well that she'd had no come-out and no Season, what with periods of mourning and then no proper female to present her, and of course Barnaby always in the wings. How the situation must have pleased Sir Vernon, keeping her from meeting other eligible beaux, gentlemen who might not be as amenable as cabbage-headed Barny to sharing her dowry. Sheltered? Yes, she'd been kept from all but the local society, but if he meant to excuse Barnaby Coombes on the count that she was a green girl, the baronet was sadly mistaken.

"I have not been so sheltered, sir, that I do not know the ways of a man with a maid, if that is your meaning."

He dismissed her words with a wave of his manicured hand. "No, no, I did not suppose you to be an ignorant schoolroom miss. That's not my meaning. I refer instead to how you have been protected from fortune-hunters and hangers-on, and shielded from slights due to your mother's, shall we say, bourgeois background."

"Mother's parents were wonderful people!"

"And wonderfully wealthy. Unfortunately, that wealth came from trade, my dear, which even your sweet innocence must recognize as offputting to anyone with pretensions to gentility. That is not quite the point I am desirous of making, either. Your mother and your Bradshaw grandparents, with my assistance, I admit, and Barnaby's, have kept you from the harsher realities of life faced by every other well-born female. The fact, drummed into the ears of each and every girl infant blessed with either fortune or breeding or merely great beauty, is simply the necessity to marry well."

Annalise twisted the fringe on her shawl. "I take it you are speaking of arranged marriages, arranged for the convenience of the families instead of for the young people involved. Titles are exchanged for riches, lands are joined, successions are assured without considering the feelings of those who must spend their lives together."

"Precisely. Great happiness is often found in these marriages, and if not"—another casual wave of his hand—"other arrangements can be made. Less regular, but highly rewarding."

"If you are suggesting that I contemplate wedding someone only to . . . to forswear my vows, then I shan't listen."

"Why, I would never suggest you compromise your morals, my dear, I am simply trying to make a bitter pill go down easier. You see, you have foolishly been led to believe that you could marry to please yourself."

"My parents did, and I intend to do the same."

"Ah, yes. Your parents, the perfect example. Sweet Caroline followed her heart—right into disaster!"

"My father—"

"Is dead, so I shall not disparage his memory. Suffice it to say that Viscount Avery was cast off without a farthing for marrying a tradesman's daughter. And not just any trade, but coal, the dirtiest, sootiest trade of them all, considering how the ton hates getting its fingers dirty. Caroline was never accepted in his world, and he despised hers. The viscount took up gaming, you must know, and only his early death saved even Caroline's vast fortune from being whistled down the wind."

"My parents loved each other!"

"That was not enough. At least Caroline had the sense to accept my offer, so that you might be raised away from the smell of the shop."

"And you did not suffer from the marriage, either. I remember Thompson Hall was in shambles when we moved here from Grandfather's, and there were almost no servants."

"Precisely. An advantageous marriage for both parties. Just as your wedding to a well-respected landowner like Barnaby Coombes will benefit all of us."

"*I* do not respect Barnaby Coombes. I do not trust him, and I do not even like him very well anymore. I shall never marry him, no matter what you say. I shall marry for love, as my mother did, or not at all."

Sir Vernon studied his polished nails. "I never supposed you to be so buffle-headed, so perhaps I have not made myself clear even yet. You have no choice, Annalise."

"Of course I do," she said with a laugh. "Other men will be attracted to my dowry if nothing else. I am not quite on the shelf, you know, even if I am one and twenty."

"But I prefer Barnaby." Sir Vernon's words were softly spoken, but Annalise caught the steel behind them.

"You cannot force me to—"

"Yes, I can. That old fool Bradshaw used to be your guardian; now I alone have the right to bestow your hand, and not a court in the land can gainsay my choice. If we were not in such a backwater, I'd have had you wed while you were delirious with the fever. Our own Vicar Harding is above such irregular proceedings, unfortunately. He would be

14

affronted at the idea of a deathbed marriage unless I suggested you and Barnaby had anticipated the wedding night."

"You wouldn't!"

"Of course I would, child. Do not doubt it for a minute. A bit of laudanum ... a tearful plea for your soul's salvation. Had I known you to be such a willful chit, the deed would be done and we'd not need this tiresome little chat. That was my error, thinking you to be a biddable female like your mother." He sighed. "I shan't make the same mistake twice, so I'll have to journey to Town for a special license. So fatiguing, don't you know."

Annalise could not believe what she was hearing. They'd never shared much affection, but this ... this declaration of cold-blooded treachery sent tremors down her spine.

"You'll never get away with such villainy," she declared.

"Oh, no? Who will stop me? The servants whose salaries I pay? Or perhaps you think the Duke of Arvenell will come to the aid of a mongrel granddaughter now, when he wrote his son out of his will ages ago. Your mother showed me the letter he sent when she advised him of the viscount's death. Arvenell *thanked* her, Annalise, for having just the one daughter, so he never had to worry about the succession falling into tainted hands. No, the mighty duke is not about to leave Northumberland to cry halt to an unexceptionable wedding of an unacknowledged chit. Don't suppose any of the local gentry will interfere, either, not when I tell them how unbalanced you are by illness and grief. They'd only congratulate me on finding you such an understanding husband."

Annalise was trembling for real now. Perhaps she was still caught in the fever's nightmares. But no, Sir Vernon was pressing Barny's ring into her clenched fingers, fingers that had unraveled half the fringe on her shawl.

"The choice is yours, my dear," he was saying. "You can accept Barny's offer and have your charming little wedding in the village chapel next month after the banns are read, or you can expect my . . . solution to the dilemma. The outcome will be the same, my dear, never doubt it. I'll have your decision as soon as I return next week with Barnaby and the special license."

Annalise was going to be long gone by then.

Chapter Three

"*H*ere's some nice gruel, Miss Avery."

"How about a little nap, Miss Avery? Are you sure you should be downstairs, ma'am?"

The servants must have been told Annalise was suffering a nervous decline from the brain fever, for they watched her and followed her about, speaking to her as if she were in the cradle or in her dotage. They were happy enough to humor her, fetching any number of books from the library, fresh flowers from the gardens, the most tempting delicacies from Cook's pantry, but not one would call a carriage for her.

"Oh, no, miss. Sir Vernon said you were much too ill to go afield. Doctor's orders, he said. Perhaps you'd like to see the latest fashion journals the master had sent from London for you?"

At least none of them objected when Annalise wanted to search the attics for old wigs and such. The entire staff knew the fate of her long blond locks and sympathized with poor miss, so gone off her looks that her handsome Mr. Coombes had ridden away in high dudgeon. Her maid and two footmen even helped carry down some ancient costume pieces, stuffing them in satchels and hatboxes, so miss could try them on later in the privacy of her room. Maybe that would raise her spirits.

Annalise raised the bandbox lid and stuffed in one more change of linen and another pair of sturdy shoes. Into the satchel she crammed her jewel box, miniatures of her parents, the jade horse, and her grandmother's journal, all cushioned by two heavy flannel nightgowns. She pulled on one of her old mourning gowns, then another on top of that. She was so thin her new riding habit, a green velvet picked to match her eyes, still buttoned over the two black dresses. A heavy wool cloak went over everything, the pockets weighted with a small pistol, a silver flask of Sir Vernon's finest contraband cognac, the contents of the household cash drawer, and as many lumps of sugar as she'd been able to pick up from the tea tray without drawing suspicion. Her own pin money was stashed in various inside pockets of the several layers of clothing, along with the thin stack of letters Sir Vernon must never find.

Annalise did leave him a note saying that she was running away to Bath to find Signor Maginelli, the music instructor who had begged her to elope with him last Christmas. She also left her entire trousseau, and Barny's ring. Adjusting the wig on her head one last time, she gathered up her parcels and locked the bedroom door behind her. She placed two wig cases outside the door to be returned to the attics, indicating that she was not to be disturbed till morning, then she crept down the stairs while the servants were at supper.

The hard part was saddling her half-Arabian mare Seraphina before the stable lads came back for their nightly dice game. No amount of sugar was going to keep the spirited animal from cavorting around in welcome to her long-missing owner.

"Hush, you silly, hush! I missed you, too. Now stand still, and we'll have a nice long run. Hush, beauty."

At last Annalise was done, the mare daintily sidestepping at the unfamiliar packages tied to the saddle. She whickered softly when Annalise led another chestnut mare into the Arabian's vacant stall. "No, she's not as pretty as you, my darling, but in the dark she'll do. Now come, Seraphina, just a few more minutes of quiet, then we can fly. No one will ever catch us."

Especially not with all the loose bridles locked in a tack box, the key tossed into a pile of manure.

They rode through the home woods, picking their way cautiously around fallen trees and rabbit holes, then cross-country over fields and pastures. At last they were beyond Sir Vernon's boundaries, with the main road just ahead. Annalise laughed out loud and Seraphina reared on her hind legs, then dashed forward, not south toward Bath, however, but north toward the market village of Upper Morden. Annalise laughed again, causing a weary farmer to cross himself and a goose girl to run down the lane, screaming about haunts in the woods. A poacher just setting out at dusk decided to return home. This was not a night to be testing one's luck, not with any White Lady abroad, riding astride like all the hounds of hell were after her and her devil horse. Worse, she was yowling like a banshee, with bundles of souls flapping beside her and a great dark cape billowing behind. She and the horse and the cape were all shrouded in an eerie white fog.

The only wig Annalise had considered suitable for her purposes was a towering edifice à *la* Marie Antoinette. Well powdered, of course.

19

She discarded the wig behind a hedgerow outside Upper Morden and tied on a close-fitting dark bonnet. She walked Seraphina right through the main street and tied her to the rear of the Findleys' Two Rose Tavern. Mrs. Findley herself bustled over to the back entry where Annalise stood, drawing the dark woolen cape more firmly over the green of her riding habit.

" 'Ere now, we run a proper establishment. We don't let none of your sort in this—criminy, Miss Avery, is it?" She looked behind Annalise as if the girl were hiding a maid and two footmen behind her skirts. "And out alone? I swann, that's a rare to-do. What's the world coming to, I want to know, when proper young females go racketing about the countryside after dark on their ownsomes?"

Annalise was gently steering the portly landlady down the hall toward the private parlors, away from the public taproom. "Please," she whispered, though not terribly softly, "I need your help. I am running away."

Mrs. Findley's mouth hung so wide, a swallow could have nested there. "I swann."

Annalise tucked a coin in Mrs. Findley's fat hand. "It's not as improper as an elopement or anything. My grandfather is sending a coach to take me north. My grandfather, his grace the Duke of Arvenell, that is. I need to wait in your back parlor for just an hour or so. Will that be all right?" She held out another coin, which quickly followed the path of the first down a slide between mounding bosoms.

"What about Sir Vernon?" Mrs. Findley whispered so loudly that only the passed-out louts in the alehouse missed her words.

Annalise hid her smile by staring at her riding boots. "You mustn't tell Sir Vernon. He . . . he wants to marry me against my will." Which wasn't a lie, just misleading. It was enough to send Mrs. Findley's massive chest heaving.

"Lawkes a mercy! That bounder! That Coombes fellow was bad, always sniffing round the serving girls, but this is outside of enough, I swann! I get my hands on that makebait, he'll wish his parents never met. You come this way, dearie, where no one'll bother you till your granfer comes. A real dook, too? I swann."

Annalise was right where she wanted to be, in the Findleys' own parlor, with its own rear door. She ate the bread and cheese a wide-eyed serving girl brought, and waited for full darkness and a full taproom, judging from the noise. She left another coin, then she stepped outside, asking a passing ostler the way to the necessary.

This time Annalise kept the mare to a quiet walk through the back alleys of Upper Morden. Then she took every deserted lane and cowtrack she knew, keeping to the trees when she heard a carriage or another horseman, until she was nearly back to Thompson Hall. At the edge of exhaustion, she rode through the home woods and down a quiet path that skirted the home farm and the tenants' houses. Annalise could barely keep her head from collapsing onto Seraphina's neck when she finally saw the glow of candles from a cottage that stood all by itself in a clearing. She smiled. Sir Vernon was wrong; there *were* people who would help her.

In times of dismay, disillusionment, and dire peril, a body needed three things: love, loyalty, and larceny. Annalise's old nanny, Mrs. Hennipicker, was sure to provide unquestioned love, unquestioning loyalty—and hot soup. Henny's husband, Rob, was a retired highwayman. What better allies could a fugitive find?

"What are you, girl, dicked in the nob? Stealin'

a horse and the household money, tellin' whiskers up and down the pike, gallopin' like a goblin acrost the countryside. And for what? So's you don't have to marry your childhood sweetheart, 'cause he's been gatherin' his own bloomin' rosebuds, and so's your step-da can't steal the money old man Bradshaw stole from the poor sods who worked his coal mines." Rob spit tobacco juice into the hearth and went back to trimming his beard with a knife. "I thought you had more sense'n a duck. Guess I was wrong, chickie."

"Whisht, Rob, leave the poor thing be. Can't you see she's plumb tuckered? You go on and hitch up the wagon. It's too cold for missy to ride home in her weakened condition."

So much for love and loyalty.

"I'll have a little talk with your Barnaby afore the wedding if you want," Rob offered, holding the shining blade to the fire's light. "Convince him of the error of his ways for you. Worked fine on that nasty billy goat old Trant used to let roam loose. Of course old Trant's nannies ain't had no kids since then. . . ."

And minor illegalities.

Bribery wouldn't work; Rob likely had three times her jewels and coins stashed away in the secret compartments of the cottage, from his days on the high toby. Threats would never do the trick, either; she hadn't cried rope on Rob for thirteen years, and they all knew she'd never go to the authorities now, even if she weren't a runaway herself. Nanny always said, "Crying don't pay the piper," so tears would be useless, should Annalise find the energy to produce them. That left only honor. It was a hard hand to play, and only one trump left.

Annalise put her high card on the table: "You owe me, Rob Hennipicker."

Rob put the knife down and winked at his wife. "I told you she had bottom, Henny, didn't I? You fatten our girl up whilst I go see about hidin' that pretty little mare."

Annalise had to use the corner of her cloak to wipe her eyes. With all the miscellany in her pockets she could not find a handkerchief. "You and Rob were going to help me get away the whole time, weren't you?"

"Of course we were, poppet, we just had to make sure that was what you really wanted." Henny put a steaming bowl of stew in front of Annalise, clucking her tongue about how those fools at Thompson Hall were letting her baby waste away to nothing. She brought over a thick slice of bread and began buttering it. "You wouldn't have called in that old debt if you hadn't been desperate. We all know that."

Many years ago, when Annalise's father was still alive, he rented a place in Brighton to be near the ton's wealthy gamesters for the summer. The viscount and Lady Avery went ahead, with the baggage and their personal servants in a second carriage. Eight-year-old Annalise was prone to travel sickness, so she and her nursemaid, Mrs. Hennipicker, traveled at a slower speed in a hired chaise. Henny was deathly afraid of being set upon by the highwaymen plaguing the Brighton road, but the hired driver and his arrogant young footman made light of her fears.

"G'wan with you," the old coachman wheezed, "most of the ladies is pleased to give their baubles to a gentleman of the road."

"Especially that brazen Robin fellow," the footman added, taking another swig from the jug he refilled at every rest stop. "The one what kisses the ladies' 'ands an' calls 'em 'chickie.' Cock Robin is what they're callin' 'im, on account a' that an' 'ow cocky 'e is, but you don't 'ave to worry none. 'E's only interested in women what got jewels or looks. All you got's an ivory-tuner's brat an' a sour puss."

Annalise stuck her tongue out at the rudesby; Henny let her get away with it.

They were not set upon by highwaymen after all. Instead, the ancient driver wheezed his last right there on the box of their carriage. The footman sitting beside him was so castaway by then, he never even attempted to catch the ribbons as they fell from the coachman's lifeless fingers. He just jumped off the box. What was a bad situation was going downhill quickly. And literally. The horses were panicky, the road was steep with a sharp curve at the bottom of the incline. The horses might make the turn; the coach never would, not without someone's hands on the brake.

Now Robin Tuthill never made it his business to hold up drab and dusty hired chaises. Not worth the risk. And he surely never made it a habit to stop runaway coaches. No money in that at all. But there was something about the screams of a woman and child, coming to him as he sat his horse at the top of the hill, that just ripped away at his heart. Before he could wonder if there'd be a reward, he was digging his heels into his stallion's sides and taking off after the careening coach. With her head out the window, Annalise could see everything, how the caped rider pulled even with the frantic horses and strained to reach the reins. How he stood in the saddle of his own galloping mount, then leapt up to the box of the coach and pulled with all his strength. How the foaming horses made the turn as sweet as pie, and the carriage barely rocked going around the corner.

"You saved us, sir!" Henny was crying as their

24

rescuer opened the coach door. "How can I ever thank you?"

"Don't fatch yourself, chickie, the pleasure was mine."

Chickie? Henny collapsed in a dead faint, right into Robin's arms. Oh, Lud, that's what a fellow got for not minding his own business. Then he looked up, and it was love at first sight—between his fierce black stallion and a tiny golden-curled moppet who was feeding the unruly beast a peppermint candy from her pocket. Now, what was an honest bridle cull to do? He couldn't go off and leave an unconscious nanny and her little charge out there with a dead coachman and, unless he missed his guess, a broken-necked groom. On the other hand, someone would be coming, there was no cover on this stretch of the road, and his own horse was winded.

At this point the debt was entirely Miss Avery's, until she led his horse back to Robin, looked up at him with innocent green eyes, and sweetly inquired, "Do you really like being a highwayman? If not, I have an idea . . ."

So Robin Tuthill, wearing the footman's livery, drove the ladies into the next village to report that the notorious Cock Robin lay dead on the road a few miles back, having fallen from his horse during an attempt to waylay their carriage. Their poor driver had had a seizure during the holdup. A new driver and groom were hired. Two months later Robin became Rob Hennipicker, Henny's long-lost husband, home from the sea with a comfortable nest egg from prize money, and a fine, full beard. After they'd all moved to Worcester, Rob built Henny a little cottage and set up pig farming.

"So now, chickie, what's to do? We can tuck you away in the tunnel beneath the cottage until Sir Vernon comes to his senses, but with the kind of blunt involved, you could sprout roots and turn into a mushroom quicker."

"It's too damp, Rob. Remember, the girl's been sick."

Annalise smiled, revived by Henny's stew. "No, I'd have to stay hidden away in your bolthole for four years, until I reach my majority. Even marriage to Barny might be preferable to that. I don't have enough money to keep myself for that long, either, not even in a tiny cottage, and no, I will not take any part of your, ah, pension. I have a better idea anyway."

Rob spit into the fire and grinned. "And here I was thinkin' I'd have to take up the profession again, it was gettin' so quiet around these parts."

"I'd take my skillet to the side of your head, Rob Hennipicker, and well you know it. So just hush and listen to what the child has to say."

"Henny, I'm not a child! I'm twenty-one, well past the age to be married and a mother in my own right. That's the whole problem, don't you see? If I hide away until I am twenty-five, I'll never find a husband." She fumbled through one pocket after another, handing the silver flask over to Rob, until she located the packet of letters. She waved them triumphantly and announced, "I am going to go live with Aunt Ros in London!"

"But, Miss Annalise, I thought you never heard from her anymore, not since Sir Vernon forbade your mother to correspond with her. That was years ago, right after they got married."

"No matter, she's been at the same address forever, and she was always inviting me to come visit. And her particular friend Lord Elphinstone is very high in the government. Surely with his influence something can be done about my stepfather's guardianship. So I only need your help in getting to London."

"Only? When every man, woman, and sheriff'll be out looking for you soon as Sir Vernon puts out the word and the reward? A' course here'll be the first place he'll look, so we don't have half to worry about, now do we, chickie? 'Sides, seems to me this Aunt Ros of yourn blotted her copybook onct herself. I'm not sure she's fit to be in charge of you and your cork-brained schemes."

Annalise refuted that argument with a snap of her fingers. "Pooh. That's just Sir Vernon's priggery. And the Duke of Arvenell's. You know what kind of man he is by the way he disowned his children. All Aunt Ros did was refuse to marry the man he chose for her. She *has* to take me in!"

Chapter Four

$\mathcal{U}$nfortunately, Lady Ros was not in London. She and Lord Elphinstone had traveled to Vienna for the peace talks and parties.

This bit of news was one crushing blow too many for Annalise. She was cold, hungry, tired, and frightened. Crying still wouldn't help, so as soon as the helpful watchman went on along his beat, Annalise kicked at the locked door of Aunt Ros's small, tidy town house at Number Eleven, Laurel Street. Then she limped back to the hackney carriage where Henny and Rob waited. The devil fly away with it, she thought, they'd worked so hard just to get to London!

They'd waited at the cottage long enough for Sir Vernon to throw Rob off his land.

"Iffen we leave afore he gets back, he'll move heaven and earth to find us," Rob said. "You can put your blunt on that. The man's mean, he ain't stupid. 'Sides, I got preparations to make."

Annalise didn't ask what those preparations

were; Henny advised her it was better not to know. Rob promised Seraphina was safe and would be waiting in London when they arrived, and that was enough. Annalise slept the time away in her hidden little cubby behind the kitchen pantry, waking only to swallow the hot soup Henny kept bringing.

The retired highwayman was right: the cottage was the first place Sir Vernon looked, after sending men north to Arvenell and south to Bath. He arrived with the magistrate and three brawny grooms.

"Don't see no writ for a search," Rob said.

"I don't need one," Sir Vernon replied, holding a lace-edged handkerchief over his nose. "It's my property."

"Seems to me just the land is yourn, on rent. You know I built this cottage on my own." The magistrate, Squire Bromley, was looking uncomfortable, so Rob went on: "No matter. I got nothin' to hide. Go ahead, boys, look your fill. You find any sweet young thing under the bed, just don't tell m'wife."

So the men made a halfhearted search, Henny following them about, threatening to comb their hair with her footstool if they so much as disturbed her pressed linens and stacked preserves.

"If she's not here, Bromley, then this man helped my stepdaughter escape, a minor female, out of her wits and sickly. I demand you arrest him and hold him till he reveals her whereabouts."

Henny started weeping into her apron, and the magistrate was shifting from foot to foot.

"And when you think about doin' that, Squire, think about what himself's done to make a gently reared female run off that way, and straight from the sickroom, too."

"The chit's dicked in the nob, that's all. Her nerves came unhinged from the fever, so she doesn't know what she's doing. It's obvious the dear girl needs a keeper," Thompson insisted. "I intend to see she's held safe and secure as soon as we find her."

"Aye, clappin' the poor lass in Bedlam'd suit you to a cow's thumb, wouldn't it? Then there'd be no one to ask about all that inheritance money."

"Why, you, you ..." Sir Vernon looked around and noticed the interested grooms. "I want you off my property, you swine. There's always been something havey-cavey about you anyway. No common seaman I ever heard of made enough prize money to live so well."

The bearded farmer spit tobacco juice, missing Sir Vernon's highly polished boots by a good half inch. "Mayhap I weren't so common. And mayhap I kept back enough of my winnings to hire me a fancy advocate, in case some jumped-up toff tries to bring false charges 'gainst me, or tries to take my land without compensatin' me."

"My secretary will bring the rent refund tomorrow morning. Be gone by the evening." Sir Vernon stomped out of the cottage.

"What about my house that I built with my own two hands?" Rob called after him.

"Take it with you."

"I druther see it burn than leave it to the likes of you."

So they burned the cottage, after packing what they could onto a wagon, and after Henny made her farewells in the neighborhood, leaving her cousin's address in Swansea. "Her man's a fisherman, you know, and my Rob's been missing the sea for all these years. We were only staying to be near Miss Annalise anyways, and with her gone, and bad feeling from Sir Vernon, it's better this way. You come visit if you ever get to Wales."

Henny cried softly despite her own advice as they

drove away from the flaming building, even though there had been no choice. They couldn't leave the cottage standing, lest Sir Vernon come find the hidden chambers.

Annalise did not see the flames or the tears. She was tucked away under the wagon's false bottom.

They traveled slowly west, just another country couple in somber clothes. They bought food in the village shops or from housewives rather than from taverns, and they paid a shilling or two to sleep in barns instead of inns. Before Hereford, Henny got down with her portmanteau and walked the last quarter mile into town, where she purchased an inside seat on the mail coach to Oxford. No one paid any mind to the nanny on her way to a new position.

Rob and Annalise took turns driving the wagon, just another country couple in somber clothes, traveling west for another half day. Then they turned south toward Gloucester, where they traded the wagon for a hooded carriage; Rob shaved his beard and donned a caped driving coat, and Annalise pinned a silk rose in her bonnet, veiled to keep the travel dust from her eyes and nose. They stopped at only the busiest posting houses, Mr. and Mrs. Robbins, off to Oxford to see the sights. They left Oxford in a hired coach, Rob and Henrietta Tuthill, taking their widowed niece to London to meet her in-laws. In the center of London they switched to a hackney, whose jarvey didn't care who the hell they were, so long as he saw the color of their money.

"Henny, have you ever seen so many people? Don't you think the smoke bothers them? Did you see that man dressed all in green?"

"Look, Miss Annalise, I swear that's the spires of Westminster itself!"

Rob frowned. "We ain't never goin' to get away

with this if you two can't remember your places. We made it so easy a goose could get it right. Annie and her auntie, and Uncle Rob. Unless you want to put a notice in the papers that Miss Annalise Avery's come to Town, chickie." He settled back on the squabs, his arms crossed over his chest.

"Pshaw, Robbie," Henny chided, "just because you're happy not to be Rob Hennipicker any longer, no reason to have your nose out of joint. I intend to enjoy my visit, see the sights, the Tower and Pall Mall and everything."

"And as soon as Aunt Ros and her friends hear my story, I'll be safe with my own name, Uncle Rob, so you can stop grizzling."

They passed through twisty, dirty streets, then broad avenues shaded with trees and wide thoroughfares choked with traffic. They saw mean slums, then vast open spaces with houses set in parks minutes apart, right in the middle of the city. After a while they left the fancier neighborhoods for narrower houses on narrower streets.

"This don't look like Mayfair," Rob grumbled.

"It isn't," Annalise answered. "Didn't you hear me give the driver the address? We're going to Laurel Street, Bloomsbury."

"Thought your aunt was Quality, knowing all the nobs. What's she doin' out in Bloomsbury?"

Henny looked out the window. "Oh, my, they sell near everything on every corner, don't they? Look at that, Robbie, fresh lavender and milk and—"

"Is Rosalind Avery respectable, or ain't she?"

Annalise answered: "I explained that the duke cast her off, remember? I never knew the whole story; it happened before my time. As far as I understand, Lady Rosalind was beautiful and in love with a handsome soldier, but her father wanted her to marry a crotchety old nobleman whose land marched with his. Aunt Ros tried to elope with her soldier instead, but they were stopped before reaching the border, but not before, uh . . ."

"I know what *uh* is, chickie."

"Papa always said she was just young and in love, like him and Mama. He said the Averys fell in love with their hearts, not their minds, but the Duke of Arvenell never did care about anything but the family name. So the handsome young soldier was sent back to the army, where he died. Aunt Ros refused to marry anyone else, which was of no account, I suppose, for the duke's choice refused to marry her since she was ruined, although there was no child. But Arvenell never forgave her, and she never forgave him, so she left home and came to London."

Henny nodded. "Leastways he didn't cut her off entirely. She had enough income to set up her own establishment, though not the first stare, naturally."

"And it was a brave thing to do, because most of her old friends cut her at first. Not all of them, though, not when they saw she wasn't setting herself up as a cyprian or anything."

Henny squealed, "Missy! What do you know about such things?"

"Enough to know my aunt would never be one! She's not invited to all the ton parties, of course, and the highest sticklers didn't recognize her when Mama was alive, but she is still Lady Rosalind Avery. Maybe they do now."

"And maybe they don't. Them niffy-naffy types have long memories."

"So what? Mama was not received, either, so I have no place in society anyway. Can you see Henry Bradshaw's granddaughter being invited to Almack's?"

"I can see the Duke of Arvenell's, for sure. And that's 'xactly what I thought I'd see when I agreed to this harebrained scheme. Not settin' you down on any primrose path with a fallen woman."

"Now, Rob," Henny put in, "Miss Annalise's mother always spoke highly of her sister-in-law, and she was real upset when Sir Vernon made her stop writing. Lady Rosalind led a quiet life, she said. I suppose she couldn't do much better on the portion she had."

"And I didn't come down in yesterday's rain, chickie. No gentry mort lives in Bloomsbury."

"Aunt Ros *is* respectable," Annalise protested, "and her friends *are* influential. You wait and see. Besides, until everything is settled, I'll be safer there, where it's quieter and away from all the gossip. No one will care tuppence about some hag-ridden female on the fringes of town."

"And when you get roses back in your cheeks and hair back on your head, chickie, what then? Where're you goin' to find any eligible part-ee to take you in hand, that's what I want to know. Not in Bloomsbury with some—"

"Mind your tongue, Robbie Tuthill."

Rob still grumbled. "Should of taken the womanizer. A little arsenic in his coffee, you could of been free in no time. That's why they call it widow powder, ain't it?"

Annalise could not look Rob in the eye when she reached the carriage and had to tell him what the watchman had said, that Aunt Ros was traveling abroad with a gentleman friend. "Of course there must be some innocent explanation," she added, wishing she had the imagination to conjure one up. More important, what were they to do now? Her friends had already given up their home for her. How much more could she ask? "Do you think we should try to find her in Vienna?"

"Thompson's sure to be having the ports watched.

'Sides, I ain't never been on no boat, and I ain't goin' on no boat now. Good Lord wanted men to swim, He'd of given us gills."

"Pshaw, Robbie, and here I've been telling everyone back home we were off to the coast so you could go fishing!"

"Cut your nattering, woman, and let me think."

"Well, do your thinking in a hurry, Robbie Tuthill, for this coach is passing damp, and Miss— Annie needs to be in a warm bed. All that jouncing around in the cold and wet, and eating what I wouldn't toss to the pigs, why, I can see my lamb fading right away."

Annalise bit her lip. Henny's shorn lamb would fare even less well locked away in some insane asylum for the rest of her bound-to-be-short life. She'd heard of such things, unscrupulous physicians taking money to declare an unwanted family member mad. Right now Annalise was so mad, she could just—

The door of Number Eleven, Laurel Street opened and a young girl in a gray uniform with white apron and cap peered out. "Was it you knocked on the door a minute ago?" she called over to the carriage. "I was on the ladder, doing the chandelier."

The maid's name was Lorna, and she allowed as how the travelers could rest in the kitchen for a bit, the younger female looking so pulled and all. Of course they had to be gone by four o'clock, when a young lord was coming to look the place over to rent, she told them, happy to have someone to talk to. And she wouldn't mind a hand with moving the heavy furniture at all, because she was hoping his lordship would keep her on as daytime help if the house met with his approval. "Of course he'll still need to hire a housekeeper and a cook and a man of all work. Was you folks interested in the positions?"

35

Chapter Five

*R*oss Montclaire, the sixth Earl of Gardiner, loved women. All women. Tall or small, lithe or rounded, haughty or shy, exquisite or plain. He loved the way they moved, the way they smelled, the way their emotions were written on their faces, the way they played off their charms for a man. Old ladies delighted him; tiny moppets enchanted him. The only females he did not enjoy were the predatory debutantes on the Marriage Mart and their ambitious mamas. Luckily, he never encountered these greedy, grasping representatives of the fair sex in his rambles through London. In fact, he avoided the polite world's piranhas like the plague. Worse, for if there were a plague, he would offer to help bury the dead; Lord Gardiner could not even bear to witness his friends' weddings.

The earl's friends, those still speaking to him after his refusal to attend their nuptials, called him Gard. The broadsides and scandal sheets called him Earl en Garde, because he was always ready. The duels they referred to were not affairs of honor, either, simply affairs: the *duello d'amore*, whose field of honor was a bed, a couch, a closed carriage, or a blanket in the woods, the eternal skirmish from which both combatants rose satisfied, if the *passage d'arms* was conducted properly. Ross Montclaire was everything proper, and he never received a challenge he didn't meet.

Like the bee that goes from flower to flower, the earl visited woman after woman, never bruising the most fragile blossom, never staying longer than the sharing of a sunbeam. He might return, but a single bloom never held him long, much to the rosebuds' regrets.

When Lord Gardiner was not paying homage to his ladyloves with his body, he was worshipping them with his pencil. He sometimes got so lost in the beauties of a woman's form that he forgot her function there in his bed for hours on end. Well, minutes on end. Heirs to earldoms seldom being encouraged to pursue artistic careers, Ross was not as fine a draftsman as more advanced technical training could have made him. Practice, however, made him outstanding in this field, too. The faces of his portraits may have been mere rough likenesses of their models, but, oh, the bodies were perfect in their infinite variations. An unexpected dimple here, a softer fold there; the earl took endless delight in his two favorite pastimes.

Ross Montclaire, my lord Gardiner, was a rake of the first order. Then his mother came to Town.

The earl was as close to his mother as most noblemen with one and thirty years in their dish. Like most of his fellows, he'd been sent off with wet nurses, nannies, and tutors, then to boarding schools and university, grand tours and a stint in the army. His later years were spent between house parties, hunting boxes, and bachelor digs, with occasional appearances at his far-flung properties and his seat in Parliament. Which is to say, Gard might be able to sketch his mother's face from memory. Or he mightn't. He did love and respect Countess Stephania, naturally. She was his lady mother; he was a proper son.

"You are the most unnatural child a woman could bear!" the diminutive dowager screeched, beating her much larger son about the head and shoulders with her cane. "Where are my grandchildren? Where is the successor to your title? Do you think I suffered with your great hulk for nine months just so you could become a byword in the gossip columns? That's not why a woman has children, you dolt! She has them so her husband leaves her alone—from the grave, you jackaninny. Your father is disturbing my rest again!"

Ross tried not to laugh as he easily fended off his mother's thrusts. The late earl, Sebastian Montclaire, often cut up his lady's peace, it seemed, especially when Lady Gardiner was dissatisfied with her allowance, her life as doyenne of Bath society, or, most commonly, her son.

"Sebastian cannot be happy knowing his heir is a profligate here-and-thereian," the countess pronounced, finally accepting an Adams chair in the Gold Parlor. "And I deserve to have little ones playing about my skirts."

The last thing the countess would have permitted, her son considered as he rang for tea, was sticky fingers on her elegant gros de Naples ensemble. Nevertheless, she seemed determined to make Ross's life a misery. She was in London, the dowager announced, to make sure he reformed. This time she would see he attended correct gatherings, met suitable females, settled down to begin his nursery.

"Your past behavior outrages and offends my every proper feeling as a mother," she continued after Foggarty, the butler, wheeled in the tea tray. Eyeing the almond tarts, macaroons, and poppy-seed cake, Lady Stephania slammed her delicate cup down in its saucer. "How can I eat, looking at my only son, knowing he has just recently left some doxie's arms?"

So Gard made sure the dowager's digestion did not suffer. He left. Since his presence seemed to displease the countess, and he was nothing if not a considerate son, the earl stayed as far away from her as possible, which was far indeed in the clubs and stews of London, and the vast reaches of Gardiner House, Grosvenor Square.

The dowager bribed the servants to discover her son's location; he threatened them with dismissal if they divulged his hideouts. Ross came in after she was abed and left before she was awake. Peace reigned. If the fifth earl walked the halls at night, the sixth one never met him in the darkened corridors.

The system worked fairly well until the night of Diccon Inwood's birthday celebration. Lord Gardiner found himself having a late supper at Hazlett's with his closest comrades and half the Royal Theatre's *corps de ballet*, the most comely half. *Esprit* was running high after the sweets course and after numerous bottles of champagne, when the guest of honor turned to his dinner partner and declared, "You're as pretty as a picture, *chérie*." Which wasn't terribly original for a gentleman hoping to entice a female to his rooms for another bit of dessert. Considering how castaway Lord Inwood was at the time, however, his friends were impressed with his finesse as he continued: "Not even Bottle . . . Botti . . . Michelangelo could capture your incredible beauty."

To which Lord Gardiner's best friend Cholly, otherwise known as the Honorable Charlton Fansoll, replied, "Gard could do her justice."

Some of the other revelers remembered Lord Gardiner's clever renderings from their Oxford days and quickly followed Inwood's plea that Gard do a portrait of his *belle amie* with clamors of their own. No one wanted to be behind times with the girls, who seemed entranced with the idea. Zeus, it was cheaper to buy old Gard another round than to spring for a pair of diamond earbobs. But old Gard couldn't do all the fair charmers' pictures, especially when they seemed to multiply in front of his eyes, so he offered an alternative. He'd give the fellows a few pointers, lend a more practiced if no steadier hand so they could each draw their own lady. The suggestion was received with applause and laughter, and quickly evolved into a bet, as was wont to occur among these bucks and sporting bloods of the Corinthian set. The best portrait would win ten pounds from each of the wagerers, half to the artist, half to the model. Gard could judge, since he was too good to compete. The only problem was that they needed more room than Hazlett's private dining parlor could provide, and a few props and drawing materials, all of which were in ample supply at Gardiner House in Grosvenor Square.

The earl was very considerate of his staff, most of whom had been at Gardiner House longer than he had. He always sent his valet, Ingraham, to bed when he left for the evening, scandalizing the old man with tales of how many times he'd be in and out of his clothes that night without his valet's assistance. Lord Gardiner also refused to permit Foggarty to stay on duty all night just to open the door, when Gard had a very fine key in his pocket, so no one met his lordship's party in the marbled hall.

They tiptoed past a gape-jawed night footman on their way to the grand ballroom, miles away from the family wing of the huge pile. The footman's only prior function, as far as Lord Gardiner could tell, was to report back to the countess what time her erring son returned and whether his neckcloth was tied correctly. Tonight the clunch could earn his keep lighting candles, laying fires, and fetching the earl's pads and charcoals. Gard and Cholly made forays to the wine cellar and the conservatory while the other gentlemen shifted a plant stand or two and helped the dancers remove Holland covers from the gilt chairs and satin-covered love seats.

"Gentlemen," Gard finally announced, "in the interest of fairness, I have established some criteria for the judging. Artistic composition and depth of expression shall be counted as well as execution."

"What the deuce are you talking about, Gard?" Cholly asked for the rest, who were shaking their heads and looking more confused than foxed.

"That it doesn't have to look like your ladybird, you gudgeon, it just has to be a good picture. That way you can use your imaginations, if you have any, even if you haven't much skill. You have one hour. On your mark . . ."

Soon there were naked ladies with roses in their teeth, naked ladies draped creatively across gilt chairs. Ballerinas had remarkable flexibility, surprising even the connoisseur earl. One dancer was wearing the gauntlets from a suit of armor and nothing else; one was en pointe on a plaster pedestal. There were more chuckles than concentration on the other side of the makeshift easels.

"Drawing class was never like this," Lord Inwood laughed as the earl made his way around the room, straightening a line, adjusting a pose. He offered a suggestion here, a bit of gauze there, a kiss

41

or a pat of encouragement to all the models. Ah, the joy of Art.

"Cholly, you've given her three arms! Nice pose, Lockhart, but you're not supposed to be in the picture with Chou-Chou; get back to your drawing. Hello, Mother. No, Nigel, you're supposed to draw on the paper, not on the model." Hello, Mother?

More lightskirts went home in Holland covers that night than in the entire history of British shipping. Someone had the presence of mind to extinguish most of the candles. They were just a tad too late, however, to prevent some of London's choicest spirits from witnessing the Dowager Countess Gardiner, five feet from the tips of her embroidered slippers to the curl papers in her silvered hair, attack her six-foot-plus son with a fireplace poker.

By way of remorse, Gard sat through three lectures about not fouling one's own nest and two secondhand visitations from his father's uneasy spirit. In the end, just to win a modicum of peace for his aching head, he even agreed to accompany Lady Stephania to a few tonnish parties and to consider—consider, mind!—looking around for a suitable countess.

The balls were as awful as he recalled, too hot, too crowded, too many rules. The refreshments were more fashionable than filling, the table stakes were low, the dance floor stakes were high. He no sooner asked a young lady for a dance than her name was linked to his in the morning's papers. Her mother was calling him "dear" and her father was telling him when he could call. And the debutantes were as insipid as the lemonade they drank, while their older sisters, the established Beauties, were as cold as the ices from Gunther's every hostess served. Raspberry, lemon, the only difference was in the color of their dresses. As for the dresses themselves, those low necklines and dampened skirts did nothing to reconcile Lord Gardiner to leg shackles. A fellow didn't choose his wife from a row of Covent Garden whores, and the whores at least provided what they promised. The price for these highborn high flyers was too costly.

Those same clinging gowns and plunging bodices did arouse a bit more than Lord Gardiner's ire, however, so he picked up a few of the hankies dropped at his feet by dashing widows and daring wives. He gathered his rosebuds where he may.

A sennight or so later, he hobbled into White's.

Chapter Six

"Deuce take it, man," his friend Cholly asked; "what happened? Did Lady Stephania light into you again? I thought you were reformed."

Gard carefully lowered himself into one of the leather chairs and signaled for a waiter. One ankle was strapped, one eye was blackened, and, most unfortunate of all in his lordship's opinion, he had a fiercesome rash where he sat. He did not bother answering Cholly's remark about the dowager: less said, soonest mended. Not soon enough for his battered skull.

Cholly was observing him through a quizzing glass. "Can't believe you turned your curricle over, nonpareil whip like you. Does the Four-Horse Club know?"

"Cut line, Cholly. You look like one of those blasted dandies. Put that silly thing away and I'll tell you what happened." Ross leaned his head back against the cushions and sniffed at the aged cognac the servant brought. "Ah," he sighed, swirling the dark liquor around in the glass while his friend waited impatiently. At last Lord Gardiner took a swallow of his drink, savoring the flavor. "I have indeed been a paragon of virtue," he finally confirmed. "No opera dancers, no chorus girls, no bits of muslin."

"What, no females at all?" Cholly nearly choked on his own drink.

The earl looked down his aristocratic nose, which was just slightly out of line. "That's not what I said. At Mother's insistence I frequented the haut monde instead of the demimonde."

"Nearly took a turn seeing you at Lady Bessborough's."

"Precisely. So all of my, ah, companions this past week have been *ladies*." He took another sip. "And see what it's gained me."

Cholly nodded his head in sympathy. "They're the devil when it comes to being crossed. Why, m'sisters—"

"No, the women didn't wreak such havoc on my body, not directly, at any rate. This"—he indicated the leg propped on a footstool in front of him—"I received when I was forced to climb out a window. The *lady's* husband came home unexpectedly. The trellis broke, equally unexpectedly, by George. My face, on another night, was rearranged by footpads."

"Jupiter, I would have thought you were too downy a bird by now to be taken like that."

"And so I thought, too, but it was four in the morning with not a hackney to be seen, if a person could have seen anything through the fog. I had sent Mother off from Lady Bessborough's in our carriage, and then accepted a ride home—her home, naturally—from a certain widow who shall, of course, remain nameless."

"Of course," Cholly echoed, searching his mind for likely candidates.

"A widow who is received in all the best drawing rooms, incidentally. I must say I was delighted with her charms, until she rudely shoved me awake and out of her bed. The servants mustn't see me there when they lit the fires in the morning. The *lady's* reputation would suffer." He took another sip of the brandy.

"But what of the footpads?"

"I think they'll be more careful picking their target in the future. Just because a chap is clunch enough to leave a warm bed in the middle of a cold night doesn't mean he's an easy mark." Lord Gardiner ran his fingers through his dark curls, wincing at the lumps and bruises. He couldn't tell which were from the attempted robbers, which remnants from the dowager's fire poker. "And that's not the worst of it," he confessed.

Cholly refilled his own empty glass. "Deuce take it, there's more?"

The earl shifted uncomfortably on his chair. He nodded. "There was one more *lady*. A regular dasher, with some old dragon living with her to lend countenance. Bold as brass she asks me to take her for a ride in the country while the dragon visits an ailing cousin. She wants me to pull in at a quaint little inn she knows outside of town. *Quaint* wasn't the word I'd have used. Rundown, ramshackle maybe, not quaint. And you know how I never stay at even mediocre inns."

Cholly was starting to smile. "And I know the way your man Ingraham is always following you around with your own bed linen and stuff. Tender skin, ain't it?"

The earl flicked a speck of dust off his dark sleeve. "But the jade says that way she can be sure no one will recognize her, so I take a room. Blast it, quit laughing, she was a convincing armful!"

"And?"

"And those sheets were so filthy, my butt's the color of a baboon's behind!"

When Cholly finished wiping his eyes, he told the earl, "What you need is a wife!"

"I need a wife like your picture of Babette needed that third arm. What's a rash compared to a nose ring?"

Cholly put his handkerchief away. "Mightn't be so bad, y'know."

"What? I can't believe my ears! Never say you're thinking of becoming a tenant for life?"

"Been thinking, that's all. 'Sides, who'd have me? I'm just a second son with a houseful of sisters, and m'brother's already filling his nursery with heirs. Ain't got a fortune, no title to trade for one, so no nabob's going to hand me his daughter. Wouldn't want an heiress anyway; don't fancy living under the cat's paw." He considered his friend's tall, athletic form and chiseled features that were only made more interesting by the purplish bruises. Then he contemplated his own short, stocky body and carroty hair. "Ain't got your looks, and never did have your way with the ladies. Still, we're not getting any younger. All I've got to offer is a comfortable income. If I found a comfortable female, I just might take the plunge."

"Dash it, marriage isn't a bath you can jump out of if the water's too cold! It's for deuced eternity!"

Cholly nodded sagely. No argument there. "If you won't take a wife, then how about a mistress?"

"What, a fixed arrangement? Hell, if I wanted to be faithful to the same woman day after day, I'd get married."

Cholly choked. "You mean you intend to be constant when you're hitched? You?"

"Why not? I'd expect my wife to be." Gard ignored his friend's sputtering. "No, mistresses are more trouble than wives, greedier and harder to please. They're always throwing jealous tantrums and they're impossible to get rid of. No wife of mine would expect me to live in her pocket, and she'd dashed better be too well-bred to get into distempered freaks. No, thank you, the carefree bachelor life suits me fine."

Cholly raised his quizzing glass again. "Looks to me instead like the tomcatting is killing you, creeping down alleys and over windowsills. What you need is an establishment of your own."

The earl resented his friend's inference that he needed taking care of. "Have you forgotten Gardiner House? It's a little hard to miss if you happen to be near Grosvenor Square."

"No, I mean a pied-à-terre, a little place you can come and go, private like. Discreet."

The earl called for another bottle. "A *bijou*. Interesting. I could fix the place up the way I like, even set up a little drawing studio. I could hire a whole new staff of servants who wouldn't carry tales."

Cholly smiled. "And who'd make sure the sheets are clean."

Gard laughed, too. "Can you imagine me asking poor old Ingraham to carry fresh linens to a house of convenience? He'd have a spasm."

"Should have pensioned off the chap years ago if he disapproves of you."

"I can't. The man valeted my own father. Frankly, it would be a relief not to see his disappointment every day. I'm getting to like your idea more and more. Still, I could make the love nest so cozy, the birds of paradise might want to take up permanent residence. They're deuced difficult to dislodge, you know."

"Blister it, you have the butler send 'em to the rightabout if you're too tender-hearted."

They both laughed at the picture of the elderly Gardiner butler giving some courtesan her *congé*. Old Foggarty was another long-time employee who refused to leave the earl's service, he and Ingraham having nowhere else to go. "Lord save me from loyal old family retainers."

Cholly stared at the tassels on his Hessians. "Seems to me you could keep any of the ladybirds from settling in if you told them right out the arrangement was only temporary, that you were just renting the place. I recall hearing that Elphinstone's digs out in Bloomsbury are for let."

"Someone mentioned that he went with the delegation to Vienna. I didn't realize Lady Rosalind went with him."

"Should have. Inseparable, don't you know."

"And you say their house is out in Bloomsbury . . . ?"

The town house could have fit into the entry hall of the earl's principal seat in Suffolk, but it was well maintained and respectable-looking. The street was quiet, with trees and flowers, and mothers pushing prams. The man who came to take Lord Gardiner's horses was middle-aged, neatly dressed, and clean-shaven. He seemed knowledgeably appreciative of the earl's prime-goers.

"Shall I take these beauties back to the mews, gov'nor, or just around the block so's they don't cool down?"

"Can you drive?"

The man carefully aimed a stream of tobacco juice between rows of pansies. "Anything with wheels."

"And can you keep a still tongue in your head?"

"I reckon so," the one-time Cock Robin said with

a grin. "If Rob Tuthill can't keep his mummers dubbed, then no one can."

Lord Gardiner watched Tuthill drive the curricle away with consummate skill. He was liking this notion better and better. He'd have to remember to invite Cholly to his first not-so-intimate gathering.

A dimpled little maid opened the door for him, took his beaver and gloves, and showed him to the parlor. "I be Lorna, milord. I come in days. Would you please to wait in the parlor while I fetch the housekeeper to show you about? We put refreshments out for you, milord." She curtsied prettily, showing the dimples again before she left.

Gard smiled back at the delightful little baggage, not that he ever dallied with servants in his employ, or such young chits, either. A pretty face always being welcome, though, he automatically added the maid to the inventory of the house's attractions.

The excellent strawberry tarts were another. 'Pon rep, he wouldn't miss squiring his barques of frailty to noisy public restaurants if the house boasted a fine cook of its own. Strange, he thought as he sipped a fine sherry and had another bite of pastry, the rental agent had not mentioned the residence was fully staffed. The fellow would have dickered for a higher price if he knew how Lord Gardiner loved strawberry tarts. Ross's blue eyes shone as he looked around the parlor that ran from front to rear of the small home, tastefully furnished yet with enough room for a deal table or two. Even had a pianoforte, although he doubted many of his guests would have the training, or the time, to play. Yes, the house was a bargain.

The rest of the place was just as pleasing. The housekeeper led him to a smaller sitting room across the hall that contained an overstuffed sofa in front of a tiled fireplace. Excellent. Next to that was a dining room that could seat ten, the house-keeper informed him. Two was enough. Beyond the dining parlor was a small apartment consisting of an office for the household accounts and a tiny bed-room, which she hustled him out of so fast, he was sure it belonged to his guide.

Below stairs he was introduced to Rob Tuthill's wife, who blushed when Lord Gardiner compli-mented her cooking. " 'Tis a joy to cook in such a modern kitchen, my lord." She rattled a stack of dishes nervously, so the earl bowed and moved on, determined not to agitate such an asset. The chef at Gardiner House threw a Gallic fit if a stranger entered his domain. Ross smiled, trying to turn the woman up sweet so he'd be more welcome in her kitchen next time. He gave cursory inspection to the Tuthills' chambers behind the kitchen and pan-tries. What he wanted to see was upstairs.

He was not disappointed. The master suite con-sisted of two fair-sized dressing rooms connected to a bedroom almost as large as his in Grosvenor Square. There was an enormous canopied bed and rugs so thick he'd have taken his shoes off right then if not for the housekeeper. Ah, yes.

There were two other pleasant bedrooms on this floor, in case Cholly stayed over. On the attic level were some unused servant's rooms, one of which could make a perfect studio. "Yes," he said, nod-ding. "Yes, indeed."

"Then you like it?" the housekeeper asked, nearly wringing her hands. "You'll take it?"

Lord Gardiner cupped his chin in his hands, de-liberating. The house was ideal for his purposes, close enough for convenience yet almost invisible to the eyes of the Polite World, ergo, his mother. The place itself was charming, inviting. He men-tally saluted Lady Rosalind's taste. Only one thing bothered him: the housekeeper, Annie Lee, *Mrs.* Annie Lee, by George, was the ugliest female he had ever seen!

Chapter Seven

The *Mrs.* had to be a courtesy title. Love might be blind, Gard reasoned, but this was asking too much. The woman had jaundiced skin and a chest so flat you could iron a neckcloth on it. She wore a black dress obviously made for someone two sizes larger, and a grayish mobcap with lappets that covered whatever hair she might have, except the three long ones growing out of the mole on her cheek. Dark spectacles most likely hid an awful squint or worse, and, since she never smiled, the earl assumed her teeth were as bad as her eyes. She stood perfectly, rigidly erect, except for the one shoulder that was permanently higher than the other.

Love would have to be deaf and dumb besides to settle on Mrs. Annie Lee. The notion of an unfortunate Mr. Lee offended the earl's sense of justice. The unfortunate notion of Mrs. Annie Lee in his cozy little love nest offended his aesthetic soul. There just had to be a way of getting the house without this housekeeper from hell.

"You seem young for such a responsible position," he began with a lie, having no way to guess the woman's age with so little of her showing. At least she had not gotten out of breath on the stairs.

"I have been holding house for years," Annalise quickly replied, happy to be telling the truth. She'd been managing Thompson Hall since her mother's death. "Hen—my aunt Henny trained me. That's Mrs. Tuthill, in the kitchen," she added. "Her, ah, rheumatics make it too hard for her to manage anything but the cooking."

Blast, the witch was a relative to the Tuthills. That meant he'd have to give up the treasure in the kitchens and that man who was a dab hand with the horses, too, just to be rid of her ugly phiz. It was worth it.

"Have you been here long?' he asked, preparatory to mentioning that he had an old family retainer in mind for the position.

Annalise knew she'd be found out as soon as he made inquiries, so she answered, "Not personally, but the family . . ." She let her words trail off.

Ross knew all about lines of service passing from father to son, mother to daughter. Hell and tarnation. Well, if he had no grounds to dismiss her on issues of loyalty or longevity, he still had the matter of remuneration. He could just refuse to pay.

"The rental agent mentioned nothing about your salary being included in the terms. I am not prepared to—"

"Oh, but we have nothing to do with the land agent. It's more a private arrangement with Lady Rosalind. Here." She whipped a letter out of her pocket, held it under his nose for a moment, then snatched it back. As far as he could tell, Lady Rosalind had abominable handwriting, but her signature was there, all right, under a line that seemed to have read, *Annie* (something), *Always welcome. Stay as long as you want. Fondly.*

"Lady Rosalind took her butler and abigail along with her, of course," Annalise went on, thinking that sounded likely, "but meant for us to stay with the house. She said any gentleman hiring the premises could be expected to honor her commitments."

That tore it. Gard was trapped with the subtle emphasis on *gentleman* and *honor*, the hag's intention, of course. He'd have to keep her on. At least his mistresses wouldn't have any jealous complaints. And she seemed surprisingly well spoken for a servant. See, he congratulated himself, there was something to admire even in the homeliest woman. "Yes, yes, I'll take the house."

"Excellent. Our salaries amount to eighty pounds per annum. Thirty for myself, twenty for each of the Tuthills, ten for Lorna, the maid. That's twenty pounds quarterly, payable in advance. Uniforms not included. Vacations and half days as per custom. Additional wages for extra servants for heavy cleaning or large parties shall be determined later. Housekeeping expenses cannot be estimated until we know the style you wish to maintain. Oh, and we require advance notice for company."

On the other hand, Lord Gardiner told himself, there was nothing whatsoever admirable about an ugly woman with the mind of an accountant and the arrogance of the royal *we*. He swallowed a sharp retort. The demands were not outrageous. Gads, he spent more than eighty pounds on a pair of boots. He simply was not used to dickering prices with servants—that was Foggarty's job, or his man of business's. He had certainly never haggled with a female employee in his life. The women he usually had dealings with were never so vulgar as to mention money at all, merely hinting at a pretty brooch

55

they'd seen or a diamond pendant. That was obviously not suitable in this instance. He nodded curtly.

Annalise released the breath she'd been holding. "Fine. When shall you be bringing Lady Gardiner around to inspect the premises?"

"Lady Gardiner? Mother? Here? When hell freezes over, Mrs. Lee!" Gads, he wondered if the woman was queer in the attic besides being ugly as sin.

"I meant your wife, my lord," she offered hesitantly.

His bark of laughter shook the hairs on her cheek. "I'm glad to see you have a sense of humor, Mrs. Lee. You were bamming me, weren't you?" She was wringing her hands again like something out of *Macbeth*. He laughed again. By all that was holy, the woman was a prude! Here he had the perfect solution, a way to get rid of the cloud and leave the silver lining. "I thought you understood, working for Lady Rosalind and Lord Elphinstone as you did. I shall be bringing lady friends here, daily, nightly, whatever. Of course I'll give notice when possible, as I agreed."

He got no response. Blast, he wished he could see behind those tinted lenses! "And I shall expect you to make my . . . friends welcome. You know, flowers, bonbons, bath salts, the kinds of things women like." Then again, perhaps she didn't know. Damn, she was nodding mutely. The woman was as hard to get rid of as a toothache. So be it.

The earl took out a roll of bills and peeled off a small fortune in pound notes. "Here are your wages, and uniform and household expenses. As you can see, I do not wish to stint on anything. I'll make separate arrangements with Tuthill about acquiring a carriage to leave here, but I wish you to purchase personal items my friends might forget to bring with them, robes, hairbrushes, et cetera. Do you understand?"

The woman was clutching her stomach as if she were about to be sick. Gard refused to feel sorry for her. Be damned if he was going to go shopping for negligees and perfumes when he was paying such a handsome wage. If she wanted the position so badly, she'd just have to earn her keep. "Oh, yes, and fetch me a dressing gown, a banyan or something. Can you do that?"

She grunted her assent, or groaned. He couldn't tell which, but she took the money from his hand. "I'll send over a change of clothes later. It will be a relief to have fresh linens on hand. I do like things clean, Mrs. Lee. That's one of the reasons I decided on this house, your excellent housekeeping. Keep up the high standards and we'll get along just fine." He could swear her lip curled, but he went on anyway. "There's just one thing more, Mrs. Lee, and then I will let you go about your duties. Understand this: you are all sacked if a single word of my involvement here reaches my mother's ears."

If a single word reached past Annalise's lips again, she'd be surprised. She was so shocked, so utterly dumbfounded, she could only nod as the elegant nobleman retrieved his high-crowned beaver hat and gloves from the table in the hall. She only just remembered to curtsy when he left to speak to Rob about a carriage.

"Try to have everything ready in a day or two," he'd said on his way out. "I'll send a message when to expect me."

"He can send his message to hell!" Annalise exclaimed, finally finding her voice twenty minutes later when Rob came back into the kitchen. "I'm sure they are expecting his lordship's arrival daily! Let him just see what kind of welcome they give him!" Not even hot tea and the last of Henny's strawberry tarts could calm Miss Avery's rage. The dastard had eaten all the rest!

Rob straddled one of the kitchen chairs and lit a pipe. "What did you think a fancy young buck like him wanted with such an unfashionable address?"

"I never thought he wanted it to set up a . . . a bordello!"

"Tain't that at all, chickie. Just somewheres cozy for him to be private-like, away from all the rattlin' tongues of Mayfair."

"He talked about bringing friends for cards and such! He'll be throwing orgies next thing you know!"

"Now, what do you know about orgies, huh, chickie? Anyways, the gov told me as I'd be fetchin' young ladies from Drury Lane and such."

"Ladies, hah!"

Rob took a deep pull on his pipe and watched the smoke rings rise. "He don't seem evil to me, just a young buck sowin' his wild oats."

Annalise pounded her fist on the table. "Not in my house, he won't!"

"But it ain't your house, chickie, that's the point."

Henny stopped banging her pots and pans around and took a seat at the table. "But, Robbie, Miss Annalise's reputation! No young lady should even know about such things, much less be living amid such carryings-on! We'll have to leave, that's all."

"Can't do it without makin' people wonder what happened and why. No, no hope for it. 'Sides, it's safer this way. Even if Sir Vernon happens to locate Lady Rosalind's address, there won't be a trace of any Miss Avery, just a swell and his sweeties."

Annalise grimaced, but she knew Rob had the right of it. "I have no reputation left anyway,

Henny, not after running away and spending all those nights on the road. No one would believe I'm innocent of nothing worse than avoiding marriage to a womanizer. Hah! This philanderer is worse. At least Barny kept some loyalty to his Sophy!"

"Maybe we won't have to stay too long," Henny said hopefully. "Just till we get word to your aunt."

"I already sent letters through the foreign office and the embassy. One of them has to reach her. I know she'll come or send for me, and I'm sure Lord Elphinstone can have the guardianship overturned. He has to!"

Henny patted her hand and poured more tea. "He will, dearie, he will."

"And meantime his lordship ain't so bad," Rob commented.

"Rob, he's a libertine!"

"He's generous with his blunt, knows his cattle, and likes Henny's cookin'. That's enough for me. I've worked for worse."

"He's a despicable, lust-ridden whore-monger!" Annalise insisted. "And you don't have to work at all if you don't want to!"

Rob made another smoke ring. "I wouldn't leave you alone here, chickie, even if Henny'd let me. 'Sides, I've a mind to see the fancy lord's fancy pieces."

Both women glared at him.

The next morning Henny was humming while she baked enough strawberry tarts for an army. Rob was whistling when he went off to the livery stable to see about Seraphina and a coach for his lordship. Miss Avery was loudest of all, gnashing her teeth.

"Ain't he the handsomest thing that ever lived?" the maid Lorna rhapsodized, skipping along at Annalise's side as they went to the shops. "He's got the broadest shoulders in all of London, the bluest eyes, and the nicest smile I ever seen."

"The man's a rake!" Annalise stormed back. "An unprincipled, immoral rake."

"Me mum says they're the only sort worth having."

"Hogwash," retorted the ladylike Mrs. Annie Lee. "You'll want a nice, steady fellow when you're old enough, not one with a roving eye."

"Yes'm," the little maid replied doubtfully, ready to agree with her new benefactress. She'd never had so much money to bring her mum at once, with the promise of a new dress and some pretty ribbons for her hair, and good smells coming from the kitchen. If this lady wanted his lordship to be Old Nick himself, Lorna would help look for his horns and tail next time he came.

Lorna had no doubts whatsoever that the housekeeper was a lady, a real lady, no matter what rig she was running. Lorna had watched the sickly looking miss who called for Miss Ros turn into the hideous Mrs. Lee, even helping tear up one of the lady's fine petticoats to making a binding for her chest and a hump for her shoulder with the rest of the muslin. She'd gazed in wonder as the cook mixed up a batch of flour and stuff to make a yellowish powder for her skin and then added a little sugar and water to affix the mole. Whatever hugger-mugger was going on, this was better than the Punch and Judy show at the ice fair. And Lorna was getting paid for being in it! She danced along at Mrs. Lee's side.

"Get ready for his friends, he said," Annalise was muttering. "I'll get ready, all right."

"Ma'am?"

"I don't care what Rob says, I refuse to live in a bawdy house! I'll show that bounder the error of his ways, or die trying!"

"Oh, ma'am, you can't be thinking of worriting his lordship. He'll up and leave!"

"Exactly. If I discourage him enough, he'll get out. We'll find proper renters next time, a family or a pair of retired schoolteachers or something."

"You'll get us fired!" Lorna wailed.

"No, I won't be so obvious."

She did not buy him a hairshirt instead of a dressing gown, for instance; she just bought him a robe at least two sizes bigger than she estimated he needed, and slippers two sizes smaller. She did not purchase dowdy flannel nightgowns for his lightskirts, just lacy ones with about a million tiny buttons. And robes with ostrich boas whose feathers got inhaled up your nose if you wore them. And the heaviest, most cloying perfumes she could find. She bought tooth powder that tasted like garlic, a hand mirror whose slight distortion just happened to add a few pounds to the reflection, a lovely bedside carafe that was sure to drip, and exquisite blown wineglasses that were so fragile, they were bound to break at the first use.

No, she wasn't obvious, but the dastard wasn't going to find Laurel Street any bed of roses, either.

There was no way on earth Annalise Avery was going to let another despicable man and his lascivious ways ruin her life.

Chapter Eight

*W*ednesday night. Almack's. The wages of sin. Gads, he'd promised the dowager he'd escort her a few places, not lay down his life for one minor indiscretion. Yet here he was, martyr to a mother's pique, clad in knee breeches, with his neckcloth starched so stiff and tied so high he'd have a rash under his chin by morning.

If this was the Marriage Mart, he'd do his shopping elsewhere—when the time came, of course. He doubted he'd ever be on the lookout for a silly female who giggled and batted her eyelashes like the one in his arms right now. The chit's only conversation consisted of her clothes. Hell, the widgeon would be a damned sight more attractive without all the ruffles and ribbons. Without any clothes at all, in fact. Firm, high breasts, soft skin . . . my lord Gardiner entertained himself throughout the remainder of the Sir Roger de Coverley picturing his mother's best friend's goddaughter naked.

Lady Jersey babbled in his ear during the waltz,

trying to get up a flirtation. She was a little ripe for his tastes, but then he envisioned himself swimming, sinking, lost in pillows of warm flesh. No bony hips, either.

Miss Kelsall romped energetically through the country dance beside him, but he saw only her enticing derriere jouncing, bouncing, joyously bare.

The stately quadrille brought him statuesque Lady Moira Campbell, aspiring widow of a spendthrift Irish laird. Lord Gardiner hardly noticed the speculative gleam in the widow's hazel eyes, his own blue eyes firmly fixed on her low neckline. It left little to the imagination. His creative mind subtracted the rest.

Another waltz, and his hand was at Miss Compton's tiny waist. Two hands could span it, Gard estimated, two hands that could stroke and caress the Pocket Venus till she reached Olympus.

The boulanger, Miss Beaumont's legs. The lancers, no. He'd embarrass himself on the dance floor with that image. So Ross drifted through the bastion of the upper crust, mentally undressing every doyenne, dasher, and debutante right down to their drawers. He floated toward the refreshments room, picturing them all in their altogethers. Shifts, chemises, petticoats disappeared like magic in his mind's eye. Laces, ribbons, buttons went flying through the assembly rooms. Alabaster flesh came tumbling out of corsets. Acres of velvety skin lay yearning for his touch, posed for his pen and pad, poised for his pleasure.

Lord Gardiner ate three pieces of stale cake with such a wide grin on his face that his mother was picking names for grandchildren. His friends were shaking their heads at the next benedict. Bets were being made on which of the lovelies had caught his interest, since he'd not danced twice with any of his partners. Every one of those partners was sure the earl's glorious smile was just for her. Every one was right.

By the time Countess Stephania was ready to leave, Gard was so randy, he leapt into the family carriage next to her and ordered Ned Coachman to spring the horses. Stopping at Gardiner House only long enough to call out his curricle, he kissed his mother's cheek, told her what a delightful evening he'd had, and that he'd be sure to accompany her next week. Foggarty was waving a vinaigrette under the dowager's nose when Ross hurtled into his curricle. He nearly ran over an urchin, a mongrel, and a streetlamp in his eagerness to get to Laurel Street.

Foresight was everything. That afternoon he'd counted on a night at Almack's being such a bore that he'd deserve a reward. Instead, it was such a . . . stimulating evening, he thanked his lucky stars for Corinne.

He'd thought to share his first night at a new place with an old friend. Not Cholly. He sent an invitation to Corinne Browne, an occasional lover who was rarely too busy to answer an invitation from a warm-blooded, deep-pocketed earl. As soon as her affirmative reply came, Gard sent a messenger to Laurel Street. Tuthill was to pick up Corinne at her rooms, rooms that often smelled of other men's colognes, to the earl's displeasure. Not tonight. Tonight Corinne would be waiting in his own rooms, just for him. Life was sweet.

"Did Miss Browne arrive?" Ross asked the housekeeper, who must have been waiting for his knock, she answered the door so promptly.

"Yes, a few hours ago. She decided to wait upstairs. You said to make your guests welcome, so I offered her some wine. Was that acceptable?"

"Perfect. You are a jewel." He was already on the

stairs. Not even the depressing sight of Mrs. Lee in her yards of black could dampen his enthusiasm.

"Mrs. Tuthill made a supper for you and the young lady," she called after him. "Filet of sole stuffed with mushrooms, duckling in oyster sauce, and a trifle."

"That sounds delightful. Thank Mrs. Tuthill for me." He took another two steps.

"I saw no reason for Aunt Henny to stay up, my lord. I hope I did right?"

"Fine. Whatever. You know best." He started to loosen his neckcloth.

"The supper is keeping warm on the stove. Shall I serve it now?"

"Deuce take it, no! That is, please hold it for later, Mrs. Lee." He took the rest of the stairs two at a time, tearing at his shirt buttons. Gard never even felt the housekeeper's scornful glance. If looks could kill, that one would leave him a soprano.

Only one candle was left burning in the large chamber. By its soft light he could see Corinne's long, dark hair spread out on the pillow. A bottle of wine stood nearly empty on the bedside table. He smiled. The flame in the hearth and the fire in his loins weren't to be the only glows this evening.

"Corinne?" She didn't move. "Corinne, my sweet?"

He leaned over the bed. Her red lips were curved up in a smile, but she was fast asleep. "I hope you're dreaming of me, my pet. I know just how to awaken a sleeping beauty."

Once in the dressing room, the earl couldn't get his clothes off fast enough. He didn't bother lighting another candle; the fireplace from the bed chamber offered enough light for him to find a maroon velvet robe carefully draped over the back of a chair. Its satin lining next to his skin heightened sensations already at fever pitch. So what if he had to roll the sleeves back a bit? The velvet in his fingers made his toes quiver. He quickly slipped his feet into the matching slippers. And winced. Ah, well, he'd go barefoot. The rug was thick, the rooms were warm. . . .

"Blast!" He immediately tripped over the hem of the robe, stubbing his toes and slamming his shoulder into the edge of the dressing table. By George, he thought, rubbing the painful joint, it would take a giant to fill this robe. He was right: Mrs. Lee knew nothing about men. Luckily, Corinne did.

"Corinne?" he called softly. Then he pulled back the bedcovers and discovered Corinne's ample charms laid out for him in a nearly transparent gown. He forgot all about housekeepers and hurt shoulders. Something was aching, and it wasn't his toes. He climbed into the bed next to her and kissed her awake.

"Huh?"

"Corinne darling, it's Gard. Wake up."

Corinne rolled away from his seeking mouth, whacking him on the chin with a limp hand as she turned. This was not quite the reception he had in mind. He put his hand on her nearly bare back, and the girl made a soft, moaning sound. That was more like it.

He trailed kisses where his hand had been, and she moaned again, louder. This time she followed the sound with a disgruntled "Oh, go away."

"Corinne?"

She pulled a pillow over her head. "I said go away. I have a headache."

A headache? He thought only wives got headaches.

Perhaps she'd feel better after a nap, he reasoned, deciding he may as well assuage another hunger while he waited. Gard vaguely recalled eating a few pieces of stale cake in King Street. He only hoped Mrs. Tuthill's cooking was as good as he'd imagined; Lud knew he deserved that something should be this night.

He considered changing back to his clothes to face Mrs. Lee downstairs but, dash it, this was his house. If she was offended by his immodesty, she could leave. Then again, no one told the old besom to wait up; she was most likely contentedly asleep on her cold, narrow pallet. Good. He was certainly capable of serving himself. If he didn't trip over the damn fool robe on his way down the steps.

He was holding up the hem like a belle making her come-out, feeling a total nodcock even before he caught sight of the housekeeper sitting by a candle in the hall. She adjusted her spectacles and put the book she was reading in a pocket before he could catch the title. Sermons, no doubt.

"You needed something, my lord?"

The blasted woman was staring at his bare feet. He released the fabric in his hand. "Miss Browne isn't feeling quite the thing."

"I am sorry, my lord. Shall I send Uncle Rob for a physician?"

"No, no, I doubt that will be necessary. She says it's just a headache."

Annalise nodded. "Perhaps she had a bit too much to drink." Then again, Annalise thought, perhaps Miss Browne had just enough laudanum. She couldn't help the tiniest of smiles from escaping. "I noticed the bottle was half empty when I checked the fire. Perhaps I should have removed it. I am sorry."

Deuce take it, the crone didn't look sorry. She looked like a cat in the cream pot. He cleared his throat. "Yes, well, I thought I'd try a bit of Mrs. Tuthill's cooking. No, you needn't fix a tray or anything, I'll eat in the kitchen."

Lord Gardiner took a step in that direction and tripped over the robe again. This time he caught himself on the hall table, merely tipping a vase of flowers which splashed cold water on his feet. Annalise continued on her way to the kitchen, pretending not to see. "Damnation!" he cursed, which she pretended not to hear. "Do you sew?"

"Of course, my lord. All housekeepers sew."

"Do you think you might hem this up for me? I'm afraid I'm not the man you thought I was," he said, trying to make a joke of it while she laid out a place setting for him at the heavy oak table.

Or perhaps you're not the man you thought you were, Annalise silently commented, wondering whether he'd have an apoplexy if a pin should accidentally be left in the sewing.

There was that smirk again, Gard noted. The witch was laughing at him, he knew it! Well, he'd have a bit of fun himself.

"I was wondering about your name, Mrs. Lee. I cannot help noticing that you wear no ring. Is the honorific merely because it is customary for your position?"

Some of the wine she was pouring spilled over the edge of the cup. Now *he* was smiling, which made the already frazzled Annalise forget her role even further. Here was this half-naked man, dark hairs showing all over his chest where the robe lay open, who had just left his doxie upstairs, making sport of her, Annalise Avery! "That's none of your blasted business. My lord," she added belatedly.

That wiped the smile off his face in a hurry. *No one* addressed the Earl of Gardiner in such insolent tones, especially not some hatchet-faced harridan who seemed to delight in his discomfiture. "Who the bloody hell do you think you are?" he bellowed. "I pay the—"

"I apologize, my lord," Annalise hastily interrupted before he could waken Henny. The fat would really be in the fire then, her old nanny seeing her charge alone with a belligerent, bare-chested man. She'd most likely reveal it all, landing them in the basket for sure. "I . . . I forgot my place, Lord Gardiner. Of course you have a right to know something about your employees. I am afraid I'm just . . . sensitive about my ring," she told him, improvising madly. "You see, after my husband fell at Corunna, I gave my ring to buy medicine for the wounded soldiers. I . . . I prayed that someone did the same for my Jamie."

Her thin, work-worn hands trembled, and she brought her apron up to cover her tears. My God, what had he done? Ross thought in dismay. He stumbled to his feet. "Don't give it another thought, Mrs. Lee. Please accept my apologies. I never wished to bring back unhappy memories, I swear. I, ah, I'll be going now," he decided, his appetite having disappeared altogether. He grabbed up a handful of the robe, inadvertently revealing muscular calves in his hurry to be gone.

Annalise only peeked a little, sobbing even louder into her apron.

Upstairs, his lordship quickly changed his clothes after checking on the still-sleeping Corinne. He left her a handsome *douceur*, for her time if nothing else, hoping she wouldn't spend it on Blue Ruin. The ring he'd intended giving her, a pretty pearl and sapphire affair, he left in the pocket of the maroon robe. The blasted thing only reminded him of poor Annie Lee and her lost ring, and the misery he just caused her. Fiend seize all women and their megrims!

Downstairs, Annalise was helping herself to his lordship's supper, falling to with the best appetite she'd had in weeks. At this rate, she'd have her weight back in no time. At this rate, she'd have that scoundrel out of her life even sooner.

Chapter Nine

"You're mighty chipper this mornin', chickie."

"Hmm," Annalise answered, peering in the corners of the stable behind the town house, where Rob was lovingly currying the horses he'd selected for Lord Gardiner's new landau. The coach was comfortable but undistinguished, just the way the earl wanted it, and the grays weren't flashy, either, just the way Rob wanted them. He'd picked the geldings more for strength and stamina, just in case he and Henny and Missy had to show London their heels in a hurry. It didn't appear that Miss Annalise, Annie as he'd better remember, was worried.

"Get a good night's rest?"

"The best in ages."

Rob figured he'd give his eyeteeth to know what went on after he went to bed last night. The dollymop he drove home this morning had hardly enough energy to make it up her stairs. Seemed happy though, and gave him a tip. Now, here was their Annie looking merry as a grig. It didn't figure after the fuss she'd made yesterday. "Guess you've got it all straight in your head now about Lord Gardiner and his bits o' fluff, eh?"

"You might say I am resolved."

"That's all right, then," Rob said, returning his attention to the horses. But Annalise was shifting bales of hay. "Did you want something there, chickie?"

As nonchalantly as possible, she answered, "Oh, no, I'm just trying to catch mice. You wouldn't want any in here with these beauties, would you?" She came over and stroked one velvety nose.

Rob looked across the gray's broad back and saw that she had an old cheese box in one hand and a broom by her side. He shrugged. Never could figure women. "Got a message from the gov'nor this mornin'. Company again tonight."

"The same woman?" she asked sharply. The horse stamped its feet. "Sorry, boy. Corinne again?"

Rob shook his head. "No, this one lives at St. James's Street. He says to ask for Catherine."

"But St. James's is where all the men's clubs are. Ladies cannot even walk there!"

"Didn't suppose she was no lady."

"And I didn't suppose she was a . . . a dealer or something from a gambling den. Actresses and dancers are bad enough."

He spit a stream of tobacco juice out the door. "Could be worse. Lot of high-priced fancy houses are set up near where the gents are like to be."

The cheese box hit the floor. "F-fancy houses? You mean . . . ?"

"Ain't for me to say." He looked closely at her, close enough to see that red was creeping into her cheeks, even under the yellowish powder she wore on top of her own still-sickly color. "And ain't for you to say, neither!"

"I do not intend to speak one word to that reprobate who calls himself a gentleman," she snapped back, snatching up her broom and the empty crate. "I intend to find me a mouse. No, a rat. The bigger the better."

Rob could only scratch his head at that. "I know Henny ain't goin' to let you serve up any rodents on the earl's dish, so I don't need to know nothin' more. 'Sides, I misdoubt you'll find any vermin here. I got me a ratter." He whistled, and a small dog trotted into the stable.

Annalise took off her dark glasses and inspected the ragged little mongrel, who was busy scratching its ear. "That? It looks more like an overgrown rat than anything. No, it looks just like a fur muff I once had that the moths got into."

"Genuine Clyde terrier he is, from Scotland. Guaranteed to catch mice."

"Catch fleas more like." She laughed as the dog performed acrobatics to get at an itch near its tail. "Wherever did you find it?"

Rob gave the horse's rump a pat. "I didn't need to go lookin' for him, I swear. Poor tyke must of been livin' off the rats here after Lady Ros cleared out. He ain't skin and bones, but he was happy enough for a biscuit and gravy. I mean to give him a bath this afternoon when I wash the carriage. Get rid of some of his stowaways, then I figure Henny won't mind him in the kitchen."

Gold flecks sparkled in Annalise's eyes behind the spectacles as she watched the mongrel scratch some more. "You're so busy, Rob, why don't I give the dog his bath?"

"You're sure you don't mind?"

"Absolutely positive. Come on, Clyde."

Clyde had the most thorough scrubbing of his short life—after he'd been fed and put to rest for the afternoon in the Earl of Gardiner's bed.

* * *

Catherine was too totty-headed to be a dealer; she said she couldn't deal *vingt et un* because she didn't know French. She was more a decoration at Fremont's gaming parlor, sometimes a distraction for the less reputable doings at the tables. Sometimes she wasn't even at the tables, taking certain high rollers upstairs for private games. Fremont didn't mind. Why should he? He got a portion of everything that went on under his roof. He got an even larger fee, in advance, when Kitty prowled under someone else's roof. She was good for business, he insisted, explaining the exorbitant price.

Her name was Catherine but they called her Kitty for her playful ways. She was small and sweet and silly, a fluffy armful with big brown eyes in a heart-shaped face. She was just what the earl needed after a musicale at Marlborough House where all the guests were as solemn as creditors at a poor man's funeral.

He'd gone to Fremont's after the debacle with Corinne. White's was too sedate for his mood; unfortunately Gentleman Jackson's was closed. Instead of getting thoroughly disguised, which was his intention, the earl became enamored of little Kitty as she stood on tiptoe to whisper in his ear, rubbing against him.

He could have had her then and there—heaven knew he was ready—but Corinne was sleeping off her drunk in Laurel Street, and the idea of trailing a strumpet up the stairs in full view of a roomful of hardened gamblers no longer appealed to him. They'd be taking bets on how soon he returned, he knew. He'd have done the same a fortnight ago. Gard supposed his mother's stay in town must be having some effect after all. Tomorrow, then.

"The wait only makes things more enticing, eh, *chérie*?"

"Oh, you wanted *sherry*. I thought you wanted an hour with me." She stuck her lower lip out in an adorable pout.

An hour wasn't going to be enough. He wanted Kitty purring the whole night, no matter Fremont's fee.

Lady Gardiner decided to leave the entertainment at the intermission, Handel be praised, so her son was able to dash across town earlier than he thought. He reached Laurel Street before Kitty and scurried around, getting ready. First he happily dismissed Mrs. Lee for the evening. The woman made him so uncomfortable, he was glad to see the last of her, even if he did have to open every cabinet door in the kitchen to find fresh wine goblets. The first two broke off in his hand, spilling wine on the lace cuffs of his dress shirt. He shrugged and drank a glass of the excellent vintage to steady his nerves. He wasn't any young sprig taking a lass out behind the barn for the first time. There was no hurry.

He still bounded up the stairs to snuff out candles and turn down the bed. Putting on his robe, he was pleased to note that it was neatly hemmed and the ring was still in the pocket. The ring was for Kitty if she pleased him, since Fremont was most likely keeping the lion's share of the night's fee.

Then he scampered back down the stairs, getting stabbed in the back of his calf only once by an overlooked pin. Well, the woman did have such terrible eyesight, it was a wonder she could sew the thing at all. He had another glass of wine. It wouldn't do to leave too much in the bottle for Kitty, not after his experience with Corinne.

At first Kitty was disappointed in the house. "I thought an earl's would be bigger." Then she giggled as Lord Gardiner chased her all the way upstairs, the belt to his robe in her hand. "I was right."

He grabbed for her right there by the hearth—the rug was soft enough; the wooden floor of the hall landing was soft enough, by George—but she danced away.

"The wait only makes things more exciting, eh, brandy," she laughingly echoed his words, pirouetting out of reach. Then she proceeded to show him how exciting the wait could be. First she kicked off one shoe, raising her hem to show nicely turned ankles, then the other. The watered-silk gown was shortly in a puddle at her feet. Gard felt he'd join it soon, so slowly and sinuously did she move, like a cat stretching. He groaned.

She tossed her petticoat over his head, after spending at least an eternity untying the tapes. He dragged the soft muslin down, then clutched it to him, as much to cover his excitement as to uncover his eyes, lest he miss an instant of her performance or an inch of her rosy skin. Kitty wore no corset—her sweet young body required none—so only her lace-edged chemise covered her from swelling breast to dimpled knee. She reached for the ribbons, winked at him, then lifted the chemise to untie one of her garters.

"No!" he growled, so she smiled and went back to the ribbons on her shift. What a painting she would make, he thought an instant later when he could breathe again, bare skin reflecting the fire's glow, the pink frills on her garters the only prop she needed. No, what a lover she would make, his body insisted, refusing to wait an instant longer. Those silly garters and silk stockings could stay on till the cows came home, for all he cared.

Ross scooped her up and tumbled her to the bed, where she still played the coquette, tickling and teasing, nibbling and nipping. Her hands were everywhere, her mouth was everywhere, his wits had gone begging ages ago. Finally he pulled her down

76

on top of him for a deep, deep kiss. Still she made tiny pinches up and down his legs, little bites on his buttocks. Only her lips were clinging to his lips and her hands were stroking his—

"Yeow!" Ross shouted, throwing Kitty off him, jumping up and beating at the bed. "I'll kill her," he raged, flailing at a pillow so hard it ripped, turning the room white with feathers, where it wasn't already blue with his cursing. "I'll tear every hair out of her head for this, I swear."

Now, Kitty might have more hair than wit, but even she was instantly able to ascertain that his lordship was no longer interested in her services. As a matter of fact, where certain parts of him were swelling up like sausages with angry welts all over, other parts of him were trying to disappear altogether. That seemed smartest to Kitty, too, who scrambled into her clothes and fled outside to call a hackney while his lordship was still calling for his housekeeper's blood.

Chapter Ten

*G*ard couldn't find the blasted belt to his robe. *It would serve that beldam right if I go downstairs like this,* he raged. Then he tugged the bellpull so hard, it ripped right off the wall. He tied *that* around his waist and stomped down the stairs, still bellowing with fury.

"You rang, my lord?"

There she was, waiting at the foot of the stairs, still dressed although he distinctly recalled dismissing her for the evening. Still wearing that shapeless black sack and hideous cap, that same infuriating smirk, Mrs. Lee was his own personal Fury, Erinys come to torment him for his sins. He hadn't done anything terrible enough to deserve her—yet.

"No, I didn't ring, blast you. I didn't call and I didn't send a message!"

"No, my lord, you shouted." Now, Annalise had never seen a man so enraged in her entire life. Sir Vernon had been cool and restrained in his anger, not like this inferno of ire. Could he get violent? Employers beat servants all the time, according to Lorna. Annalise took a step back. But no, she told herself, she was made of sterner stuff. She wasn't about to let any great, roaring bear of a man intimidate her. She'd faced her first naked chest the evening before and survived; she was not about to be sent scurrying off to her room by a wrathful earl, especially not over a few pawky flea bites. Even if half of his body was uncovered again.

Annalise was too tired for all this nonsense anyway. She refused to go to bed with all the muck on her face, and feared to remove it until his lordship left the house. With just cause, as events proved. The sooner he got it all off his chest—and some proper clothes on his chest—the sooner Miss Avery could find her own rest. She kept her eyes lowered, but she did step closer to the earl to inquire, "Was there something you wanted?"

"Yes, Mrs. Lee, there was something I wanted!" The framed prints in the hallway vibrated from the force of his shout. "I wanted to wring your scrawny neck! I *wanted* a clean house! Just look at this!" And he made to whip aside his dressing gown.

Annalise shrieked and threw her hands over her glasses.

"For the love of—I am not quite that depraved, Mrs. Lee." But he was red-faced all the same. "Take your hands down and look at my legs. No, I wouldn't want to offend you. Look at the welts instead. Do you know how they got there—and everywhere else? Bedbugs, that's how! After I particularly told you to make sure the house was immaculate. You are relieved of your position, Mrs. Lee, and I don't care how many appeals to my honor you make."

Annalise had nothing left to lose except her temper and her pride. She raised her chin in the air.

"Honor? You talk about honor? Then look a little further before you place all the blame, my high and mighty lordship. You said yourself you rented this house because the premises were spotless. Well, they were before you started bringing your straw damsels here. You want to know how those bedbugs got in your bed? I'll tell you: You lie down with dogs, you wake up with fleas!"

"What the devil is that supposed to mean?"

"It means that it took me hours to scrub the face paint off the sheets after Miss Browne, and now this! It means that if you bring home girls of the night, you have to be prepared to pay the consequences. Be thankful it was parasites and not the pox!"

Annalise clapped her hand over her mouth, shocked at the words that had spewed forth. The earl never noticed her action, being too outraged to see anything beyond his own shaking fist. He'd never in his life struck a woman; there was a first time for everything.

"How dare you!" he thundered instead. "Not even my mother would dare to speak to me like that!"

"Perhaps she should have!"

"You are an insolent old bat!"

"You are a licentious, loud-mouthed fribble."

And they continued to stand in the dimly lighted hall, glaring at each other, until Lord Gardiner felt an unavoidable urge to scratch his nether regions. He couldn't, not in front of this green-glassed she-dragon. A gentleman could curse and carry on in a female's presence under certain circumstances, but some things were simply beyond the pale. The housekeeper crossed her bony arms over her flat chest, almost challenging him. So he did it, he scratched his arse, right there in front of her. Then he was ashamed when he heard her gasp at this ultimate insult.

"Told you I had sensitive skin," he muttered, looking away and so missing the smile Annalise couldn't hide.

"Oh, stop whining about it like a sulky child," she told him, almost feeling sorry for what she'd done. "I'm sure Henny has something in her kitchen for the itching, or else I can mix something up from Grandmother's book of receipts."

He grunted something that may have been a thank-you.

She didn't wait for him to follow. That way he couldn't see the grin on her face; she didn't feel quite so bad, now.

Gard sat down in one of the kitchen chairs, and immediately jumped up again, squealing like a stuck pig. Or peer. He pulled a needle out of the back of his robe.

"Oh, is that where I left the silly thing? I searched high and low for it, too. Thank you," Annalise said sweetly, putting a pot of water on to boil before returning to her search through Henny's medicine shelf. "I'll have to consult Grandmother's book. She kept an excellent stillroom, so we can only hope Henny—Aunt Henny—stocks the right ingredients. Tea will be ready in a minute."

"Wine," he grunted, scratching his leg.

"I'm afraid alcohol will only heat your blood, making you itch more. How about some lemonade? And don't scratch, that makes it worse, too."

What was it they used to do with witches, Gard wondered, burn them at the stake? That was too good for Mrs. Lee. Here he was, in the middle of the night, in his charming little love-lodge, swollen and spotty and being lectured at by a shriveled old prune. He leaned back in the chair and closed his eyes, defeated and disheartened. And despising Mrs. Lee the more for seeing him thus.

Still, the lemonade did cool a throat parched by

shouting, and the damp cloth she placed on his forehead while she mixed her potion was refreshing.
Maybe a heart did beat in her narrow chest after
all.

"I think you are supposed to bathe in the stuff,
but we don't have enough of some of the wild things,
like dock, so I'll just spread some on, like this."

"Like this" was burning hot. His lordship yowled
and jerked his foot away.

"I thought men were supposed to have a code
about stoicism, stiff upper lip and all that. Why,
you're worse than a colicky infant."

So the earl sat there, suffering as silently as he
could, while his housekeeper tortured his already
agonized limbs. He muttered almost to himself: "I
bet Mr. Lee threw himself in front of the French
cannons on purpose."

"You leave Jake out of this," she said, applying
a measure of the hot salve with unnecessary vigor.

"I thought his name was Jamie."

"It was. James Jacob Lee." She kept spreading
the stuff on his feet and ankles.

"He must have been a rake of the first order."

"That's a shameful thing to say, my lord. Why
ever would you think a thing like that? Don't you
believe any man can be constant? Or do you just
doubt that any man could be faithful to me?"

"You're putting words in my mouth. I just
thought he must have been a womanizer, to have
you so set against the breed. You obviously do not
approve of me or my life-style."

"That's not for me to say, my lord."

"And that hasn't stopped you before. What, did
you suddenly remember your place? I'm asking you,
Mrs. Lee, as your employer, why are you so bitterly
resentful of a man having a bit of fun?"

"I am not in your employ any longer, my lord.
You dismissed me, remember?"

Gard remembered. But that stuff she was spreading on his legs was working on the itch, after the initial sting, and Mrs. Lee apparently had a gentle touch when she wished. Besides, he noted as he watched her work, the housekeeper's wrists were perhaps the thinnest he had ever seen on a woman not begging in the streets. If she lost this position, no one would hire the harridan, and then what would become of her? The earl did not want her wasting away on his conscience. "Perhaps I was a bit hasty. I'll reconsider, if you swear to rid that room of its wildlife. And if you answer my questions."

Annalise nodded. "Very well, I shall fumigate the bed chamber, and no, I do not approve of your ways."

"You do not believe in innocent fun?"

"Innocent fun is sleigh-riding and picniking, not your hellraking. My lord."

"Come now, hellraking? I don't go around raping innocent women and ravishing the countryside. My, ah, companions are all willing, nay, happy to spend time with me."

"So happy that Kitty flew out of here as if she'd been scalded, and Corinne had to drink herself into oblivion before facing you?" Annalise got up to mix a fresh batch of the ointment.

"Those were two instances out of many." He spoke angrily, to her back.

"Many. Exactly. You make a travesty out of what should be a sacred act of marriage. You have no faithfulness, no loyalty, no real love."

"Lud, how did a moralist like you ever get on with Lord Elphinstone?"

"I, ah, had few dealings with his lordship, but Lady Ros always spoke highly of him. Trust and respect, that's what they share. And friendship, of course."

"Friendship? You cannot be bacon-brained enough

to think that's all Lady Ros and Elphinstone share!"

Annalise had nearly convinced herself such was the case. She absentmindedly dabbed at the earl's knees with the freshly heated salve as she explained: "Lady Rosalind lost her heart many years ago in a tragic romance. She remains true to her first, dead love. That's why she and Lord Elphinstone could never marry."

"You've been reading too many novels, woman," he said through gritted teeth. "That's a touching story. Perhaps you should tell it to Elphinstone's wife."

"Wife?" Annalise let the cloth she was using fall into the bowl. That explained a lot. Poor Aunt Ros was being exploited by another no-account libertine, just like the one grinning at her discomfiture now. Annalise thrust the bowl into his hands. "You can finish the rest yourself."

He kept grinning. "I was wondering when you'd reach that point. Do you think you could force yourself to put some of that stuff on my back, though, where I cannot reach?"

Annalise could not refuse such a reasonable request. She took the bowl while he turned around, straddling the chair, and shrugged the robe down over his shoulders. Annalise tried not to think of those broad shoulders or wavy muscles. "Lady Ros is no trollop!" she stated instead.

"I never said she was. I never heard a rumor of her going with another man, Annie."

Miss Avery stiffened, there behind his back. First he was half naked, now he was getting familiar. In her most haughty, lady-of-the-manor voice she declared, "I did not give you permission to use my given name."

He laughed. "I don't need your permission,

ma'am, now that you're back on my payroll. Lud, you're not like any servant I ever knew."

And the situation was like no other he'd been in since he was five and some nursemaid or other had pulled nettles out of his hide. She'd put on the same smelly concoction, too, most likely. She never aggravated him or taunted him or made him feel like the lowest kind of reptile. He could feel the housekeeper's antipathy through the slaps on his back. "By George, I'm only being friendly. You'd think I was asking for droit du seigneur or something."

"I am finished, my lord," she said, slamming the bowl down on the table. "And of course you can call me what you will, my lord. As you said, I work for you. However, I do not wish your glib friendship. Save your honeyed words for the women who accept money to listen to them, *my lord*."

Gard turned around in the chair again and began to daub at the welts on his chest. "Don't be so quick to condemn those women and the men who support them. You have an honest job now, but where would you be if you had no position and no family to help you?"

"I'd find some way other than selling my body!"

"You'd have to," he said without even looking up to see the rigidity in his housekeeper's stance.

"If men would keep their minds more on their business and less on their pleasures," she snarled at him and his bare chest, "they'd be better able to provide for their daughters." Affront was interfering with Annalise's breathing, that and knowing the robe was draped just across his hips and thighs. She took a deep breath. "For men to use women so is deplorable. There is no excuse for lives based on satisfying lower appetites, lives ruled by vulgar passions." She gasped as his hand moved beneath the robe's covering. "And don't think you can force your unbridled lust on me!"

85

Lord Gardiner laughed till tears came to his eyes. "You can rest assured, Annie Lee, that is the last thing in the world I'd ever do!"

Chapter Eleven

*H*is lordship went to Suffolk to nurse his wounds while the Laurel Street lodgings were being de-infested. "Estate business," he claimed to Lady Stephania, making his excuses to visit a place where he could wear loose clothing.

"But Lady Martindale and her daughters are coming for dinner Tuesday next, and we are promised to the Ashford-Farquahars' come-out ball on Friday. Twins, you know. Both well favored and fabulously wealthy. And that Irish widow, Lady Campbell, called again this afternoon. She said she wanted your advice about buying a carriage. Encroaching female, coming to tea as if she were one of my boon companions, but you did make an offer to help, it seems. What shall I tell them?" Her cane rapped the floor, fractions of an inch away from his toes. "What shall I tell your father when he wakes me in the middle of the night to ask why you are not paying court to any of the reigning Toasts?"

"You may tell Lady Martindale and her fubsyfaced daughters to go hang. And that goes double for the Ashford-Farquahar twins. You may tell Lady Campbell that I shall call as soon as I return, although a visit to Tattersall's is not quite what I offered. And you may respectfully tell my father not to worry about finding his ice skates. Hell will freeze over before I dance attendance on one of the spoiled society darlings you keep tossing at my head."

"But you gave your word to look around for a countess!"

"I gave my word to show more responsible interest in the earldom, my lady. That's what you wanted, and that's what I shall be doing in Suffolk."

This time the cane caught him firmly in the ankle. "I meant in providing it with heirs, you lobcock, not giving the estate managers advice they neither want nor need!"

Miss Avery, meanwhile, was stalking rats. She'd burned pastilles in the master bedroom, boiled all the linen, beat all the rugs, changed the mattress. Now she and Clyde were on the hunt.

Mangy rats, she sought. Plague-carrying rats. Red-eyed, yellow-toothed rats as nasty as the vermin who had the nerve to laugh at her. There she'd been feeling sorry for the cad, all lumpy and swollen. Then he'd called her Annie. What was she supposed to call him? Gard, as his friends did, according to Lorna? He was so arrogant, so self-assured, he most likely preferred to be called God. Heaven knew he had the same morals as those old Greek basket-scramblers. He even looked like a god with his dark curls and ripply muscles and finely detailed features, flea bites notwithstanding. Still, he was a rodent.

"Whyn't you just put down some poison, chickie,

if you're so worried about pests gettin' into the house? Get rid of the problem onct and for all."

So she consulted Grandmother's stillroom book, took her market basket, and stomped off to the apothecary. When he read her list, the assistant there gave her an odd look, undecided whether to call for the manager or the constable. Annalise glanced over both shoulders, the high one and the low one, to make sure no one overheard, then whispered, "Mistress runs a school for wayward boys. Springtime, don't you know."

The assistant put the powders and salts in a sack. "This should take care of the problem for her."

Her house in order, or soon to be, Miss Avery went riding in the park. Smuggling Napoleon out of Elba had to be less complicated.

At seven o'clock in the morning, Rob walked Annalise the three blocks to the Holborn road. No one in the neighborhood who was awake at the time saw anything unusual about the new servants from Number Eleven setting out on their errands. They were used to Tuthill the stableman and his widowed niece who kept house because she was too ugly to get lucky twice.

The pair was met at the Holborn road by a hackney carriage, a former associate of Rob's at the ribbons. The housekeeper entered the coach, a black cloak covering her from collar to toes, a black coal-scuttle bonnet concealing most of the rest of her.

When the carriage pulled up at a livery stable behind Cavendish Square, an establishment also owned by a friend of Rob's in his earlier days, an elegant young woman stepped out. There was no question that this was a lady, not with her noble bearing and obviously expensive green velvet riding habit in the latest military style, which she filled to admiration since the habit's alterations.

She wore a veil over her face, attached to a shallow-crowned beaver hat with green feathers at the side; only the tiniest hint of silver-blond curls peeked out beneath the brim. Just in case there was any doubt of the Fair Incognita's status, the biggest, brawniest groom in the stable bowed low, assisted the lady onto the back of her prancing mare, and followed her down to Oxford Street and hence to Hyde Park. The fraternity of the road was a loyal bunch, or Rob would never have let Annalise out of his sight.

Miss Avery had a glorious ride, feeling freer than she had in ages. It was almost as if she could outride her problems, just gallop away on Seraphina and leave all of the distress and uncertainty behind. Nothing could destroy her sense of release this morning, not even the gentlemen just returning home from an evening's carousal who were stopped dead in their wobbly tracks by the vision of a goddess flying past on her Arabian mare. They may have been tempted to try to stop her, to talk to her, but the fellow riding behind on a rangy bay looked like he'd be more at home on a gibbet than on a jaunt in the park. If Clarence's scarred face and thick arms were not discouragement enough, the pistol tucked in his waistband was. The wastrels doffed their hats and reverently watched her ride away.

One fellow was not so polite, or so wise. A sporting mad young buck out exercising his stallion decided to make a race of it with the veiled equestrienne. He tried to pull ahead on his barely controlled mount so he could cut her off and force her to a halt and an introduction before any of the other early morning riders got to her. Ignoring the warning from the lady's groom, he made a grab for her reins, shouting suggestive offers at the same time.

Annalise could not have been more disgusted if

one of the park pigeons had left its calling card on her shoulder. She reached over and brought her riding crop down on the scoundrel's gloved hand, then, when he pulled back, down on his horse's flank. At the same time a pistol shot rang out. The unruly stallion snorted, lifted all four feet off the ground, did an about-face, and departed a few days early for the Newmarket meets. His rider didn't make it as far as the park gate. He stood, rubbing the part of him that had landed hardest and contemplating the bullet hole in his hat. He made one last try as Annalise rode past: "You could kiss it and make it better, sweetheart!"

At least no one could see the scarlet color creeping into her cheeks. Her pleasure in the day had been stolen by the insufferable coxcomb, however, another male with as much control of his passions as over his horse. Men! Faugh!

She returned home by Rob's prescribed circuitous routes, confirmed in the righteousness of her plans.

The earl's problem was not getting Lady Moira Campbell alone; it was putting the fiery redhead off long enough to send a message to Laurel Street to make sure the place was ready.

"I don't think this afternoon is the proper time to discuss your new carriage, my lady. My mother frowns on discussions of horseflesh over tea. Why don't we wait for after Mrs. Hamilton's card party tomorrow evening? That should break up early, so we'll have ample time to make sure I know what you want."

"I like my horses big and dark and not too tame," the lady murmured. The dark-haired earl stirred his tea with added vigor. "Strong ones that can run all night."

Lord Gardiner blotted at the tea on his fawn

inexpressibles. "I'm certain we can find just what you're looking for."

Lady Moira was statuesque, Junoesque, Reubenesque—one escargot away from plump. She was also one escapade away from being cut from polite society and even closer to drowning in River Tick. She couldn't afford a coach and four. She couldn't afford a bag of oats. And she definitely couldn't afford to let Ross Montclaire, Lord Gardiner, slip through her fleshy fingers. The earl was said to be on the lookout for a bride. With his reputation, no milk-and-water miss would suit him, not like a mature woman who could match his passion, yet still bear him sons. Stranger things had happened than a well-breeched young nobleman falling for a well-formed young widow's lush charms. He might just succumb. If not, he was known to be generous to his ladyloves. She might stave off her creditors a bit longer; she might even put off forever her acceptance of that rich old satyr with damp lips and clammy hands. She much preferred a lusty young centaur with deep pockets. Oh, yes, Moira Campbell was eager to please his lordship.

"Good evening, my lord, my lady." The earl's message to the house had stated very clearly that he was bringing a lady; Annalise was not impressed that he was associating with a higher class of doxie, although she did wonder if his choice reflected their last conversation.

The housekeeper curtsied deferentially as she took the woman's wrap. This blowzy female may be a lady, but she was certainly no better than she ought to be, with her black crepe gown cut down to there. The widow's vibrant coloring looked spectacular in black, Annalise thought sourly, looking at her own hanging black bombazine with disgust. She might look like the hag she meant to imitate, but

92

at least she was decently covered. "You must be chilled, my lady, it's such a damp, cold night. There's a nice fire in the small parlor. And, my lord, I think I made a good find in some excellent Burgundy. I'll need your opinion, of course, before purchasing the case. If you'll come this way?"

The parlor was snug; the Burgundy was superb. The earl had two glasses finished and half Lady Campbell's buttons undone when he heard a scratching at the door.

"Yes? What is it, Mrs. Lee?"

"I'm sorry, Lord Gardiner," she said from the doorway, her eyes carefully averted, "but Robbie thinks there might be a swelling in one of the horses' forelegs."

"Blast!" But he went to check his precious cattle.

"Would you care to wait upstairs, my lady? Perhaps you'd enjoy a relaxing bath while his lordship is busy with the horses? These things can take awhile, as I am sure you know. I can have hot water upstairs before you can say Jack Rabbit."

When Gard came back, complaining that he found no swelling and no stableman, either, Annalise was quick to tell him that Rob must have gone to the livery stable to fetch ingredients for a poultice. "You know he would not take a chance with the horses. Oh, and Lady Campbell is having a bath."

She only raised her pointed chin a little, as if to say this was part of her tidy housekeeping. He nodded curtly and went to stand by the fire, cold again. He welcomed the glass of wine Annie put in his hand.

Annalise ran upstairs to help Lady Campbell with her bath, downstairs to tell the earl just a few minutes more and pour him another glass of Burgundy. Upstairs, downstairs. "Will that be all, my lord?"

"Yes, thank God. Ah, thank you, Annie. I'll see to the lady now."

Annalise's lip curled. He'd see her, all right. The trull was lazing in the tub surrounded by bubbles, waiting for Lord Gardiner to watch her leave the water, like Venus rising from the sea. Or a fat pink sow shaking off a puddle. Annalise went back to her own rooms. Gard flew up the stairs.

Now, there was a sight that could warm any man's blood. Except that Ross was still a trifle chilled. He held the towel and Moira flowed into it, not so quickly that he couldn't see she was a natural redhead after all, disproving his doubts. But that rosy skin, that fiery triangle. Ah, the heat rose in his face, at least.

"Come to bed, my centaur," she urged, unbuttoning his marcella waistcoat, letting the towel fall to the floor between them. Soon his shirt followed. "Hurry, my charger, I want to ride." And his dove-gray pantaloons. "I want to gallop with the wind, my noble mount, my stallion." Finally his small-clothes. My gelding?

Moira shrugged. The earl took another drink from the bottle he'd carried upstairs. "Just a little cold," he apologized.

"I'll warm you soon enough," she said, getting into the bed and holding out her arms.

'Faith, she was inviting. Not just a tasty morsel, she was a whole feast, laid out just for him. Why was his appetite not rising to the occasion? Because instead of her lush charms he saw his blasted housekeeper's sidewalk-straight chest. Instead of flowing auburn locks he saw an awful, dingy cap. And instead of Moira's full red lips he saw Annie's pursed-up, pinched-together mouth, frowning in disapproval. Or worse, smirking in secret enjoyment. Let the old stick enjoy this, he thought, throwing himself into Moira's eager embrace, returning kiss for kiss, caress for caress.

Soon they were both damp and breathing hard. Moira had twice crested the great steeplechase hurdle and feigned a third. The earl had not yet left the gate.

"My Earl en Garde," Moira panted in his ear. "I have yet to be pierced by your famous sword. Show me your weapon," she gasped. "I long for your forged steel."

Unfortunately, that particular dagger stayed in its scabbard. The earl's lance couldn't have made an indentation in a feather pillow. Blade, bayonet, broadsword—there wasn't enough mettle to make a butter knife.

Moira did not give up. Her hair hanging in moist tendrils, she tried tricks no Haymarket whore would do, to the embarrassment of them both. Nothing. Then she laughed. And kept laughing all the way down the stairs, where Annie held the door open for her.

Chapter Twelve

*H*is life was over. There would be no pleasure. Ever. No children. Ever. So this was his punishment for a life of sin, being cut down in his prime. He should have listened to his mother and ensured the succession years before. Now, most likely his father would come visit *him* in the middle of the night. Lord knew, no one else was going to.

Gard checked under the covers. No soldier stood at attention. "Traitor!" he cried. "Deserter!" Near tears, he drank straight from the bottle of wine, not bothering to find a glass. Maybe he should see a physician? Maybe he should join a monastery. Lord, the closest he'd ever get to a woman again was with a drawing pencil—one with lead in it! If he got up, he could go visit the foundling hospital on the other end of Bloomsbury, see all the little nippers no one wanted—no one but a man who would never have his own.

No, he thought, if he got up, he might have to

face Annie and her knowing smile. His life was hard enough. It was the only thing that was.

Jupiter, how was he ever going to face Lady Campbell? She wasn't some chance-met cyprian he'd never see again. She was part of the beau monde. He was bound to encounter her at every ball, rout party, and breakfast his mother dragged him to. The theater, the opera, not even the farthest-flung of his properties was far enough away to make a safe haven. The woman was always invited to country parties. What could he say? What could she say? Then again, she might find a lot to say—to everyone else. What if Moira Campbell were a gossip?

Oh, God, all women were gossips!

It was all Annie Lee's fault, of course, that he'd picked a prime article from the polite world instead of his usual opera dancers and actresses. Hell, Corinne could have slept through the whole debacle and woke with a smile on her lips. But no, there was Annie with her long-nosed insinuations that his soiled doves were befouling her roost. Her roost! He laughed, but it came out more a sob. Quit whining, she'd said when he complained about the flea bites. Would she tell him to keep a stiff upper lip now, too?

Gard drank the last of the wine and lay in a sodden stupor, telling himself that he'd get up and go home when he was sure the old bat had gone to sleep. He stayed awake, breathing in the nauseating mixture of sweat and heavy perfume, afraid to shut his eyes. He knew he'd hear Moira's laughter in his nightmares, that and Annie's "Good night, my lady. Thank you for coming."

"All right, missy, I want to know what you did to that poor bloke. I brought me a peacock and his game pullet to the house, and I took home a cackling hen. Hours later I get to half carry a bird what's like to cock his toes up. Plucked and ready for the pot, he looked. I want to know what's going on, chickie."

Annalise was in her riding habit, the black cape buttoned securely over it so no green showed. She was getting warm in the stable, warm under the ex-highwayman's steady regard. "Don't be silly, Rob. I just keep house, remember?"

"And I've known you since you was in pinafores, remember? I mistrust that dancin' light in your eyes. Tells me you've been up to no good. Just how bad have you been, is what I want to hear." He made no move to follow her when she stepped impatiently to the door, just stayed seated on an upturned keg, polishing harness.

So Annalise told him. About the sleeping powder in the wine and the fleas in the bed.

"And?"

"And . . . I gave the earl an inhibitor."

"An inhibitor?" Rob sounded it out. "You gave him something to inhibit his—gor blimey, you didn't, girl!"

She nodded and picked up the harness he'd dropped.

"You took the charge out of his pistol? The wind out of his sail? The fire out of his furnace? That's downright evil. Why, I knows body snatchers as wouldn't sink so low."

Annalise shook the reins under her friend's nose. "He is not going to carry on in this house while I am under this roof!"

Rob shook his head. "Little harmless fun is one thing. Give him somethin' to think about besides his rod. But diddlin' him out of it altogether is a whole nother kettle of fish, chickie. I ain't going to be party to filchin' any fellow's manhood."

"Gammon. I didn't steal anything. I didn't even

borrow it! That insufferable man's manhood is the last thing I'd want! I simply discouraged him, temporarily, so maybe he'll go away and leave us in peace."

"And maybe he'll kill hisself. You didn't see the look on his face. A fellow loses his pride, his confidence."

"Oh, pooh. You're making too much of it, Rob."

"And you're making too little." His face split in a grin, till he remembered the unfortunate earl, and his audience. "Deuce, chickie, you don't know what you're talkin' about, innocent miss like you. You ask Henny. At least she appreciates a man for what he is. No matter. Whatever old-maid notion you've got in your pretty head, I won't stand for any more of this tinkerin' with his, ah, virility. You find some other way of keepin' his bed empty or him out of it, you hear me, missy?"

"I hear you, Rob. Now can I go for my ride?"

He went back to polishing the tack. "That's another thing. You're stirrin' up talk with your rides in the park."

"But I don't speak to anyone, and I have your friend Clarence with me. No one has bothered us since that first time."

"No, but they've noticed. Can't help it, you ridin' neck or nothin' like you was born in the saddle."

She smiled. "Well, I was, practically. And you taught me everything else." Clyde came in, so Annalise bent down and scratched behind the little dog's ears.

Rob looked up, and his weathered face creased in a grin. "Howsomever, you do look a picture on your horse. And all veiled like that, you create a kind of mystery for the paper-skulls with naught else to do but gawk."

"Those fops and fribbles are harmless enough.

The others who are out exercising their horses know better than to come near."

"Aye, but they're talkin'." He turned aside and spit into a bucket halfway across the floor. "London's a great place for talkin', you know. Clarence says he heard mention of a lady in green in the pubs."

"So let them talk." Annalise kept petting the dog.

"Thing is, I have one of my chums on the look-out. Sir Vernon's sent orders to the Clarendon, where he keeps rooms and a staff. Keepin' it mum about any missin' heiress so far, but he's got men out askin' questions."

"But none of his London people know me, and he's never seen this green habit. And I make sure every morning that Clarence remembers to paint the three white stockings and blaze on Seraphina. There is no way Sir Vernon's people can recognize me."

"Ain't many women ride like the wind, chickie."

"Oh, Robbie, don't say I shouldn't go!" she pleaded, taking the harness away from him. "I cannot attend parties or the opera. I must not visit the fashionable shops or booksellers where the ton gathers. I can't even go sight-seeing except dressed as an old crone. Please don't say I have to stay indoors all day, feeling as depressed as I look!"

"Reckon you'd only get up to more mischief that way, anyhow. Suppose it'll do, leastways till we hear Sir Vernon hisself comes to town. I'll have Clarence take another groom along. And maybe you should get to the park an hour earlier, afore the young bucks get there."

Annalise laughed. "Then we'll certainly have to convince his lordship to go home early at night, won't we?"

The earl went home and soaked in a hot tub to get rid of the stink at least, if not his despair. His spirits did not rise, however, nor anything else.

He sent his disapproving valet for a bottle of brandy. "But, my lord, it's barely gone seven."

"Morning or evening? No matter. Just fetch the liquor, Ingraham."

Then Ross decided he'd never drink again. Men were often ruined by strong spirits; he'd always heard it was so. Who'd have thought it could happen to Lord Gardiner, though? He'd been a three-bottle, four-barmaid man in his salad days. Obviously his salad was wilted.

Hell, he reconsidered, if he could never go wenching anymore, he may as well drink himself into oblivion. He started as soon as his man returned with the bottle.

Ingraham was shocked. "But, my lord, we have an appointment with Gentleman Jackson for this morning, and we are promised to attend a Venetian breakfast this afternoon with Lady Gardiner. Then there is dinner at White's with Mr. Fansoll."

"*We* aren't going anywhere. Certainly not to be pummeled by any sparring partner or fawned over by those simpering misses. And as for White's . . ." He shuddered, thinking of listening to the latest *on-dit*, knowing there was a special place in tattlemonger's hell reserved just for him. "You can make my excuses, Ingraham. Tell them I'm below par, out of sorts, under the weather. Incapacitated." He shuddered again.

Ingraham attempted to put his hand on the earl's forehead to feel for a fever. He was roughly pushed aside. "Shall I call a physician, my lord?"

"No, just leave me alone." Then Gard regretted the real concern he saw on his old retainer's face. "I just need a few hours' sleep. Been trotting too hard, is all. Don't worry, I'll be right as a trivet tomorrow."

Ingraham smiled in relief. "That's all right, then.

A day's rest should put the starch back in your step."

Too bad that wasn't where he needed it.

Annalise put the mare through her paces, wishing there were a jumping course, a real challenge. As it was, her mind was only half on controlling the playful chestnut. The other half of her thoughts were on Rob's words, what he'd said about his lordship.

Taking the lustful Lord Gardiner down a peg or two was as satisfying as this morning's hard gallop on the deserted paths. On the other hand, even she had to admit he was a handsome devil, exuding manliness with every breath. It would be a sin to cause such a virile man permanent damage, even if he was a rogue. Gelding a fractious stallion was one thing, but Annalise never meant to end Lord Gardiner's career as a rake altogether, just while he was in her vicinity. His morals or lack of them were his own affair, as long as he kept his affairs out of her house.

Unhappily for Miss Avery's conscience, her grandmother's directions were not quite as explicit as Annalise could have wished. Most likely the older woman never had occasion to use that particular formula.

Annalise was thinking so hard about his lordship's condition that she never heard her name called.

"Miss Avery? Miss Annalise Avery?"

By the time the name registered, she and Seraphina and their two escorts were far beyond the caller. Clarence and his cohort were not aware of her real name in any case, just knowing her as a connection of Cock Robin's. Ma'am, she was to them, or Miss Robin. They never looked back.

Annalise knew the danger and was able to ride on without registering the slightest start at hearing her name, not the smallest jab at the reins to disturb the mare's easy gait, not the tiniest stiffening of her own erect carriage. She did turn back at the fork in the path, though, cantering effortlessly the way she had come, trying to spot her adversary in order to get a good description of him for Rob. The man called out again as they passed, and she looked right through him, through her veil, with the same haughty rise of her chin she gave the few pedestrians who sought to engage her in conversation. One man whistled and another rudesby tipped his hat and offered compliments on her riding. She kept going, knowing that anyone who sought to follow would be deterred by her companions.

Annalise knew better than to flee the park immediately, so she continued with her ride although her peace was cut up. She thought she'd acquitted herself well, but now she had something else to worry about in addition to Lord Gardiner's sex life.

Chapter Thirteen

Lord Gardiner slept the clock around. He awoke at dawn refreshed and optimistic. The morning waters always—no, the tide was still out. He decided to go riding despite the dismals. A horse just might be the only thing he'd ever mount again.

Expecting to have the park to himself, he was astounded at the small knots of riders and carriages he saw along the tanbark. Even Cholly Fansoll was out, and Cholly never stirred before noon.

"What's toward, Cholly?" Gard asked, pulling his black stallion to a halt alongside his friend's curricle. "A race or something starting here?"

"Where have you been that you haven't heard the latest—oh, forgot. Sickly, your man said. How are you feeling, then?"

"Fine, fine." He didn't want to talk about it. "What's this about, some new marvel?"

Cholly just smiled. "Wait."

All eyes were directed toward the avenue along the Serpentine, so Gard looked that way, too, holding his restive horse in check with a firm hand. "I know you want to run, Midnight. Soon, boy."

In a few minutes a collective sigh went up from the gathered gentlemen as a perfect vision cantered down the path.

"My word, what a magnificent creature," Gard exclaimed.

"And the horse isn't half bad, either. Part Arabian from the neck and the small head. She's got enough speed to give even your Midnight a run for it, I'd guess from the way she's been showing all the chaps her heels."

"Who the devil is she?" the earl demanded, interrupting Cholly's continuing enumeration of the chestnut mare's fine points, from the three white stockings to the white blaze on her forehead.

"Dashed if I know. That's what all the commotion is about. Fellows are determined to find out. Intrigue fires 'em up, don't you know. Lady in Green, they're calling her. Don't talk to anyone, won't stop for anything. Bets are on whether she's just another pretty horsebreaker trying to stir up interest and a higher price, or visiting royalty trying to remain incognito. Eccles has a monkey riding on her being someone's runaway wife. Alvanley thinks she's just some demirep with a horrible scar, and that's why she stays all covered up."

"I'll lay my blunt on the princess."

"But you can't see her face!"

"She's just got to be beautiful. Look at that figure. Besides, only a beautiful woman carries herself with such assurance. And none of the Fashionable Impure would ever be seen with two such thatchgallows in tow. Or a veil. Or without her manager, if she's looking for a new protector. No, she's a lady."

"Someone's wife, then?"

"No one in his right mind would let her out of

his sight, and someone would have identified her by now if she was married to any of the peerage. She's a princess, all right. There's just something about her." And something else about her, perhaps the defiant way she raised her head and ignored the stares and whispers, perhaps just the silly green feathers trailing along the cheek he couldn't see, appealed to him so much that he felt a current stir in himself he feared was dead. He shifted in the saddle and grinned. "I think I'm in love."

"In rut, more like," his friend commented ruefully, out of long habit, "though how you can be without ever seeing the female is more than I can say. Still, glad to see you're takin' an interest. Some odd stories going a—"

Gard rode forward, to see better. He knew the path the lady was on, but so did the others. He couldn't get near.

Annalise was getting nervous. All those men, all the carriages. Her tension was reaching Seraphina, making the high-strung animal jittery. Annalise turned to her escorts to tell Clarence to close ranks, to ride closer, they'd be leaving the park. But a high-perch phaeton somehow darted into the narrow path between her and her companions. When she looked forward again, a racing curricle was sideways across the roadway in front, and riders and men on foot lined the grass verge on her right side, with the river hemming her in on the left. Seraphina pranced in place uneasily. Annalise stroked the mare's neck, but her own tension was like a hammer pounding between her ribs.

"A moment of your time, pretty lady," the driver of the curricle called to her. He was what Robbie would have called a curst rum touch, she could see from his snuff-stained shirt, the pouches under his eyes, the evil grin that showed blackened teeth. She said nothing, allowing Seraphina to back and circle in her fidgets.

She could hear Clarence bellowing behind her, and the sounds of a scuffle where her other guard, Mick, should have been. She did not take her eyes off the dissipated driver in front of her.

"Your name, fair one, that's all."

At first Annalise did not understand what kind of game the men were playing. Surely these gentlemen—and she labeled them thus from the expensive equipages she saw and the unmistakably Weston-tailored apparel on many of the leering pedestrians—never meant to offer harm to a well-bred female in broad daylight. Robbie was right, she concluded. She had made herself too mysterious to these profligates with nothing better to do than tease an unprotected woman. They were just curious. She could give them Miss Robbin or something, and they would let her pass.

Then a man in a puce waistcoat, on a winded bay, shouted to the man in the curricle, "No, Repton, that ain't all. Ask for her price."

One of the other men who bordered the path, cutting off a possible retreat through the wooded area, yelled, "I'll match it, whatever you bid."

Her price? Were they thinking Seraphina was for sale?

Then she heard another voice from behind her. "I say we get a look at her face, see what we're bidding on."

Dear Lord, they were discussing her, Annalise Avery, as if she were a horse on the block! She looked again at the man in the curricle blocking the roadway. His eyes were glinting and he licked his lips. He actually thought she would go home with him if he paid enough! Annoyance gave way to insult, tinged with fear. That man, Repton, they'd said, did not look like he'd accept a polite refusal.

One of the riders darted out of the crowd. "I'll uncover the masterpiece," he bragged, reaching for her veil.

Annalise backed Seraphina again and raised her whip.

"Watch out, Hastings, she already caught Jelcoe with the whip." There was coarse laughter from the group nearby.

The man called Hastings answered, "That's all right. I like a woman with spirit. I don't mind using a whip myself on an unruly filly."

More crude comments and advice were sent to Hastings and Repton, most of which Annalise did not understand, blessedly. She had heard more than enough, however. Anger overcame her fright. "Animals!" she screamed. "You are all worse than beasts! Have you no respect, no honor? Not all women are for sale, you dastards!"

Lord Gardiner had managed to push his way forward through the ranks of horsemen. "Bloody hell," he swore when he saw one of the lady's bodyguards on the ground, wrestling with four times his number. The other was still on his horse, but with a pistol held to his head.

Some of the other men were turning back, shame-faced and muttering. Like Cholly, they'd come only to see the latest comet in London's sky. No one wanted to have it out with Repton, though. He was hot at hand when it came to issuing challenges, and he was a crack shot with a pistol. In addition, he held a lot of the younger men's vouchers. They started drifting away.

Gard, however, was determined to go to the lady's rescue. If this wasn't a damsel in distress, he'd never played at St. George. Besides, he owed her for the boost to his morale. Then, too, he'd do his damnedest to get any female, even his housekeeper Annie Lee, out of the clutches of this pack of dirty dishes. Peep-o'day boys and ivory tuners, they were all loose screws. Repton was the worst.

The earl's plan was simple: beat the hell out of Repton and move the curricle from the lady's path. Before he got near enough, she let loose a stream of invectives that stopped him in his tracks. Then, while he and the others were still absorbing her magnificent fury and vitriolic message, the woman pulled back on her reins, causing the mare to rear. The chestnut backed up, still on her hind legs only, until her tail was almost touching the phaeton behind. With the lightest of touches the lady brought the mare down to all fours and then, with a leap and a bound and burst of speed forward, the two sailed right over Repton's curricle and away. If the old roué hadn't ducked, they'd have taken his head with them. As it was, his hat went flying.

Lord Gardiner leaned down from his stallion and retrieved the hat while most of the other spectators were still staring at the cloud of dust kicked up by the lady's departure. One or two started clapping. Ross turned back to them and sneered. "Would you have clapped so hard if she'd broken her neck trying that amazing jump? What if she'd lamed the animal, trying to get away from you?" Eyes shifted to study the ground. "And you call yourselves gentlemen. I am ashamed to be one of your number."

"Come now, Gardiner, just a bit of fun. No harm done." Repton was sitting up again, getting his color back. He held his hand out for his hat. "Since when has Earl en Garde developed such nice scruples when it comes to women anyway?"

Someone, Hastings, he thought, snickered. Lord Gardiner studied the hat in his hands. "Scruples?" he drawled. "Do you know, in all my years I never had to terrorize a single defenseless female into agreeing to warm my bed. I wouldn't quite call that scruples. Not even common decency. I don't suppose you'd recognize either, Repton. By the way, I don't like your hat. It's filthy and smells rank." And he threw the offending article as far as he could, into the Serpentine. "If you have any complaints, I'll be happy to oblige."

Repton was not about to challenge the earl, not with Gardiner's prowess with a sword. Cloth-headed gapeseeds who didn't know an épée from an epergne, those he would challenge. They had to choose pistols. Of course, if Lord Gardiner challenged him ... "Want her yourself, do you?" he taunted.

The earl did not take offense. "I might not be the beast the lady called you, Repton, but I am still a man."

"Are you? I heard rumors ..."

Gard clenched his fists. The muscles in his jaw worked so hard, they twitched. He'd kill the bastard. Then he'd strangle Moira Campbell. He started to dismount. "I won't call you out, you muckworm. The field of honor is reserved for gentlemen. You'd make a mockery of it. I'm just going to beat you to a pulp."

Repton did not need another invitation. He cracked his whip over his cattle and was gone before the earl's foot touched the ground.

Gard turned to the other men. "Anybody else have any questions about my manhood?"

No one answered. Ross Montclaire had challenged Oxford's champion boxer while at school, and won. He still sparred with Gentleman Jackson himself. No one forgot that.

"Then let go of the lady's escort before I forget that I am a *gentle*man."

The man who was covering Clarence put his pistol away and stood back, but not far enough or quickly enough that Clarence's heavy boot didn't catch him in the jaw, knocking him flat on the ground. The rowdies who had tackled Clarence's partner hurried into the woods, some with spilled claret, some with daylights already darkening.

A spotty-faced sprig in yellow pantaloons brought the fellow's horse. He coughed and stammered an apology.

Lord Gardiner nodded. "We all, and everyone who considers himself a gentleman, owe you an apology. And the lady, of course." He directed his words to the two grooms, but spoke so all of the remaining members of Repton's plot could hear. "Please convey our humblest regrets for this deplorable event. And please tell your mistress that she will be perfectly secure in the park from now on. 'Twould be a shame if such a spectacular horsewoman were denied her ride. Inform the lady that I, the Earl of Gardiner, guarantee her safety." He looked around, frowning awfully, making sure the makebaits all understood that he would exact dire retribution on anyone who caused her more distress. The cowed expressions he read satisfied Gard. "The Lady in Green can ride as unmolested as my own mother. If she is still fearful, tell her that I stand ready to escort her, with no expectations or demands or disrespect. On my word of honor."

Chapter Fourteen

Annalise was shaken. She didn't know how she got home, by which route she made her way back to the livery stable, or what she told the men when they asked for Clarence and Mick. There were more insults along the way, she recalled, for a solitary woman with no escort who was galloping madly down the street as if all the hounds of hell were at her heels. They were, as far as she was concerned. Lord, was there no safe place for a woman in this whole city? If two reformed hedgebirds were not enough to protect her in the public park, she could never ride again. Now, when her looks were finally coming back so that she didn't frighten herself in the mirror, she could never come out of her crone's guise. It wasn't that she was vain about her looks; she never considered herself a beauty or anything, though Barny had been wont to call her pretty. She simply hated being the antidote Annie Lee, from whose appearance grown men turned and little children hid behind their mothers' skirts. Annalise hated being ugly. She hated being afraid. She mostly hated the feeling that she was a fox forced to go to ground, with the hunters waiting at every burrows' end, day after day.

Rob had taken Henny on errands, luckily for him, for Miss Avery was damning every male alive. She wouldn't even share her uneaten, crumpled roll with Clyde the dog.

The day got worse. As Annalise sat with trembling hands around a cup of steaming tea, looking fully as ugly as her mood, Lorna reported a man at the door.

"He's nobbut a cheeky footman, I'd guess, passing hisself off as some nob's secretary or something, all so's he doesn't have to use the back door. He's asking for the mistress, and I 'spose that's you, ma'am. I tried to send the fellow away, seeing as how you're looking blue-deviled, but the coxcomb says he won't leave a message or anything, and he'll come back another time. Thinks a lot of hisself, this Stavely."

Stavely was a moderately good-looking knave with slicked-back hair and padded shoulders. He was also the man who had called her name in the park yesterday—was it just yesterday? He was Sir Vernon's man.

If she gave him short shrift, Annalise considered as she watched him preen in the hall mirror before he was aware of her presence, he'd be suspicious, wondering why his questions were going unanswered. A pretty fellow like this would be used to getting his own way among the serving girls. Also, even if housekeepers like Annie Lee were often autocratic, deeming theirs among the highest rungs on the servants' ladder, it would never do for Annalise to come over as haughty or arrogant. She didn't want this popinjay going back to her stepfa-

113

ther saying he was shown the door by a house-keeper who was putting on the airs of a lady. Sir Vernon was too clever. So Miss Avery gathered her shaken poise and gushed like a moonstruck tweeny as if her life depended on it. It most likely did.

"Come along, dearie. We can talk about your er-rand over a nice cup of tea. Or else maybe you'd fancy some of the stable man's ale. I was just say-ing to myself, Mrs. Lee—I'm a widow, don't you know—wouldn't it be cheery to have some company on a chill morning like this? Handsome company, too."

The footman gulped. His Adam's apple bobbed above his necktie. There was a nice reward if he found any information for his employer, but no tip was worth cozying up to an old hunchback hag like this. "No, ma'am, thanks for the offer, but I can't stay. On important business, don't you know. I'm after news of a young miss what might of come your way."

The witch cackled. "We get a lot of young misses hereabouts. A different one every day, or night. The master's a regular billy goat, he is. Of course, he's not to home right now, so don't feel obliged to stand out in the hall." She made to take his tricorne with her emaciated fingers. He snatched it out of her reach. "What did you say your name was, ducks?"

"Ah, Stavely, just Stavely. Thing is, I've got a lot of places on my list to ask."

"Oh, yes, your missing gel," the housekeeper said with disappointment in her voice.

"I only wish," he replied, equally as disap-pointed. "The wench is way above my touch. She's a lady, a real lady."

Annie sniffed. "No real lady would be caught dead here. There's some as calls themselves ladies, but I ask you, would a fine, well-bred female come to bachelor quarters like this?"

"No, but this one's a relation of some kind to Lady Rosalind Avery. She's got nothing to do with the buck you've got sporting here now."

"Ah, now, that's a different kettle of fish. I'm right sorry I can't help a likely looking lad such as yourself, Stavely, but I wasn't in charge here until Lady Rosalind left. I had no call to pay attention to the comings and goings of the company."

"And no young ladies have come looking for Lady Rosalind since she left?"

"Nary a female comes looking for anyone but Lord Gardiner. But I'll keep a lookout for you, Stavely my boy. How old is this lady and how'd she come to be lost?"

"She's twenty-one, used to be a real Diamond, they tell me, but maybe fallen off her looks. And she left her stepfather's household 'cause she's all about in the head."

Mrs. Lee clutched her flat chest. "Lawks a-mercy, should I call the Watch, then, if I see her?"

"No!" George Stavely exclaimed. "That is, no, ma'am. She ain't considered dangerous. The family wants her back, is all."

"Seems to me they're well rid of her if her attics are to let. What do they want her back for?"

"Sir Vernon says he wants to take care of her." He put his finger alongside his nose and grinned. "Word below stairs is that she's an heiress. Sir Vernon locks her away—for her own safety, don't you know—and there's no pesky husband to claim her dowry."

"Ah, that's a man after my own heart!"

"Here's his card, if you hear anything. There's a nice bit of silver in it for you if you find the chit."

"Hmm, might be I'd claim my reward in other ways, eh, bucko?"

George left in a hurry.

* * *

Annalise didn't bother with tea this time. She went straight for the Madeira. Near spasms, she decided she must have become another person with this disguise. In less than twenty-four hours she'd stopped a seduction, been the intended victim of a seduction, and simulated the seduction of a slimy footman. In her whole twenty-one years she'd never even contemplated such a thing. She hardly recognized herself at all! Four more years of such deception and she'd be depraved indeed.

Her friends told her she did well. Henny clucked her tongue and busied herself at the stove, but Rob thought she had a great future in the criminal world.

"Never seen a sweet young gal turn to cheatin', lyin', cussin', and committin' mayhem with such a flair. We sure could of used you in the old days. And just think, you get tired of hidin' out here in Bloomsbury, you can make a career on the stage."

"Don't tease, Rob," she said tearfully. "I know I've made a rare mull of things."

Rob lit his pipe, since Henny refused to let him chew his tobacco in the kitchen. He could chew it, that is, but he'd have to swallow the stuff. She wouldn't tolerate spitting in this fancy house. When he got the pipe going to his satisfaction, after much puffing and poking, he winked at Annalise. "Things is workin' out for the best. They allus do."

"For the best? You didn't hear about the incident in the park. I'll never be able to put off these blacks again. Poor Seraphina. No more rides for her, either."

Henny put the bottle of wine back on its shelf and substituted a cup of coffee in front of Annalise. "That's just the wine talking, missy. We'll come about. You'll see."

"Oh, no, Henny. You weren't there. Those men . . ."

"Ain't goin' to bother you again," Rob told her, pulling on his pipe. "We had the story from Clarence. Pay it no never mind, chickie. You have a protector now."

"A protector? Who in the world . . . ?"

Rob slapped his knee and grinned. "Lord Gardiner, that's who! Our very own rake is after protectin' some unknown lady's virtue. Yourn!"

Annalise just shook her head. "I have no idea what you're talking about. How could Lord Gardiner protect me—and why?"

"Seems you left the park in a hurry. Missed the gov'nor tryin' to come help you. By the time he got close, you'd already saved yourself and got away. He stayed to give them clodpates a regular beargarden jaw about honor and stuff. And he vowed to watch over you from now on."

"Me?"

"That Lady in Green they're all talkin' about. Claimed you'd be safe as houses and dared any of them to say him nay. He nearly ate them alive if they blinked, says Clarence. All the milksops backed right down, he's got such a reputation for a handy set of fives. So nary a one of them—and none of the other gents at the clubs—will dare touch a hair on your head."

Annalise didn't credit a word of Rob's story. "Have you seen it, Rob? It's finally growing back. My hair, that is. Except it's silver, not blond anymore."

"Pay attention, chickie. This here's the answer to your problems."

She sat up straighter. "What, I should become his lordship's convenient? That would certainly save me the effort of scuttling his romantic interludes. And think how . . . convenient for him: a housekeeper by day, a bed partner at night. I could have been married to Barny. That's all he wanted, besides the money."

"There wasn't no mention of any arrangement like that. In fact, the gov'nor swore he means to be your escort only, nothin' more."

"And King Arthur is asleep in a cave somewhere! Robbie, chivalry is long gone, and Lord Gardiner wouldn't recognize it if Sir Lancelot bit him on the nose."

"I'd bet his word is good. But don't be so hasty either way. Think on this: After today your steppa's bound to hear about the dasher in the park, the one with the good seat and no connections. But he won't think twice if he hears she's in Earl en Garde's keeping. No way that piece of easy virtue could have anything to do with a female who left her fiancé in a huff over his particulars. You'd be safe as the Bank of England."

"But safe from Lord Gardiner?"

"I ain't suggestin' you accept a slip on the shoulder, chickie. He gave his word as a gentleman. I trust him."

Suddenly Annalise felt better; things weren't so bleak. For some ungodly reason, contrary to all the evidence and everything she believed, she trusted Lord Gardiner, too. Then she laughed out loud. Sir Vernon must be right: She was ready for Bedlam after all.

The topic of the conversation, meanwhile, was sitting in his book room with a sketchpad on his knees and a dreamy smile on his face. He was trying to capture the graceful, soaring flight of the woman and her mare as they leapt the curricle. Of course he had no face to put on the female's form, but he recalled enough of her trim waist and rounded bosom to fire his imagination. Hell, if he had no face to depict, he might as well leave off the clothes, drawing just the female at one with her mount.

Zeus, he needed a woman!

Chapter Fifteen

The beau monde went on the strut in Hyde Park at four in the afternoon. So did the demimonde. The ton came to see and be seen; likewise the muslin trade. The ladies of fashion came to make plans to meet their gallants at the evening's parties. The Fashionable Impure came to make sure their dance cards were also filled, so to speak.

Both groups of females gathered in little knots along the paths or sat in carriages under the trees. One group had more color to their faces and gowns, fancier coaches, and no dowagers, dragons, or dogs-berries among them. They also had more of the young gentlemen surrounding them.

Lord Gardiner tooled his curricle along the road-way, studying the various delectables like boxes of bonbons set out in a sweet-shop window. He doffed his hat and bowed to his mother's friends and their milk-and-water misses. He nodded and smiled at a few widows with waving hands and a few wives with wandering eyes. The curricle picked up speed.

There was no way the earl was going to dally with a lady. Not till his confidence was back, at any rate. He looked, though, with a connoisseur's eye at this one's swanlike neck, that one's narrow waist.

If truth be told, Lord Gardiner was searching for the lady from the morning. He didn't think she'd show herself here, not after her efforts at concealing her identity, but she might be playing some deep game after all. She might even be someone of his acquaintance, or soon-to-be acquaintance, if he had any say. There were females with erect postures and stylish ensembles, but none he could identify as the elegant horsewoman who rode through his mind. Gard followed a lady wearing a feathered bonnet over short-cropped curls that turned out to be brassy blond. He halted the curricle when he saw a flash of emerald green behind a hedge: the foppish Viscount Reutersham was relieving himself.

Finally the earl's eyes lighted on a maiden sitting on a bench, twirling her parasol. She was nothing like that other female, being shorter and rounder and brunette. She was also entirely alone. Something about her appealed to Lord Gardiner, reminding him of another quest in the park that afternoon. Perhaps it was her ready smile mingled with the touch of wistfulness he saw about her eyes. Perhaps it was just that the sunlight playing on the folds of her lime-and-jonquil-striped muslin reminded him of spring, and sap rising. She'd look pleasing on canvas. She'd look pleasing on a bearskin rug.

The earl got down, handing the ribbons to his tiger. "*Bonjour, mademoiselle*, may I join you on your bench?"

It was not long before the earl had his *belle de nuit* and the female had hopes of her month's rent being paid, although nothing as vulgar as money was mentioned. Addresses were exchanged, times were arranged, and both parties were eminently satisfied. Except the lady did not want to be confused with Haymarket ware.

"I don't want you thinking I do this regular like. It's just that my usual beau is below hatches right now. I ain't looking for a new protector, either, my lord. He'll come about soon enough, I'm sure."

The earl grinned wickedly. "Let us hope not too soon, eh, *chérie*? At least not till tomorrow morning."

If oysters were the food of love, kindly Mrs. Tuthill was offering Lord Gardiner sustenance enough to pleasure a harem. Or she knew about his equipment failure. And Annie knew, who was bringing course after course to Lord Gardiner and his companion. Raw oysters, oyster bisque, smoked oysters, roast duck in oyster dressing. And Tuthill knew, having mentioned with a wink that he'd made a special trip to the fish market that morning. They all knew. Gard's hand shook.

In addition to the oysters, very little wine was served, not enough to enfeeble a fly. Gard wondered if he should check for ground-up rhinoceros horn. Rob's fellow feeling he could understand, but why did Annie Lee suddenly feel sorry for him, sorry enough to provide encouragement, when she was the one who deplored his wenching? Did she take pride in her household, like his valet refusing to send him out in anything less than prime twig, claiming it was a reflection on the man's skills? Gads! It was bad enough the polite world discussed his performance; Annie Lee keeping score was enough to dull any man's desire. He almost choked on his last forkful of prawns stuffed with oysters.

Gard couldn't imagine what dessert might be. If there were oyster tarts, he'd dismiss them all. Still, his dinner partner seemed to be taking it all in good part, licking her lips, licking her fingers, licking his fingers. He might be mortified, but he was still interested, thank heavens.

"Do you wish dessert, Sophy, or shall we wait for later?"

Sophy? No, it couldn't be, Annalise considered, a bubble of hysterical laughter welling up inside her. London was just too big a place for that. This girl looked younger than her own twenty-one years—though Annalise had never considered the proper age for a man's mistress—and she was not the great beauty Annalise assumed Sophy would be. Still, her name was Sophy and she was a lightskirt.

So Annalise spilled some of the oyster sauce on Sophy's sleeve. "Oh, I am so sorry, miss! The plate just seemed to slip. Please, if you'll just come with me, I can sponge that off in a trice before it stains. Oh, do forgive me, miss. Right this way." Then she added for Lord Gardiner's sake, "Mrs. Tuthill is preparing a special dessert right now, one that won't keep. She just needs ten minutes more. I'll be sure to have Miss, ah, Sophy restored by then."

They were gone before Gard could offer to see about Sophy's dress himself, and to hell with dessert.

While she worked, Annalise was profuse in her apologies. "I could not be more sorry, ma'am. Such a lovely gown, too. I once saw one like it on a woman in Drury Lane and said to myself, what a handsome frock, especially with the lady's brunette coloring. Why, now that I think of it, it could have been you. Did you ever wear this gown to the theater? Not that I mean to pry, mind."

While Annalise worked, Sophy was surveying the amenities in the lady's dressing room of the master suite. "Some women can afford a new gown each time they go out," she answered with a hint of petulance, examining the silver comb-and-brush set laid out for visitors' use. She was not immune to the housekeeper's flattery, though. Poor old dear likely never got any thrills but for seeing her betters at the theater and such. "I may have worn it to the Opera House a time or two."

"No, I never go there. Can't understand the words they're singing."

"La, no one listens to the music. They just go to be seen."

"For my money, I like to see a show *and* the nobs. Still, the lady I recall at the theater was with a right handsome gentleman. Of course, I was just in the pit and they were in the boxes, but he seemed fair-haired and solidly built. Lovely couple, I thought at the time. Wouldn't that be a coincidence if it was you, and here I am wiping your sleeve."

"Oh, that must have been me and the Barnacle. Barny Coombes, don't you know. I call him that 'cause he's a clinger. When he was flush, that was fine. We used to go to all the fanciest places."

"And now?"

"Oh, now he's badly dipped. Rusticating until he can find an heiress or something. Aren't you done yet? I don't want his lordship getting restless, not with him swimming in lard."

"Just finished." Annalise held up the gown for inspection. "As good as new."

"Nothing is as good as new, ducks. I'll tell you what, if his lordship keeps me around a bit, I mean to get a whole new wardrobe. You can have this rag, since you seem to like it so much."

Annalise could hardly bear to touch it, but she helped Barny's mistress into the gold sarcenet. So Lord Gardiner could help her out of it. Miss Avery seethed behind her dark glasses. "Too generous, ma'am," she murmured.

Sophy clapped her hands and cooed when the housekeeper carried in the dessert, a peach flambé, blue flames licking at the edges. Lord Gardiner had the idea of feeding Sophy himself, sharing his dish, his spoon, and bitefuls of the brandy-soaked fruit, then sharing her tasty kisses. A dessert leading into the real dessert, as it were.

Annie had other ideas, quickly shoveling two servings into dishes and slamming them down at their places at opposite sides of the table.

A manservant would have known better, Lord Gardiner thought. Tarnation, a woman with any blood in her veins would have known better. She stood now at the sideboard with arms folded across her non-chest, waiting to see if they needed anything else. Like a carrion crow at the banquet, Lord Gardiner reflected sourly. "That will be all, Annie," he told her.

"Poor thing," Sophy said, wiping a gob of cream off her chin as Annie curtsied and backed out of the room.

Poor thing? What about him, who had to put up with the Friday-faced, cross-grained creature? Ross did *not* want to think about her tonight. Especially not tonight. "Can I offer you more of the sweet, my sweet?"

Sophy did not need his fingers drumming impatiently on the tabletop to hurry her along. Evidently his lordship's hunger had not been satisfied by the meal. "No, thank you, my lord, I've had enough. My compliments to your chef. Shall I, ah, leave you to your port?"

"Not on your life," he growled.

"Then perhaps you'd be kind enough to give me a tour of the house," she said with a wink. "I just love seeing how various rooms and things are decorated."

The drawing room got decorated with his neck-cloth and her shoes. The smaller parlor was soon strung with silk stockings, and the hall stairs received a hail of hairpins along its length. The guest bedrooms each received a cursory visit, and a bit of muslin here, a waistcoat there. By the time Gard and Sophy reached the large bedroom, there was very little sight-seeing left to be done.

Sophy's body was as luscious as his mind had imagined, and his own—well, his mind and his body were both ready, willing, and able, thank whatever saint watched over weak-kneed womanizers. Thank the oysters. And thank Sophy for molding her contours so exquisitely to his.

Intending to show Sophy just how grateful he was, Gard stepped out of her embrace to fix the bed. She swayed against him, though. "A moment, my pet, let me turn down the bedclothes."

She stared at his naked body, and her eyes snapped shut.

He kissed her and she groaned.

He touched her breast. She clutched her stomach. He turned to extinguish another candle. She turned green.

"My lord, I . . . I think I'm going to be . . ."

She was. On the bed, on the floor, on the fastidious Lord Gardiner.

"Annie!"

The earl tried to help at first. But the smells, the sounds . . .

Annie took one look at him and raised an eyebrow in scorn. "I know, you have a sensitive stomach, too."

Gard shrugged his shoulders helplessly. "I'm a regular Trojan when it comes to blood and broken bones. But this—my stomach gets tied in knots. I'm

126

a fine sailor, until everyone else starts hanging over the side."

Sophy started making gagging sounds again. Gard fled downstairs before he looked worse in Annie's eyes, although he didn't know why he should care what his housekeeper thought. He found that he just did, especially when he saw how hard she worked all night, making frequent trips up and down the stairs with slop jars and buckets and mops and fresh linens. All he could do was wait and see if a physician was needed. Tuthill could have ridden for the doctor, of course, but the earl had too fine a sense of responsibility for that, even if he was useless in the sickroom.

Annie tried to tell him to leave, saying she did not even need Mrs. Tuthill's assistance, for the stairs would be too much for her aunt. Besides, according to Annie on one of her trips from the kitchen, the older woman was devastated to think that her cooking may have been responsible.

"She checked the oysters ever so carefully, my lord. But you never can tell with them."

"Nonsense, I feel fine—except when Sophy makes those noises. And oysters are chancy. Everyone knows that."

Close to morning Annie reported that he should take Sophy home now. She might be more comfortable in her own bed.

Annie looked so exhausted, it appeared to Lord Gardiner that even the hump on her raised shoulder was drooping. She had every cause to be tired, he thought thankfully, for he couldn't have done half what she had this night. He tried to express his appreciation.

"I'm dreadfully sorry you had to go through this, Annie. I don't know what I'd have done without you, and that's a fact. I won't be bringing company tomorrow, so you can rest, and I'll leave something extra for you to buy yourself a gift."

Annalise smiled at him, more in charity with the rakeshame earl than ever before. He didn't have to stay, she knew. Most other men would not have made themselves uncomfortable for a straw damsel they hardly knew, not when they had paid servants to do their dirty work. That's what servants were for, she'd heard Barny say time after time. She repeated it now, "That's what servants are for, my lord. I was just doing my job," so he wouldn't feel the least guilty. After all, what had he to feel ashamed over? He wasn't the one who'd given poor Sophy a dose big enough to purge a pony. She smiled at Lord Gardiner again.

So astounding was the occasion—a smile from Annie Lee—and so sweet was the smile that Gard took special notice. Her lips were not quite as thin and parched, and her cheekbones no longer stood out like a skeleton's. He couldn't see her eyes, of course, and there was still that three-hair mole on her cheek and the dreadful mobcap, but Annie was definitely looking better.

Hell and damnation, he swore to himself later. He'd been without a woman so long, even the hag of a housekeeper was beginning to look good to him!

Chapter Sixteen

He sent Sophy home in the closed carriage with Tuthill driving after all. She sat huddled miserably in the corner of the carriage, wrapped in blankets and one of Annie's black gowns. She wouldn't look at him, not even when he tucked a roll of bills into the blankets.

Gard went home, bathed, shaved, put on his buckskins and boots, and rode to the park through a thin mist. She never came, the woman he was sworn to protect, but he gave himself and his stallion a good workout, searching. No woman who would jump a carriage from a near standstill could be hen-hearted, he convinced himself. She'd be there tomorrow. The drizzle must be keeping her away.

The weather did not discourage that dirty dish Repton and his cronies from gathering near the park gate, making assignations with the pretty exercise girls parading their horses and their wares.

"What happened, Gardiner, your little bird flown so soon?" Repton called over.

Gard turned his back on Repton's taunting grin.

"Maybe she didn't take him up on his noble offer," Repton gibed to his passenger, another loose-screw lordling, but in a rasping voice loud enough for Gard to hear. "I wouldn't be surprised. I understand our eager earl is losing his touch."

Lord Gardiner went home and went to bed. Alone. Again.

His mystery lady was sleeping the sleep of the just. Well, if not the just, at least the satisfied. Lord Gardiner's nefarious designs were foiled for another night—two if he was staying away this evening also—and Sophy was well paid for her avarice. And for one night's agony, according to Rob, who carried in the roll of soft for the bedraggled baggage. Sophy was already recovered, but Lord Gardiner could never be interested in her again, not after seeing his would-be paramour looking like something even the cat wouldn't drag in. Vengeance was sweet.

And a whole day and night without worrying about the devilish lord! Annalise was too tired for her ride, but if she slept the day away, then maybe she'd get to Drury Lane or the Opera House after all. She'd be dressed like a scarecrow and seated in the pit, but it was time Miss Avery got to enjoy something of London.

The Earl of Gardiner was in his box at the theater. He was definitely not enjoying himself. Where the ton was used to seeing the most stunning of dashers at his side, dressed in jewels to rival the crystal chandeliers, they now saw a tongue-tied young chit in pastel-pink muslin with a white net overskirt that was covered with bows. She wore a lace fichu lest anyone's blood be roused to lust by the sight of her insignificant attractions, and a single strand of pearls around her short neck. She may as well have *virgin* written on her forehead.

In case someone in the audience this evening missed the significance of seeing the earl with a demure young miss, her parents sat behind them, beaming. The Duke and Duchess of Afton were having a delightful time of it, waving to their friends, planning the nuptials of their Araminta to this nabob of a nobleman. Gard's mother was also in alt, sitting on his other side, pinching his arm in its blue superfine whenever his attention wandered, which was often. Unlike his usual demireps with their scintillating flirtations, this chit had no conversation at all. She was so overawed by his presence, she answered all of his polite efforts at setting her at ease with monosyllables, except when she said, "Whatever you think, my lord."

He thought he'd rather be at Laurel Street, eating tainted oysters. Maybe he was losing his touch after all.

Lady Araminta did provide a moment's divertissement halfway through the farce. She fainted when a little chorus girl blew Lord Gardiner a kiss as she made her exit. Countess Stephania nearly wrenched her son's arm off in her outrage when he suggested perhaps the wench may have intended her gesture of affection for His Grace, Lord Afton. That's when Her Grace, Lady Afton, fainted, too.

After Their Graces' departure, Gard just smiled angelically, nodding to acknowledge the crowd's delight in this tempting morsel for tomorrow's scandalbroth.

The next interval brought him an invitation to the Green Room which he would have ignored, except for the desire to escape his mother's continuing diatribe on his wastrel life. On his way out of the box, Ross managed not to trip on the cane she extended in his path.

The brazen chit wasn't waiting for him in the Green Room as he expected; the theater manager was, with an offer offensive even by Lord Gardiner's standards.

"I'm giving you first choice," the man, Bottwick, oozed. " 'Cause the gel seems taken with you."

"With my money, you mean." Gard did not like dealing with procurers. Women earning their way giving pleasure was one thing; men living off their labor was another. He knew this man took an interest in more than his actresses' welfare, and was repulsed.

"I prefer to make my own arrangements, thank you." He was polite, but he was not interested.

"But this one's different. She don't know how to make those kinds of arrangements, so she asked me to help. Her first time, don't you know," he added slyly.

Gard was even more disgusted. The price would be skyrocketed for the dubious pleasure of deflowering a virgin. He thought of Lady Araminta. "Sorry, innocents don't appeal to me. I don't believe in ruining maidens, not even opera dancers."

"Everybody's got to have a first time." Bottwick rubbed his stubbled chin reflectively. "And Mimi can't make her rent on what I can afford to pay her. She's just a chorus girl, after all. Some talent, but needs training. Lessons cost money, too." He shook his head regretfully. "It'll have to be some swell or other, sooner or later. May as well be one as has the blunt to pay for the privilege. Too bad it can't be a real gentleman like your lordship. Guess I'll have to take Lord Repton up on his offer, then."

Repton? With that saucy bit of fluff? Gard hadn't studied Mimi until she blew him that kiss, but he remembered a taking little thing with flowing blond

132

curls, big eyes, and shapely ankles as she pirouetted off the stage. Mimi in Repton's arms was a sacrilege.

"Very well, and I'll meet your price, but never again. I never want to hear about your sordid little transactions or your supposedly chaste young ingenues. Do you understand?"

Bottwick bowed. " 'Twas Mimi's choice, not mine."

"Very well. Tomorrow. I'll have a carriage meet her after the performance." He turned away, then gave the man another dark scowl. "And don't think to sell her to Repton tonight, or I'll have your hide. Her maidenhead won't have time to grow back by tomorrow, so I'll know."

Annalise loved the theater, except for Lord Gardiner's making a buffoon of himself during the farce. The notion that she disliked his looking foolish in front of others did not bear close examination, especially since she seemed to devote her own energies to that very end. That was different, she told herself.

The fact that the man was a prize fool besides being a prime profligate didn't keep Annalise from her ride the next morning. Both she and Seraphina needed the fresh air and exercise, and she did not have to talk to the nodcock anyway.

He was astride a large black stallion, waiting by the park gates. Annalise gave the merest nod, barely acknowledging his presence, although she did note how other riders stayed away and none of the early morning strollers made comment, as had been their custom. Clarence and Mick fell back at a glance from the earl, who took his place at her side with a "Good morning, my lady." When she simply moved her head, he let the silence fall between them, not hostile or awkward, simply accepting that was the way she wanted it. He followed her lead, kept her pace, all without another word. Annalise could feel his gaze trying to penetrate her veil, but he made no effort to press her into conversation, thankfully, since his curiosity would have put paid to the excursion. The ride was exhilarating, even for a tame park outing, yet Annalise was constantly aware of his presence at her side—and the note that had come for Rob first thing that morning. Company tonight. There were preparations to be made.

She made a jerking motion with her head, indicating the ride was over, then nodded again in dismissal when they reached the gates.

Lord Gardiner bowed from the waist. "My pleasure, ma'am. Tomorrow?"

Annalise made her voice low, hoarse-sounding. "Yes, please. Thank you."

Gard watched her ride away, memorizing every detail of this intriguing woman and her horse. The mare had the three white stockings he recalled from his first view of the superb pair, two in the front, one in the rear. Oddly enough, he could have sworn they were the other way around the day she jumped the curricle, one in front, two in the rear. His incognita might be a lady, but there was something deuced havey-cavey about her. No matter. He had plenty of time to unravel the mystery, a mystery that only added to his fascination.

At an excruciatingly boring reception at Carlton House that evening, Lord Gardiner's main entertainment was fending off flirtatious matrons, since the fledglings and their mamas were giving him a wide berth after the Drury Lane incident. He'd have to remember to reward Mimi for that bit of deliverance. His other amusement was in seeking his riding companion among the assembled ladies of Quality. Too short, too round, too dark, too blasted talkative—none had her innate dignity or grace of carriage or that delicate, almost fragile look that was belied by her easy handling of the spirited mare.

Oh, well, she would keep till morning. Mimi wouldn't.

No one answered his eager knock at Laurel Street. He pushed the door open and stepped inside. No cheerful fire glowed in the parlor, no wine stood ready to be poured. Only one candle burned in the hall. In the kitchen no pots bubbled on the stove, no enticing aromas came from the ovens. The only food in sight was a big wedge of cheese being shared by a pair of mice in a cage on one of the chairs. It looked like the mice were going to have a better supper than he was, unless the mice *were* his supper.

"Annie?"

The housekeeper met him at the bottom of the stairs. She was wearing what he was coming to recognize, to his regret, as her damn-your-eyes pose: immovable, implacable, stick-thin arms crossed over nonexistent breasts, pointed chin up in the air, spectacles twitching on wrinkled nose as if she smelled something rotten—him.

"Filthy lecher," was her evening's greeting.

So much for the warmer, kinder feelings of two nights ago.

Chapter Seventeen

"Debaucher! Despoiler of children!"

Evidently, Mimi had arrived.

Gard had thought her a trifle young himself, and he never had been entirely comfortable with the situation. Still and all, dash it, he wasn't going to give his head for washing to some blasted servant. A servant, moreover, who was not some old, loyal family retainer. A servant he didn't even like!

"Enough, woman!" he thundered. "I am not in short pants to suffer your scold. Nor am I a child molester, dammit. The girl is old enough to know her own mind. She chose me and she chose this way of life!"

"She had no money and no family and the manager threatened her position at the theater if she did not take a lover to bring in more cash," Annie raged right back, not backing down an inch from the black anger in his scowl. Grown men might take cover at Lord Gardiner's temper, but Annalise Avery was made of stronger stuff. Besides, she was right. And somehow she was not frightened by this towering storm of male wrath, even if she could see his hands clenching and unclenching at his sides, knowing they were aching to get around her neck. She had principles on her side, Annie reminded herself, going on: "She had to have food and clothing and a roof over her head. Do you call that a choice, sirrah?"

"She didn't have to choose the life of an actress, deuce take it! She could have gone into service, a hundred things. Instead, she decided to use her looks and what talent she possesses to better herself."

"Better? You call this"—wildly waving her arms at the house, the darkened hallway—"better? You call selling a young girl's body better than honest work?"

"I call it the way of the world! And your sanctimonious ranting isn't going to keep her out of my bed, because that's where she wants to be. If not mine, someone else's."

Annie stamped her foot. "How can she know what she wants? She's just a frightened little girl. But that man is forcing her into prostitution! He gets a share! Did you know that?"

Gard knew he was on shaky ground here, so he blustered even louder, shaking his fist in front of Annie's spectacles in case that old bat was even more nearsighted than she was narrow-minded. "Of course I know the man is paid. It's deplorable, but that's how these things are handled, the same as an agent takes a share from an actress's salary for getting her the role. That's his job, to handle the details. The theater manager will keep any rough customers away from her"—at the thought of Repton, Gard was not even sure of that—"when he can."

"And give her to villains like you instead!"

"Otherwise she'd be in a brothel, giving a bigger share to an abbess, or walking the street, prey to every pimp, pervert, and footpad." He was satisfied with Annie's horrified gasp. At least he'd managed to shock the virago into silence. "You might find that terrible to consider, but I find it outrageous when one of my own employees considers me so steeped in sin that nothing is beneath me! I'd dismiss you in a minute if I thought you'd leave. You're like a burr beneath my skin, Mrs. Annie Lee, and I've a mind to end my irritation!"

"That's right, pick on me when your position is indefensible." She sputtered in outrage. "Oh, you are so righteous in your indignation, so noble, so honorable. By all that's holy, my lord, what did you plan on doing with that child, read bedtime stories?"

He flushed, but gamely persevered. "I didn't plan on raping the chit, you shrew. I wasn't even looking forward to taking her maidenhead, if it truly exists. Some men thrive on being the first, you know, so a virgin is considered a delicacy; the fee is commensurately higher. There are even specialty houses that cater to such desires, houses which I have never visited, blast you for thinking the worst of me. I happen to prefer women who know all about pleasure and pleasuring a—"

Annie clapped her hands over her ears. "I couldn't think that badly of you! I didn't even know such horrors existed," she screamed like a fishwife. "I have learned more about debauchery in this last sennight than I've known in all my twenty-one years!"

That took him aback. "Twenty-one years? You are one and—"

"In all my twenty-one years of service, of course." Annie took a deep breath to calm herself before she made any more errors. Before the earl could ask another question, she went on the attack again. "How can you live with yourself, leading an innocent into your life of sin?"

"Deuce take it, the girl isn't as pure as driven snow. Your chaste little Mimi blew me a kiss in front of half of London. All this nonsense about her innocence is pure fustian."

"She was raised in a convent!"

"Gammon. You fell for her Banbury tale, that's all, and you are quick to blame me. Why she sought your sympathy, I don't know, except she must have figured you'd take anyone else's side but mine. She'd have done better to come to me if she wanted to inflate the price."

"This is not about money, you . . . you . . ." His raised eyebrows belatedly reminded Annie that she was theoretically in this man's power. "Your lordship."

He shook his head, half in wonder that he didn't beat the infuriating female. "I'll never understand how you keep your naive morality in this house, Annie, but money is precisely what this is all about, not any act of conscience or otherwise. There is no way in hell that woman—not child, mind you—does not comprehend and approve what she is doing."

"Then why is she upstairs right now, crying her eyes out?"

Lud, the girl did look like a babe, lost in the big bed. She was sixteen at the most. Hell, maybe fifteen. Ross's stomach twisted. She was sleeping and her flowing blond locks were in schoolgirl braids on either side of pale, tear-stained cheeks. She was wearing a voluminous flannel nightgown—undoubtedly one of the housekeeper's—instead of the flimsy lace thing laid over a chair.

"Damn and blast!"

The girl's eyes snapped open. They were as large

as he remembered, a pretty blue even, but red and swollen. He took a deep breath. "Mimi—"

She sobbed once and reached out for Annie, who gathered Mimi into her thin arms and sat on the bed, glaring at the earl. At least he supposed she was glaring through the spectacles. He would be, in her place. Tarnation, the chit was afraid of him! "Mimi, *chérie*, please do not be frightened. No one will harm you. I swear."

She looked up uncertainly, clutching harder at Annie. "Mignon, *monsieur*. That is my name. Mignon Dupres."

"Mignon? You are the same girl who waved to me from the stage, aren't you?" Maybe there had been a terrible mistake. And maybe the theater manager would live till next week. Both were doubtful.

"*Oui*. They called me Mimi."

The earl looked triumphantly at Annie, still holding the girl's hand on the bed. "And you knew what that meant, that I might seek your company?"

"*Oui, monsieur.*"

She spoke softly, but he made sure Annie heard. "Why did you do that, *mademoiselle*, if you didn't want to, ah, become—"

"*Monsieur* Bottwick said I must, to pay for the voice lessons, *n'est-ce pas*, so he could give me a bigger part in the next play."

"Was there no one else to help with the cost? Your family?"

"Gone," she whispered. "Papa was a wine merchant. But he was a royalist."

It was a common enough story, except the Dupres family were not decadent members of the aristocracy, they were solid, middle-class citizens. The ones with all the morals. Oh, Lord. Annie was wearing that smug half smile he hated. Ross had to be sure. "This"—indicating the bedroom, the filmy negligee, his own presence—"is not what you want?"

While Mignon sobbed again, Gard felt his same presence looming larger and larger in the room, clumsy, overbearing, *de trop*. Annie handed the girl a handkerchief. After Mignon blew her nose, she looked up at him with watery eyes, full of fear.

"You can tell me, *petite*, tell me what you do want."

"I want to marry a nice man and have babies of my own."

Gard ran his hands through his already disturbed dark hair. He turned, not able to look in Annie's direction, and muttered, "Why the bloody hell did you have to choose me?"

He thought it was a rhetorical question, but Mignon answered, "Because they said you were, how do you say, *impuissant*?"

"I know how to say it, blast it! And it's not true!"

Annie staggered into the dressing room, her hand to her mouth. Gard couldn't tell if she was laughing or embarrassed or merely sparing his blushes. He grimaced, feeling the heat in his cheeks. Blushing at his age, and in front of a puritan and an infant! What a damnable coil.

Mignon hiccuped and sniffed and gave him a valiant smile. "Then if it's not true, *monsieur*, I shall try to be brave." She scrunched down in the bed, her eyes screwed shut, her arms rigid at her sides.

"Blister it, I don't take unwilling women! Or children."

"Then that *chien* Bottwick will find someone else," Mignon told him in a pitiful little voice.

It was true. That's how the whole hobble began, trying to keep her from Repton. Devil take it, the girl's fate was sealed anyway, he could at least make it as pleasant for her as possible. At this moment, however, he felt about as much desire for the chit as he did for Annie.

"No, dash it, there has to be another way. I'll find one somehow. Heaven alone knows where. You don't move from here till I decide what to do," he ordered sternly, making it plain that while he was taking responsibility for her, he was not best pleased. The door slamming behind his departure reinforced the message.

Annie came back into the bedroom and hugged the girl, not even noticing when her eyeglasses became dislodged, she was so relieved. There was nothing she could have done for the girl, nowhere she could have sent her, and not enough money to keep her from harm's way for long. Lord Gardiner had done the honorable thing. He may have needed a nudge in the right direction to get his attention above his britches, but true nobility won out. "He'll take care of you, Mignon," she reassured the girl. "You can trust him, once he gives his word."

She knew it to be true. She smiled and went down to give the mice another bit of cheese.

Cholly was concerned about Lord Gardiner's problem. Not Mimi, just the odd rumors, and now this French ladybird Gard couldn't talk around.

His round face puckered in consternation. "Wasn't expecting to see you here tonight." "Here" was White's, where the earl found his friend sprawled in a comfortable leather chair with a book, a glass of port, and a cigar. "Mean to say, I've got a houseful of sisters, nowhere I can go to blow a cloud. Thought you had other plans."

"They didn't work out." Gard sighed as he lowered himself into the chair and signaled for a glass.

"Want to toddle over to Mother Ignace's? I hear she's got some new girls."

Gard shuddered, thinking of those new girls,

tender young females, crying their innocence away. "No!" Cholly looked startled at his vehemence, so he explained, "Imagine your sisters lost and hungry. Maybe in a place like that."

Cholly sat up and frowned. "That's revolting, Gard. I'd call a man out for saying such things if he wasn't my best friend. And a better shot."

"No offense meant, Cholly. Just, oh, blast, that little French warbler turned out to be a littler French Cit. Selling herself instead of starving, with that bastard Bottwick's help. I just can't stomach it."

Cholly loosened his neckcloth. "I see what you mean about m'sisters. I might wish them to the devil, but still and all, mean to take care of them."

"Still and all, they are all somebody's sister! Or daughter, or something! I never thought about it much either till this blasted Mignon turned into a watering pot in my bed."

"So what are you going to do with her?"

Gard took a sip of his drink. "Damned if I know. Imagine if I took her home to the countess. She'd skin me alive. And if I adopt the chit, pay for her singing lessons and stuff, no one will believe I'm not keeping her anyway. She'll never find that husband she wants. For sure I can't throw her back to that shark Bottwick, either." He had another drink.

"What can she do?" Cholly wanted to know.

"You mean besides stir up hornets' nests? She sings a little, and that blasted convent must have taught her something. Needlework, pianoforte, I'd guess." He laughed. "If you're thinking of recommending her for a governess, I'd add that she speaks French like a native."

"Not a governess, exactly," Cholly deliberated, puffing on his cigar. "You know, m'sisters could use a little polish. Trying to fire all five off at once was a mistake. Told my mother, but they're all of an age, or near enough as makes no difference."

"I danced with one of them at Almack's, didn't I? Sorry, I can't remember which. She had your color hair, though."

"Carroty. They all do. And no one can tell them apart, and not just the twins. They're pretty enough, and all have respectable dowries, but they've got no style. Just country girls, after all."

"Young misses aren't supposed to cut a dash, Cholly."

"Yes, but m'sisters get lost there with the Incomparables and the heiresses," he noted dismally. "They need something to set them apart."

"Something like a French doxie? Your wits have gone begging!"

"You said she's innocent, and I never did see a Frenchwoman without a good sense of fashion. Told m'mother the chits needed dressing up, but she's more interested in her roses and dogs."

"You really think you could hire Mignon on as some kind of fashion adviser?"

"Got to do something if I'm not going to have all five of them around the rest of my life! She'd be more like a companion or something. You know, go about with the girls, show them how to go on, music lessons, a little French. M'mother won't care that the chit's been on the stage; she ain't so strait-laced. She's only concerned with bloodlines for her hounds."

"But what about the expense?" He knew his friend wasn't plump in the pocket, but Gard couldn't give insult by offering to pay Mignon's salary, although he'd gladly pay it, twice over.

"Well, m'brother—he's the head of the family now, don't you know—holds the purse strings for the girls' come-outs. Guess he'd be as happy as I am to do anything to get them off his hands. I could tell him it's an investment."

"And I'll convince Mignon she'll be happy as a grig." Gard leaned back in his chair, his muscles finally relaxing. "What would I do without you, Cholly?"

Cholly was still thinking. "Can't take her around to parties and the like, but maybe we can find her a clerk or something to marry."

"And I'll throw in a portion for the chit!" the earl declared happily, raising his glass to Cholly's in a toast to their plan. "I'll send her round in the morning, then, after my ride."

"Still seeing that veiled charmer in the park? Have you found out who she is yet? Everyone's waiting for the word so they can settle the wagers."

Lord Gardiner smiled, a slow, sensuous grin. "No, not yet."

Cholly smiled back in relief. "That's more like it. You had me worried there, old boy." The earl cocked an eyebrow in inquiry. "You know, how your name is coming up a lot in conversation."

"But, Cholly, my name is always coming up a lot in the gossip. What's the worry?"

"Worry is, seems your name's the only thing coming up."

Chapter Eighteen

*W*as she wearing the same green habit so he would recognize her, or because it was the only one she owned?

How long before his honorable intents gave way to his lustful nature and he made her an improper offer?

So many questions, so few answers. They rode silently again, enjoying the ride, but very aware of the other's presence. As they neared the park exit Lord Gardiner spoke up: "We have never been formally introduced, ma'am, and I should not want you thinking I am some unmannered brute. I am Ross Gardiner, at your service. My friends call me Gard." He looked to see if she was acknowledging his offer of friendship. Blast, what was with women these days? They were all making themselves unreadable in their spectacles and veils.

Here it comes, Annalise thought, disappointed but not surprised. Here is where he starts casting his net. She ignored him, pretending to adjust her skirts.

Ross laughed. "Very well. I may be Gard later. Today I am merely the honor guard, sworn to shield you from insults and advances. I am, indeed, honored that you accepted my offer to lend you protection. I hope that someday you will honor me with your name."

The silver-tongued devil! "I—"

The earl held up a gloved hand. He could tell by her hesitation that whatever name she gave would be a lie. He was jumping his fences. "No, I am not asking. I gave my word to respect your privacy. I find I do not like addressing my riding partner as miss or ma'am, however. May I call you Miss Green?"

Annalise kept her voice low, husky. "That will be fine, my lord."

"And your horse?"

Her horse? Why should he want to call her horse anything, except as a way of tracing her identity? Regrettably, Seraphina was too uncommon, and the mare was not likely to respond to an alias. "Beauty," she whispered a pet name for the horse softly, and Seraphina blessedly flicked her ears.

"Perfect." The earl nodded approvingly. "Although I might have thought you'd call her Socks, or Bootsy."

"My lord?"

"Her white stockings. If I might be so bold as to offer a word of advice, strictly in my role as protector, do have a word with your grooms, Miss Green. I know they are loyal, courageous chaps; I saw them fight in your defense. But I think they have taken too many blows to the head. Yesterday Beauty had one white stocking on her rear legs, her right rear leg to be exact. Today her left leg is white. It's a wonder she hasn't four stockings, or two."

Annalise laughed. What else could she do? "I am afraid I have no aptitude for hugger-mugger either. Thank you, my lord. I shall be more careful in the future."

Her chiming laughter was a delight, lighthearted yet refined. Youthful. Not childish, he amended to himself, thinking of Mignon, just young. But a young lady of breeding, riding out with two ruffians as guards? He was no closer to solving the mystery than he was yesterday. More important than that, he realized, was his real desire to win her trust—and to keep her from harm if the reason for her secrecy was actually perilous. "Miss Green, I know that we are hardly acquainted, but I believe the deceptions and disguises you are forced to practice are against your nature."

If he only knew, Annalise thought, laughing again, this time to herself, in despair.

"If—nay, when—you come to trust me, please believe that I will do everything in my power to assist you."

To assist her into his bed, Annalise still believed. The man had endearing moments of nobility, though, for a cad.

"I have recently come to a better understanding of women's plight," he continued, and she believed him. Now, if he just stopped using her home as a house of convenience, if he found a lady from his own class, married, and stayed constant for thirty or forty years, she just might change her opinion of him.

While he was out, Lord Gardiner decided to ride over to Drury Lane. Bottwick was not well pleased to receive an irate nobleman, nor the information that Mimi would not be coming back, except to fetch her belongings.

"You can't do that, no matter who you think you are! I got my rights to the wench!"

"Oh, yes? Rights such as slavery? I believe there are laws about that, as well as regarding child prostitution," the earl quietly informed him, eyeing the smaller man through lowered brows. "I should not like to hear of another underage chit being pushed along that path." Gard flicked his riding crop against his highly polished Hessians, giving Bottwick time to digest the unspoken words. "Have I made myself clear?"

As clear as any member of Parliament, a patron of the theater, and a pupil of Gentleman Jackson's needed to be, especially when he held a whip in his hand. Bottwick mumbled his assent, not loudly enough for Lord Gardiner's satisfaction. The earl punctuated his disapproval with a quick right jab that got him the desired promise.

On Gard's way out of the theater, one of the actresses not quite accidentally bumped into him. He automatically reached out to steady her, and somehow found his hand on a bit of flesh that would tempt any anatomy student.

"Oh, la," she squealed, "sure and I should watch where I'm going."

Gard looked into brown eyes with soot-darkened lashes, under hair a yellow color never seen in nature. The amplitude of her endowments, however, were more often found in dairy barns. He grinned. "Sure and you didn't see a wee fellow like me."

She winked, laid a hand on his arm, and drew him aside. "I couldn't help overhearing your argle-bargle with that spalpeen Bottwick, me lord. 'Tis a shame, it is, about the young 'uns, and I admire a fine gent like yourself for not taking advantage. Bessie O'Neill, I be, and I didn't come down in the last snowfall."

Or the one before that, he'd wager. Bessie was

definitely not a child, definitely not a lady, and definitely not unwilling. And he was needing something to get his mind off the woman in the park before he became totally obsessed with her and her intrigues. Besides, Bessie's bountiful curves would be spectacular on canvas. He'd hardly done more than a sketch, Gard calculated, since the night of the infamous drawing party in the ballroom. By all that was holy, he hadn't had a woman since then either!

"Are you free tonight after the performance?"

"Free? No, not even for a bonny laddy like you, but I'll be waiting for you after the show."

Next he went to discuss Mignon's future with the girl. Leaving his stallion with Tuthill in the stable, Gard walked through the back door of the town house. Mrs. Tuthill was busy at the stove, and Annie sat at the kitchen table having her breakfast, her back to him.

"Good morning," he called, noticing the way Annie snatched up her spectacles from the table and shoved them on her face before jumping up to curtsy. "No, don't let me interrupt your breakfast. I just wanted to tell Mignon I think there's a solution to her dilemma."

Annie remained on her feet, looking regretfully at her plate. "She's still asleep, poor child. Should I go wake her?"

"No, I can explain to you, and you can tell her when she gets up. Do eat your food while it is hot."

He looked so enviously at Annie's piled plate that she was forced to offer him something to eat before she could enjoy her own meal.

"Thank you," he said when Mrs. Tuthill brought him a cup of coffee and two slices of dry toast. He looked over at the housekeeper's plate, where reposed fluffy eggs, warm muffins, a rasher of ham, a helping of kidneys, then back at his spartan fare. So he was still in Mrs. Tuthill's black books, was he? At least she was feeding Annie properly; the woman no longer looked as if the first wind would blow her over. He watched her butter her muffin with the delicacy of a duchess and wondered again about this peculiar woman. He shrugged. Give him a female like Bessie any day.

"You were going to tell us about Mignon, my lord," Annalise interrupted his musings. "Have you found a place for her then?"

"I think I have the ideal solution." And he proceeded to relate his conversation with Cholly, about the five plain sisters and negligent mother, the absentee heir who paid the bills. "So she'll have a home and companions and an income. Perhaps she'll find she has a flair for being a ladies' maid or companion. Cholly thinks we ought to be able to find a husband for her. He's the best of good fellows, so you needn't worry on that score, or that there might be anything harum-scarum about his household. I'll keep an eye on the infant myself, of course."

"An excellent solution, my lord," Annie congratulated him, and Mrs. Tuthill placed a large steak in front of him. Now this was more like!

"Yes, and I've already been backstage. No one will bother Mignon when she goes to pick up her things. Make sure Tuthill goes inside with her anyway, just to make sure. I would take her myself, but it wouldn't do for her to arrive on Cholly's doorstep in my curricle. Not even Mrs. Fansoll is that open-minded."

Next Ross had the unprecedented honor of basking in the glory of Annie Lee's approval. He was clever and kind and wise. Gads, that it should come to this, that he cared what an ugly old housekeeper thought of him! "Oh, yes, I've already informed

Tuthill about the company this evening. He'll fetch the lady. I may be delayed. I know you'll make her welcome; you were very kind about Sophy and again with Mignon. We do not always agree, Annie, and I still believe you are an odd kind of employee, but I do appreciate your efforts."

Annalise ignored the flummery and Henny's cough. "A lady?"

He found himself coloring. "Her name is Bess. She's from the theater."

Annie stood. "Well, then, there's a lot to be done. If you are finished, my lord?" And she took his plate away before he could protest. He had not gone halfway through the excellent steak, cooked precisely the way he liked it, and now she was feeding it to the ugliest little dog he had ever seen. It figured.

Mignon was tearfully thankful when Annalise told her of the plan. Those were her very favorite things: fashions and sewing, music and speaking French! How could she not be happy, with five young ladies to teach how to flirt! "And I shall do such a fine job of it, they will all marry dukes, no? But not so soon, I think, that I find myself with no position. Ah, *mademoiselle*, I owe you such a debt!"

Annalise was annoyed with the earl, to put it mildly. Still, she had to give him the proper credit. "You owe me nothing. It is Lord Gardiner you must be sure to thank."

"Milord is the true *gentilhomme*, no? Yet I think he would never have come to help Mignon without you. Please, what may I do to repay your kindness? I would do anything for you."

"Anything? Very well, you may tell your friends in the cast, especially the one called Bessie, that his lordship has the pox!"

Mignon's eyes grew round. "The pox? *Mon Dieu!* That is better than the other thing, I suppose. But

152

milord has been so good to me, *n'est-ce pas*, how can I play him such a trick?" She studied Annalise, tugging the spectacles and the awful cap away. "You pull the lamb over his eyes, no?"

"The wool, Mignon. Yes, but you mustn't tell. There are good reasons."

"My lips, they are sealed. But how can I tell such lies about the *grand monsieur*?"

"It's for his own good, I swear! You'd be saving him from a life of sin, the way he saved you."

Mignon looked doubtful, a world of wisdom in her young eyes. "I don't think it is the same, *mademoiselle*. I don't think it is the same at all."

Chapter Nineteen

$\mathcal{B}$essie came prepared. When Annie led her upstairs to show her where she might wait, the bleached and painted actress plucked two sausage casings out of her reticule. At least they looked something like sausage casings to Annalise. She averted her eyes.

"In case that rumor is true," Bessie said with a loud laugh, noticing where Annie couldn't look.

"His lordship . . . that is . . ." Annalise began, forcing herself.

"That other muckle rumor? A brae, lusty lad like himself? Don't worry, m'dear, Bessie's never lost a patient yet." She slapped her knee and laughed herself into a coughing fit.

Between trying not to glance at the items on the nightstand and trying not to stare at Bessie's expansive figure, wondering how a scrap of lace at the neckline could keep all that quivering flesh restrained, Annalise had nowhere to focus her eyes. So she looked under the bed. And behind the dresser, in the water closet, beneath the chintz-covered boudoir chair.

"What's that you're after, dearie?" Bessie wanted to know.

Annalise's muffled reply came from inside the wardrobe. "Mice. We're overrun with the pesky beasts. You're not afraid, are you?"

"Bessie O'Neill, afeared of a wee rodent? No, we have them in and out of the dressing rooms all the time. Takes more than that to send me scurrying. Now, snakes is another thing. I cannot abide the slimy things. Can't even be in the same room with a picture of one. Makes my skin crawl."

Snakes? Where was Annalise to get a snake in the middle of the night? In the middle of London? She might be able to locate an eel, perhaps, if she could bear to handle it. Somehow she doubted that Lord Gardiner would believe that one just happened to appear in his bed chamber, like the plagues falling on Egypt. If he ever suspected—no, that did not bear thinking on. She'd seen the man in a temper, and it was bad enough, thank you. One of his rages would be nothing compared to what would happen if he discovered her conniving against him. But this vulgar woman was taking her shoes off and sprawling on the bed, appendages bobbling about like melons in a basket.

"You know his lordship might be very late, don't you? Surely you'll have to get back for rehearsal."

"Not to worry. Rehearsal's not till three tomorrow, and I know my part so well, I can skip it. Now, beauty sleep is another matter. I'll just catch me a little nap while I wait, dearie. Be a pet and blow out some of the candles, won't you?"

"Ah, miss, you wouldn't by chance believe in ghosts, would you?" It was worth a try.

"Nary a bit, dearie. Old Bess believes in two things: having a good time and getting paid for it."

So Annalise paid her. She always hated that bracelet anyway.

The earl strode up to the door with a jaunty tread, a large pad under one arm and a box of charcoal drawing crayons in the other. He'd made a special trip to the art supply dealers on New Bond Street to find just the right shade of yellow for Bessie's hair. He also purchased a new pencil of emerald green.

Annie opened the door to his eager face, wiping the smile right away with her words: "I am sorry, my lord. Miss O'Neill was called away. A sick relative, I believe."

Gard looked at the pad in his hand, then he turned and pounded his head on the open door. He never even got to touch this one!

"My lord?"

He straightened up and adjusted his neckcloth. "Yes, Annie. Thank you."

"Mrs. Tuthill is fixing supper. Buttered crab, vol-au-vents of veal, braised duckling, and one of her special custard puddings. Will you be staying?"

It was better fare than he'd get at his club, and the temperamental master chef he kept at Grosvenor Square would resign if Gard woke him to cook a late-night snack. It did occur to the earl, and not for the first time, that in some ways he was more at home here than he was at home. Of course, he'd never spent the night upstairs in that bed which looked so inviting, but there wasn't all that kowtowing and ceremonial toadying, either. Even the outrageous tirades from his ill-behaved housekeeper were more mentally challenging than his mother's nagging harangues. At least Annie never dragged forth his father's ghost. At Laurel Street Ross could eat in the kitchen if he wanted—which was what he decided, in fact—instead of dining in state at Gardiner House. He ruefully acknowledged that if he kept eating instead of partaking of his usual exercise, he'd be fat as a flawn in no time.

He sketched Mrs. Tuthill while she bustled around the kitchen.

"Why, it's me to the inch! What a gift you have indeed, my lord. My Robbie will think it's a treat! Why, you could be one of those fancy portrait artists, I swear."

"Most likely no one would pose for me, either," he mumbled under his breath, not realizing Annie was beside him, setting the table for his meal. She camouflaged a giggle with a cough. The earl looked up. "Should you like me to do your portrait, too, Annie?"

Her exultation fled. She did not want him staring at her. Even his quick glances made her uncomfortable, and not just because he might see through her disguise. He was so handsome; she was homely. She slammed the plate down in front of him so hard, the sturdy table shook. "What for? I know what I look like, and no one else cares to look at an ugly old hag."

"I think your face might show a great deal of character, Annie, if you removed the spectacles. At least consider it."

"Mrs. Tuthill will serve your dinner, my lord. I have accounts to look over."

"I didn't mean to insult her," the earl told a frowning Mrs. Tuthill after Annie left.

"She's sensitive about her looks," the older woman replied, banging pans together.

"I suppose it cannot be easy, seeing beautiful women come and go"—mostly go, he mused—"in a place like this. I wonder if that's why she's so prickly, if it's not jealousy instead of moral indignation after all."

"Beauty is as beauty does," Mrs. Tuthill advised

157

tersely, then exclaimed, "Oh, drat, the custard burned. You weren't waiting for dessert, were you?"

Then again, in Grosvenor Square he wasn't sent to his room without dessert for being naughty. The earl sighed and got up. "Thank you for an excellent dinner, Mrs. Tuthill. I think I'll have my port in the front parlor, by the fire."

He *thought* she grumbled, "You'll do as you please and be damned for it," but he had to be mistaken. Servants just did not behave that way, not even in Bloomsbury.

Gard lounged on the sofa. He was comfortable, warm, moderately well-fed, and bored. He was restless—hell, he was frustrated! He felt like a stallion who knows there's a mare in season somewhere, if he could just get out of the blasted stable. Staring at the flames, drumming his fingers on the inlaid table next to him, the earl contemplated a visit to Mother Ignace's after all.

"Your port, my lord," Annie said, putting the tray down with an audible thud that startled Ross into wondering if the witch could read his mind. He sat up and caught himself reaching to check his cravat. No, no deuced servant was going to reduce him to schoolboy status once more, in his manners or his morals. He sprawled back again, satisfied. Except that she was leaving, and he'd have no one to talk to at all, blast it. Even her viperish tongue was better company than his own unsatisfied thoughts.

"Have you finished the accounts? That is, must you go?"

"My lord?" If bats had established residence in his belfry, she couldn't look more surprised, glasses or no.

He stared around in desperation, till his eyes alighted on the pianoforte. Sheets of music were unfolded on the stand, sheets that had not been there the last time he looked. "Did, ah, Bessie play the instrument?"

"No, my lord," Annie replied, cursing herself for being a skitter-witted noddy, leaving the music out that way. She knew what was coming next.

"Then it was you," he stated, not asking a question at all, and not the least astonished that his housekeeper could play, no matter that no servant in his experience had ever done so. Annie hadn't done the expected yet. "Will you play for me?"

Annalise surprised even herself by agreeing. Why give his suspicions more foundation? Why spend one instant more in the skirter's company than she had to? Possibly, she answered herself while sorting through the music, because he looked so pathetically forlorn there on a couch made for two, and so devastatingly handsome with his collar loosened and his dark hair tousled. As she struck the first tentative chords, she told herself this was the only charitable thing to do, since she had bought off his evening's entertainment.

"I am out of practice, my lord," she apologized beforehand.

"I am no expert, to be criticizing your technique, Annie. I just like to listen."

She nodded and started off with a few country ballads, a delicate Irish air. He relaxed against the cushions, shutting his eyes in quiet enjoyment of her pleasant competency. Then she switched to Mozart and Handel, and played well. Better than well. Better than any servant with a few hours of free time to practice. He sat up and studied Annie, even as she became lost in the intricacies of the piece she played so masterfully.

Gard quietly took up his pad and a pencil without disturbing her concentration. The pencil stayed poised in air. From his angle the flaps on her cap hid most of her face, whatever the rims of the spectacles did not cover. And the sagging black gown only emphasized her figure's deficiencies. So he focused on her hands as they flowed over the keys.

The fingers were long and elegant, easily reaching the spread of ivories, not the bony talons they used to resemble. Her hands were not as red or work-roughened as he recalled, nor were they the cracked and lined and spotted hands of an older woman. Annie Lee was not old enough to have been in service for twenty-one years. He doubted if she'd worked very long at all, since she definitely had not managed to acquire a servile attitude. Most likely her soldier had left her in dun territory. How long since Corunna? "Do you miss James very much?" he asked when she reached the end of a piece.

Annalise was caught up in her music, the first time she'd really had to play in ages. And she was trying to play her best, for him. "Hmm? James who?"

"Your husband. James Jacob."

Her fingers hit a discordant note. "Oh, yes, him. Of course. Um, yes. That is, not so much anymore. Why?"

"No reason in particular. I was just wondering if the redoubtable Annie Lee ever got lonely like us poor mortals. Then, too, you don't appear quite settled in your life of servitude."

Annie shrugged. "I'll do." And she immediately swept into a piece by Beethoven, playing louder than necessary, eliminating the possibility of conversation. He sketched.

When she reached the final deafening crescendo, Lord Gardiner applauded. "Excellent, Annie, excellent. Rest awhile," he told her, placing a glass of wine in her hand, then sitting back down, his legs crossed in front of him. "I had a visit from the real estate agent," he mentioned casually, then paused as she choked on her wine. "He wanted to know if everything was satisfactory here."

Annalise put down the glass lest she spill it. "And what did you tell him, my lord?"

"That all was up to snuff. There was some puzzlement about the household staff. The man seemed to think Lady Rosalind took her servants with her."

As nonchalantly as she could, Annalise responded, "I believe I mentioned that Lady Rosalind did indeed take her butler and footman and abigail with her." She waved her hand, dismissing the man's confusion as beneath notice. It was a gesture more in keeping with a marchioness than a maidservant, if she but knew it.

The earl ran his finger around the rim of his glass. "He was also curious about some missing heiress. A relation to Lady Rosalind. Do you know anything about that?"

Annalise's hand accidentally struck the keyboard. She winced at the sound. "Only what I heard from a man who called here for information. He said he was looking for the stepdaughter of a Sir Vernon Thompson, who was also Lady Rosalind's niece. I told him all I knew, which is nothing really. Lady Rosalind has not been in contact with us, and neither has the niece."

"I see."

As he turned the pages of his drawing pad, Annalise wondered how much he really did see. "Seems a pity," she commented hurriedly, "about the girl, I mean. Dicked in the nob, the man said."

"Not to be wondered at if she's any connection to Thompson. The fellow's a curst loose screw. I pity the chit even more for that. Of course, it was a goosish thing to do, a young girl running off like she did. Any protection is better than having a gently bred female out on her own. Just look at what happened to Mignon. The girl's most likely bachelor fare by now, especially if she's knocked in the cradle, as you say."

Annalise returned to her music, pounding the keys into submission, her back even more rigid than usual.

Gard started to sketch her that way, in hard, jerky lines mimicking her agitated motions. He put in the cap, ear wings flapping like a hound's in the wind, and he put in the flat chest. He started on that stiff back which was not quite as flat as her front, due to the hump over her right shoulder. But wasn't it over her left shoulder yesterday? He tried to picture Annie sitting with Mignon on the bed, or giving him what-for in the hallway. Gard shook his head to clear it. First those white stockings on the mare, now the housekeeper's deformity. Lack of sex must be addling his mind.

Chapter Twenty

"Lack of sex addles a man's mind, chickie. Let me tell you, the fellow's wastin' away with unfulfilled desire."

"Fustian," Annalise replied as she and Rob Tuthill walked toward the hackney waiting to drive her to the livery stable. "It's good for his soul. Think of all those monks and saints and martyrs."

Rob spit at a streetlamp. "Them holy sorts chose that way of life. The gov'nor didn't. And I say keepin' a man from his pleasure ain't good for him, besides bein' cruel and heartless. It ain't like you, chickie," he said, shaking his head in sorrow.

"I say it builds character, and his needs it! Did you get a look at that last harlot, that Bessie O'Neill?"

Rob grinned. "An eyeful, all right. But frustration don't build character, missy. That's just a tale the preachers made up to keep the peasants from overpopulatin' the countryside like rabbits. Hell, all frustration builds is aggravation and aggression—

like two male dogs meetin' in a dusty street. I don't like what you're doin' to him."

"I haven't touched him! I promised I wouldn't." Annalise kicked at a pebble in her way. "Besides, you can stop worrying about your randy friend. I am running out of ideas to discourage his particulars. I can't keep giving my jewelry away to every loose woman in London." She kicked harder at the pebble, sending it flying into the roadway. "And I'm sure he'll find every last one of them."

"It's good that you're givin' up. We'd be seein' the whites of his eyes soon else, and then watch out. Red-blooded fellow like the earl's bound to explode from pent-up feelin's and unused energies. You can't mess with life's drivin' forces, chickie, without stirrin' up a mare's nest of trouble."

"Oh, pooh," Annalise pronounced, but she did ride a little farther away from Gard that morning, as if he were a bonfire about to go up in smoke with the slightest touch. He was quiet, thoughtful, paying little attention to her after his usual polite greeting. His lack of interest should have contented her since she did not want him getting up a flirtation with her, nor asking questions to ease his curiosity. Neither reason sat well. Piqued, she even considered initiating conversation.

Then a man stepped onto the path and called, "Miss Avery? Miss Annalise Avery?" It was that same man again, Sir Vernon's unctuous footman, Stavely. Outwardly Annalise stayed calm, but Seraphina took exception.

"Are you all right?" the earl asked when she had the mare under control again.

"Yes, that peculiar person just startled my mare. I, ah, wonder what he was about."

Grimly, the earl declared, "I intend to find out." He gestured to her bodyguards to close ranks around her and the mare, then rode back along the path and dismounted, tying his stallion's reins to a park bench. In three long strides he was next to the pomaded footman, who shrank back, but not in time to avoid being grabbed around the neck and shaken like a rag. "What the bloody hell do you think you're doing, jumping out in front of horses that way?" Lord Gardiner demanded. "You could have caused a serious accident."

"Not if she's Miss Avery, I couldn't," the dangling servant said, valiantly trying to defend his actions. "She's supposed to be the best horsewoman in the shire."

"What shire might that be, sirrah?"

"W-Worcester, where she and Sir Vernon Thompson reside, my lord."

"Well, I assure you, and Sir Vernon, that the young woman with me is not his ward. I do not now and never will dally with wellborn ladies. Next thing I knew, some maggot like Sir Vernon would be demanding I marry his repulsive relation. This lady—and I am informing you just to make things clear, not that I have any intention of discussing my personal affairs with the likes of you or your obnoxious employer—is Miss Green, and she is in my keeping. I will take it seriously amiss if you disturb her again. Do you understand?"

How could the man not understand, with a fist like iron wrapped around his neck and his feet off the ground? "I'll tell Sir Vernon, my lord. Your lady's not a lady."

There, Annalise thought, watching from a distance, Robb was wrong. Lord Gardiner didn't explode, just quietly restricted himself to minor mayhem, which was not entirely undeserved, in her estimation. She smiled and rode on, missing the murder in his eyes when he joined her.

"Excuse the disturbance, my dear, it will not happen again."

See? He was the perfect gentleman. She was building his character after all.

She smiled cheerfully during the rest of their ride. His lordship gnawed on the inside of his cheek.

Rob's news about more company that evening destroyed Annalise's good humor. Not even a visit from an exuberant Mignon could restore her mood, nor the young girl's news that Bottwick had a broken nose. Instead of showing noble restraint in not skewering the scoundrel, Lord Gardiner's actions now seemed to reflect his lordship's savage nature, a nature that gave in to every base instinct.

"That dastard!"

"Bottwick?"

"No, Lord Gardiner."

"*Monsieur* the earl? But no, he saves my life, *vraiment*. He makes that pig Bottwick give my back wages. And he sends me to stay with my new family, the Fansolls."

With an effort, Annalise managed to get her mind off the invidious earl. "You are content with your new position, then?"

"How not?" Mignon said, grinning. "My young ladies are *très charmantes*, and I have a room all to myself, so I can come and go like tonight, once they are out to their balls and parties. *Madame* Fansoll is *aux anges* to be relieved of worrying over the fashions and invitations and dancing lessons. Me, I take charge." She giggled and whispered confidingly, "Someday I plan to take charge of *Monsieur* Fansoll, too."

"Charge of him, the earl's friend, Cholly?" Annalise echoed, unwilling to voice her fears.

"Oh, la, marriage, *certainement*. But he does not know it yet."

"Lord Gardiner admires him exceedingly, and I am sure he is a praiseworthy gentleman, but do you think . . ." Annalise was not sure how to proceed. She did not want to hurt the girl's feelings; neither did she want Mignon to get her hopes up.

"That he will marry a penniless orphan who once acted on the stage?"

"And who now is in his employ as companion to his sisters, yes," Annalise concluded sadly. "Don't you think you might be flying too high?"

Mignon settled back with her chocolate, one of Henny's macaroons, and a grin. "Ah, but Cholly is a second son."

"Whose brother is a marquis."

"Who has as many sons as Cholly has sisters! *Mon cher* Cholly says he wants only to be a farmer on his small property, once his sisters are settled. He is not high in the inseam."

"Instep."

"Whatever." The girl shrugged and had another macaroon. "*Eh bien,* now we have settled my future, what shall we do about yours, *mademoiselle?* This disguise is abdominal, no?"

"Abominable, yes. But necessary. I do not want to get you involved, Mignon, so I cannot discuss it."

"Can you not go to milord for help? He was kind to me, no?"

Annalise sipped her tea. "Yes, he was, but this is different. He'd be furious, not just that I tricked him, but that I am a lady he might feel honor-bound to offer for, since I have been living under his roof. And if my real identity became known around, I'd be ruined forever." She didn't mention that she'd be hauled back to Thompson Hall and locked up. That was too dismal a burden to lay on Mignon's young shoulders.

"I think there is much you don't say. *Tiens,* my head aches from these complicated matters. Still, I do not understand why you ruin milord's pleasure."

"I cannot live here in a house of sin if I am to

have any reputation at all. Surely you must see that! Besides, his pleasure seeking is wrong! Every child learns he cannot have every desire gratified. It is time Lord Gardiner learned temperance, moderation, patience. It is good for his soul."

Mignon nodded wisely. "*Enfin*, you want him for yourself."

The cup Annalise was holding clattered back in its saucer. "That's outrageous! I despise the man. He is nothing but a wicked, wanton sinner. What do you know anyway? You are just a child."

"I am not so much younger than you, *oui*? I think I have seen more of the world. Milord Gardiner is a nonpareil, no? How could you not want him? If not for Cholly, I might set my sights on him myself. But no, milord is too proud for one like me."

"He is as proud as Lucifer. An arrogant, swaggering, insufferable man. Having his wishes thwarted once in a while will make him more humble, more human."

Grinning again, Mignon asked, "And you have a plan?"

Well, no, Annalise was forced to admit, she was fresh out of plans. She had this pair of mice, fat and friendly little fellows, but the women Lord Gardiner seemed to choose were made of coarser weave. And her plan to pay them off and send them on their way before he ever got near enough to smell their cheap perfume was not working. In fact, now the tarts thought they could earn an easy wage just by showing up at Laurel Street! One of the other actresses at Drury Lane had had the nerve to write to Lord Gardiner, suggesting a liaison. Rob had taken the perfumed note around to Grosvenor Square and waited to carry the return message. Now he was assigned to convey the hussy to Bloomsbury this evening.

"Which actress is it, do you know?" Mignon asked.

"I think her name was Lilabette. Do you know her?"

"Ah, that one. She had leading roles, so was too grand to notice us poor girls in the chorus. She had to have her own dressing room, and a carriage to pick her up and take her home. Do not worry, my friend, Mignon shall get rid of her for you."

Annalise stared uncertainly at the gamin grin on the petite blonde's face. "How?"

"I think you do not want to know, my dear Annie."

"May I show you upstairs to refresh yourself before dinner, ma'am?" Annie asked the Exquisite in the hallway, taking her ermine wrap.

"I'll be right back, darling, don't go far," Lilabette told the earl, not deigning to acknowledge the housekeeper's presence except for an abrupt "I am sure I can find it myself" as she slithered up the stairs in her red silk. Annie busied herself in the parlor, poking at the fire and fluffing up sofa pillows, taking surreptitious peeks at the earl in his form-fitting evening clothes that accented his broad shoulders and well-muscled legs. Then she heard the shrieks.

"What the blazes?" Gard yelled, starting for the hall. Lilabette met him, coming down the stairs. She smacked him across the cheek, grabbed her fur from Annie, and flounced out of the door.

"What the blue blazes?" the earl repeated, rubbing his cheek, but Annie was already up the stairs before him. Following, he halted at the doorway to his chamber—his unused, unchristened chamber— to see Annie's black-clad derriere sticking up from under the bed.

Bemused, he asked, "What the devil are you doing?"

"Mice" came back the muffled reply. "Maybe that's what frightened her."

So she slapped him? She must have hit him harder than he thought, for he was content for now to contemplate his housekeeper's hind end.

Annalise meanwhile was staring at Mignon, but a Mignon she hardly recognized, with painted lips, rouged cheeks, frizzed hair, and a diaphanous nightgown. To her horror, this jezebel whispered, "I told her we'd share!"

Now Annie shrieked. The earl ran over, she jumped up, they bumped heads.

"What is it? What the deuce is going on? Mice, you say?"

"No, no. Just a spider. I was frightened when it ran over my hand, is all. I am sorry, my lord." She looked around, making sure he noted that not a cover was out of place, everything was as it ought. "The lady must have seen it, too."

So she slapped him?

After another excellent repast—this time he even got a syllabub for dessert—Lord Gardiner tried to relax on the sofa while Annie played. Relax? His body was as taut as a bow string! And all Annie was playing were jolly, lilting country songs. What the devil did she have to be so blasted cheerful about?

And by all that was holy, what in tarnation was happening to him? Once or twice in his later years he'd been disappointed in an assignation. Zeus, carriages broke down, women became ill. But *every* woman? *Every* night? Something was dreadfully, absurdly wrong. He'd get to the bottom of this tomorrow night or his name was not Ross Montclaire. If he didn't, he'd likely slit his own throat shaving.

Gard was promised to his mother for Vauxhall Gardens the next evening. Surely he'd find a warm and willing companion down one of the dark walks there.

That comforting thought was all he had to take to bed with him that night, along with the refrain of Annie's music.

Chapter Twenty-one

So, was his riding partner the missing heiress? Gard rather thought so. Rumors were starting to percolate around town, and while no one actually claimed to have seen Miss Avery, her description was on everyone's lips. Tallish, a Diamond of the first water although recently ill, a superb horsewoman with golden hair and green eyes. The woman riding so handily next to him had silvery curls, from what he could see—perhaps bleached?—but that emerald habit had to have been created for a green-eyed wench. No one else suspected, it seemed, for once the Lady in Green was firmly established as his mistress, she was ignored by the ton.

The real coil was what he was going to do about it. The best solution, Ross told himself, was to marry the chit. Somehow the idea did not stick in his throat as it usually did. His mother was right, it was time for him to set up his nursery, especially after that last scare. And he'd never fall in love with any of the brainless twits his mother paraded past him with such regularity. At least this lady would not jabber his ear off, he considered, finding that he liked her quiet, reserved ways. Miss Avery's breeding was not quite what an earl might consider, but the taint of a grandfather in trade was balanced by a grandfather who was a duke, albeit an unaccepting one. The merchant connection was also deceased, leaving Miss Avery a considerable fortune, both of which were frequent causes of memory lapses among society. The heiress might be his answer.

As for Miss Avery, her reputation would be restored and her deliverance guaranteed from whatever scheme that muckworm Thompson was plotting. And she'd be getting one of the premier bachelor catches of this and many a London Season. Yes, it would serve. Unless the woman at his side really was a Bedlamite, or had run away to join a lover, or was not the missing Miss Avery at all. The first thing to do was place the chit under his mother's chaperonage, which would eliminate any chance of dalliance as well as calm the gossip. In truth, one did not wish one's future countess considered fast.

"I am getting up a party for Vauxhall this evening, Miss Green," he told her. "Many ladies there wear dominoes, even on non-masquerade nights. Might you consider attending with me?"

Annalise knew all about Vauxhall, thanks to Lorna and Mignon. How dare he ask such a thing of her after his promise of respect? She raised her chin in a gesture Lord Gardiner was coming to recognize as affronted dignity.

"With my mother, of course, as chaperone. No insult intended, ma'am."

Annalise was astounded. "You would invite a stranger to sit with your mother?" she asked, trying to remember in her incredulity to lower her tone of voice. "What if I am not respectable?"

"I refuse to believe that. I think you must need some diversion, an evening of fun, no matter what hobble you are in."

"Thank you. I should enjoy it, I think, but I must refuse. It would be too dangerous, and unfair to expose your mother and guests to possible unpleasantness."

"Spoken like the true lady I know you to be," he approved. "Perhaps you will reconsider when they hold a true masquerade there, just the two of us?"

She shook her head sharply no and tapped Seraphina lightly to pick up the pace. Gard stayed right beside her. "I do wish you would let me help you, my dear, whatever the problem is."

"I cannot. But thank you. You have already given me a great deal of pleasure by accompanying me on my rides. I will understand if you wish to discontinue the association, however, since nothing can come of this. No other relationship is possible."

"Deuce take it, I am not pressuring you into anything you dislike. I told you I would not. I am satisfied with your company, Miss Green." For now, he told himself. "I am not a wild beast, you know, who needs a physical relationship with every female he meets."

Annalise almost fell off her horse, which effectively cut the ride short.

Maybe she wasn't the missing heiress after all, Gard thought.

Annalise rode home more frightened than she had been since leaving Sir Vernon's house. Her reputation was already in shreds, no matter as a housekeeper in a rake's house, or mistress in the same rake's keeping. Everyone assumed the latter anyway, she knew, from the smiles she received when he was by her side and from the way the occasional lady out exercising her horse looked away when they passed. She had no future anywhere, except perhaps with Barnaby. There was nothing her aunt could do, either, especially not with Lady Ros's own blotted copybook.

Her worst fear, though, was one that had kept her up all night and stood fair to muddle her dreams for many a night to come. She was sorely afraid that Mignon was correct, that besides losing all hope of happiness, she really had lost her heart to an unprincipled rogue.

Lord Gardiner did not have to seek a woman for the night among the frail sisterhood who haunted the Dark Walks of Vauxhall Gardens. One of his mother's guests, the only female over eighteen in the box, was Mrs. Throckmorton, whose eyes smoldered into his over the arrack punch. Whose bare toes massaged his thigh under the table during the shaved ham. Whose hand—whose husband passed out before the fireworks.

Why wait to get to Bloomsbury? the earl conjectured. The small Greek pavilions were scattered about the place for just such occasions. Zeus knew, he'd used them often enough. But Mrs. Throckmorton professed that she was there to chaperone her niece, one of the beruffled belles his mother had in mind for Gard. Mrs. Throckmorton insisted on discretion, which was fairly impossible for his lordship at this juncture anyway unless he remained seated.

So he scribbled the Laurel Street address on a card and whispered that they should meet there as soon as he dropped his mother at Grosvenor Square and she delivered her husband into his valet's hands. "Oh, yes," he added while another starburst went up. "Let me know if you notice anything peculiar about the place."

Having arrived just moments earlier, Mrs. Throckmorton was taking sherry in the parlor, according to Annie, who took the earl's cane and gloves, curtsied, and disappeared. For once she was acting the proper servant for the situation, Gard noted with relief, joining his guest.

The parlor was fine, too, he figured, eyeing the thick rug by the fire as Mrs. Throckmorton's clever hands continued their explorations. But, "Why don't you give me a minute or two before joining me upstairs?" she murmured to him, chuckling softly. "Hold the thought," she cooed, "but not too tightly, mind."

Those were perhaps the longest two minutes of his life, so he cheated. At the count of sixty Gard was up the stairs and on the landing outside the bedchamber, where Mrs. Throckmorton stood clutching her magenta dress together and screaming: "Peculiar? I'll give you something peculiar, you unnatural animal!" And she kicked him.

At least he wouldn't be wanting a woman for the next day or two, was his last coherent thought.

Annie stepped over the earl as he lay writhing and groaning on the wooden floor, with nary an ounce of pity for his plight. This time Mignon winked at her from inside the wardrobe, and bowed. Which was not inappropriate, since the grinning minx was wearing nankeen shorts, a schoolboy's jacket, and a short, curly wig.

"Anything?" Ross managed to grit his teeth and ask when Annie stepped over him again on her way out.

"No, perhaps the colors clashed with her gown."

* * *

One of Lord Gardiner's more fervent prayers was answered the next morning. No, Annie did not get on her broomstick and fly away, and no, Miss Green did not send him a billet-doux begging for an assignation. Instead, it rained. It rained so heavily that there was no chance of a ride in the park, thus no need to try to explain why Lord Gardiner was not in the saddle. He stayed in bed.

By midday his dreams were of the emerald rider and the mare: the perfect conformation, the supple movements and muscular strength and stamina, the graceful neck. And he wouldn't mind having the mare in his stable, either. Such dreams quickly gave rise to the conclusion that the good Lord obviously loved a sinner, for Gard suffered no permanent damage.

"Do we have an engagement for this evening?" he asked his mother over tea.

Hers must have had too much lemon in it, from the sour look the dowager gave her only son. "We were supposed to entertain Lady Barringdon and her granddaughter for dinner. The gel is a baroness in her own right, from one of those old land-grant titles that can pass through the female line, along with acres and acres in the Downs. They cried off for some silly reason." She looked at him through her lorgnette. "You didn't do anything to give 'em a disgust of you, did you?"

The earl couldn't imagine what. "I've been a paragon of virtue. And I don't even know the chit. Have we been introduced?"

The dowager struck him across the knuckles with her glass. "Scores of times, you clunch. A mother is always the last to know, but you must have done something terrible to keep Lady Barringdon from coming. The chit would have to be half dead before they'd give up a chance at a wealthy earl. Your father is not going to like this."

Lord Gardiner was not listening, sucking his knuckles and already planning on how to spend his delightfully free evening. There was nothing he could do about the Avery business, but he could positively get to the bottom of the problem at Laurel Street. All he needed was a willing woman.

The first three courtesans he approached in the park turned him down. Two had prior engagements, one a permanent jealous protector. Felice, a one-time associate of Harriet Wilson's, had an inflammation of the lungs. She cleared her throat a few times to prove it. At least the flower girl on the corner winked at him. How the mighty were fallen, he thought, considering the wench. She was pretty and reasonably clean, but he couldn't do it. Instead, he bought all of her wares and had a boy deliver them to Felice with his get-well wishes.

Two of the actresses at Drury Lane slammed their dressing room doors in his face, and one of the chorus girls laughed at him for asking if she was busy. What was wrong? Had he suddenly lost his fortune and no one told him? He caught a glimpse of his reflection in a shop window as he walked down Bond Street. He still had all his hair and all his teeth. Had the world and all its females suddenly gone daft?

And speaking of females, where the devil was he supposed to find one for tonight at this late hour? A shopgirl, a tavern wench, a denizen of one of the finer bawdy houses? Was that what Lord Gardiner was reduced to? He was the one who was so fastidious, he had to invest in his own love nest! He was determined to have a bed warmer tonight at any cost, because he couldn't think straight or keep his mind on the various intrigues that surrounded him. All he could hear was his own body's insistent clamoring.

Then he noticed a woman, an attractive woman,

staring into a millinery-shop window. She was dressed in the kick of fashion, and she was alone. She looked vaguely familiar, although Gard believed he'd last seen her wearing a ribbon around her middle—and nothing else—as she posed in his ballroom. The earl seldom forgot a pretty waist.

"Maudine, *ma belle*?" It was as easy as complimenting her taste in hats, assuring her no lady ever looked finer in that bird's nest of a bonnet, and paying for same. As down payment, it was understood.

He did not send a message to alert the staff in Bloomsbury of his arrival; he did not send for Tuthill to fetch the lady. Gard handed her into his curricle, sent his tiger home, and drove across town himself, determined not to let the female out of his sight. Maudine sat stiffly, one hand nervously clenched around the seat rail, but she smiled gallantly at him and touched the feathers on her new bonnet when the earl reassured her they were not likely to overturn.

Annie was polite, to Gard's surprise, despite the lack of notice of company. Dinner was undistinguished, mutton and kidney pie, served with a stony demeanor indicating this was the Tuthills' own meal, and now Mrs. Tuthill was going to have to start over again. She'd most likely start with the ingredients purchased for his dinner, the earl surmised from her pursed lips. Let the staff eat lark's tongues and pigeon's feet, he didn't care. Just let Maudine finish her raspberry trifle before he burst.

Just when she'd licked the last pink drop off her soft pink lips, just when he was about to lead her upstairs, Annie waylaid him with a message about a note being delivered. His mother came to mind immediately, right after Miss Avery. Gard followed Annie back to the door, where a small lad in short pants with brown curls and an oversize cap handed him a folded note in exchange for a coin. Gard started to open the message on his way to join Maudine then stopped with a curse. "Blast, this note is for a Lord Gortimer, not Lord Gardiner. You go on up, my dear, I'll just bring this back to the housekeeper to get rid of."

He met Maudine in the middle of the stairwell. He was going up, she was going down, fast. The wide-eyed look on her face made him pause. She raised her hand, he immediately took his off the stair rail to protect his privates. She put her hand to her mouth, gasping, "Don't touch me!" The chit was petrified—of him! Gard automatically took a step backward. And toppled down the stairs.

He knew he was alive because he could feel the breeze where Maudine had left the front door open and because someone had placed a damp towel on his forehead. He didn't bother getting to his feet in a hurry; there'd be nothing to see upstairs anyway.

So he missed watching Annie scurry around the bedroom stuffing whips and chains and manacles back into a cloth satchel.

Chapter Twenty-two

"*Y*ou look like the devil. What happened, did the dowager light into you again for not coming up to scratch with one of her choices?"

"Cut line, Cholly," the earl said as he carefully lowered himself into one of White's most comfortable chairs. "I do not wish to talk about it. I need a drink."

"Ah, another rash," his erstwhile friend concluded knowingly as they waited for the waiter to come take Gard's order.

"No, I do not have another rash. I fell down the stairs in that blasted house you convinced me to let for the season."

"What, Elphinstone's little hideout? Mean to say the place is decrepit?"

"No, I mean to say the place is haunted!"

Cholly shook his head. "You've been getting some deuced odd notions lately, and daresay I'm not the only one to notice." His round face cleared when the waiter brought a glass and two bottles. Cholly already had an empty one in front of him. "I bet the second bottle is a gift from Calthorpe, for winning his wager for him."

Gard lifted his glass to the foppish Calthorpe, who bowed back from across the room in a flourish of lace. Gard wrinkled his aristocratic nose. "What wager might that be?"

"You needn't put on that high-toned act with me, you know. It won't wash. Thought we was friends, though. Least you could have done was let me have a hint."

"Hell and damnation, Cholly, are you castaway so early in the night? What are you blathering about? I swear, I'm in no mood for anything to do with that queer nabs Calthorpe."

"Devilish glad to hear it, old fellow, though I never believed half the—" He caught the earl's lowered brows and changed tack. "Uh, the wager. You remember, I told you they were laying odds on the Incognita in the park."

The brandy was not sitting well on Lord Gardiner's stomach. "And?" he asked quietly, menacingly.

"And Calthorpe bet she was just some rich man's exotic bird of paradise. He followed her back from the park yesterday when you were done with your ride. Seems she leaves her horse near Cavendish Square and gets in a hackney, which meanders around a bit. You'll never guess where the hackney drops her, eh? You could have told me when I asked you, don't you know. Pockets are always to let and all, I could have used the extra blunt. All you said was not yet! Fine friend, Gard, be damned if I let you have one of m'sisters after all. Not sure anyway, with all the stories flying 'round."

Ross pushed the decanter out of Cholly's reach. "You've had enough. If you do not tell me where the hackney dropped the lady, I shall personally pull out every red hair on your head."

"Why, to your little love nest, of course, or did you think the ladybird was playing you false already?"

"And Calthorpe?" the earl ground out through clenched jaws.

"Well, you are as rich as Golden Ball, so he won. He's over there collecting now, counting his money."

Gard slowly stood and poured Calthorpe's bottle into one of the ferns. "You can tell him for me, Cholly, that if he ever goes near the lady again, or mentions her name, that he'll be counting his teeth next, in a glass beside his bed."

So Annie and the Tuthills were hiding Miss Green at Laurel Street, Lord Gardiner deduced. This conclusion explained a lot, especially if Miss Green was indeed the missing heiress, which was more and more likely. The fact that everyone else considered Miss Green his mistress was all that kept them from making the connection, while he knew for certain the woman had no ambitions along those lines. Heaven knew he'd dropped enough hints.

The real estate agent was right then; Lady Rosalind had not left any of her staff behind. The Tuthills and Annie must be Miss Avery's own loyal servants, that they would lie through their teeth for her. That also explained Annie's instant antipathy toward himself: The old family retainer deemed him a threat to Miss Avery. Naturally Annie also wished to discourage any inquisitive females from snooping around the premises, hence his disappearing demimondaines. Gard had no idea how Annie and the others were getting rid of his companions, but was certain they figured eliminating the women would eliminate his own troublesome presence. He rubbed the lump on the back of his head. Ha! They weren't going to deter him so easily!

Miss Avery knew of the plot all along, then, might even have been hiding in a cupboard somewhere while he toppled down the stairs. She must have been laughing up her sleeve at him every time she saw him. Blast, the chit was not so innocent after all. Perhaps marriage to her was not such a downy notion.

Ross was determined to have it out with Miss Avery that very morning during their ride, promise or no. Blister it, if she wished to stay at Laurel Street, let her do so openly. Everyone already believed he had installed her there. Then he thought of the parade of women through the house. Granted, they never stayed long—not nearly long enough—but, Zeus, that was not what a fellow wanted his future wife to see. 'Twas a poor reflection on his character, he supposed. Then again, he'd never considered himself good husband material, and a little conniver like Miss Avery would be satisfied with his wealth and title. If he decided to offer them to her.

Annalise arrived at the park before Lord Gardiner, so she decided to trot some of the fidgets out of Seraphina on the carriageway right by the gates. She was circling to come back when a man jumped out at her again, grabbing for the reins. This time Clarence was off his horse and had the man pinned to the ground before he could shout her name. The man was not a frippery footman, however; he was stocky and sandy-haired and full of bluster.

Annalise signaled Clarence to let the man up. "Hello, Barnaby. What brings you to London?"

"Jupiter, Leesie, you know dashed well what

brings me to London! I've been searching high and low for you, out to Bath and halfway to Wales, and here you are, bold as brass, riding in the park!" He angrily wiped the seat of his pants, which were now mud-streaked. "Or did you think I wouldn't recognize Seraphina, even with those ridiculous painted stockings that come off in the dew, when her sire was my own Altair?"

"Frankly, Barnaby, I didn't think you'd care."

"Not care? Not care when the woman I love is making a byword of herself in Town, even if no one knows your name?"

"That's a farrago of nonsense, Barny. You never loved me at all."

"I am fond of you, Leesie, more than that reprobate you've taken up with ever could be. I cannot believe you'd get in a pother with me over Sophy and then attach yourself to the most depraved man in all of London! The stories, Leesie! Why, they say the Hellfire Club is child's play compared to Gardiner's debauchery."

"That's ridiculous. His lordship has led an exemplary life since I've known him"—not with his cooperation, true—"and has always treated me like a lady."

Barny ran muddy hands through his hair in exasperation. "You never used to be such a goosecap. The man hasn't an honorable intention in his body."

"And you do?" she asked scornfully. "I suppose you think it more honorable for a betrothed man to keep a mistress than for a bachelor?"

Barny flushed, the red color blending into the dirt on his face. "I always intended to marry you at least. Still do. I gave up Sophy, I swear it."

"You mean you can no longer afford Sophy without my money. No, Barny, we shall never see eye to eye on this." She started to back the mare away from him.

"That's right, ride off, enjoy your tryst with the evil earl while you can. Just how long do you think it will take Sir Vernon to get back from Northumberland?"

Annalise again halted the mare, who pranced in place. "What is Sir Vernon doing in Northumberland?"

"Making sure you didn't take refuge with your grandfather. Not even Thompson would dare call a duke's granddaughter batty, at least not to his face. Arvenell was your only safe refuge, Leesie. Now I am. Your stepfather has the right to lock you away, and he means to do it. I expect he'll be here by week's end. You can't hide in London, and he'll chase you down anywhere else. Don't you understand, people notice veiled women as easily as they notice beautiful ones! And the mare! You might as well send out notices of your new address to the newspapers. Marry me and at least you'll be able to ride at will. You'll have a home and a family, your freedom."

"But what about respect?" she started to say, when she saw Lord Gardiner approaching at a furious pace, thinking she was being harassed.

Barny didn't see him. "I'll take care of you, Leesie, you know I will."

At which words Lord Gardiner leapt off his horse, grabbed the other, heavier man by the shoulder, spun him around, and planted him a facer. Barny went down in the mud again. He took one look at the blood in Lord Gardiner's eye and decided to stay down. He did call out one more message to his former fiancée: "I'm at the Clarendon, Leesie. I'll give you three days, then I'll tell Sir Vernon where you are myself. Three days."

* * *

"You know you are going to have to let me help," Gard shouted to Miss Avery's back as she tried to outride her devils. "Shall I call that nodcock out for you?"

Annalise pulled Seraphina up sharply. Distraught, she cried, "You wouldn't!" Dear heavens, if she had to fret about Lord Gardiner losing his life or being wounded on top of her other worries, she'd have a seizure for sure. "I forbid it!"

The earl raised an eyebrow. "I do not think you are in a position to forbid me anything, Miss Avery."

Her quick gasp told him his barb had hit home. "Yes, I know your identity and I feel certain everyone else shall in—what? Three days, was it?—when Sir Vernon comes to town and starts making louder inquiries. I really can help, you know. I have properties where no one could find you, a yacht to get you out of the country if you are set on bolting." He grinned. "A handy set of fists and excellent aim if you wish to stay to face the challengers."

"You do not know what you are saying. There is no reason for you to get involved in this coil for me."

"There is every reason, none of which I feel like discussing on horseback. The only reason you need understand at this moment is that you need help."

Annalise put her hand to her head. "Oh, I cannot think now!"

Gard reached across the horses to take that hand and give it a comforting squeeze. "And no one shall force you to. You have today and tomorrow to decide what you wish to do. All I ask is that you hear me out before you decide. Will you come with me tomorrow? We could ride out to Richmond, with your guards, of course, to play propriety. No one will know you, no one will distress you. Fresh air, flowers, we'll pack a picnic lunch. Things will look better there, I swear."

Annalise knew she shouldn't, knew with every drop of blood that raced through her body at that slightest touch of his hand that she should stay at least a mile and a half away from this man. She knew it would be harder to marry Barny after one more minute in Gard's company, much less an entire day. And marriage to Barny was looking more and more like her only choice. It wouldn't be a terrible marriage, she told herself. He'd be pleasant enough most of the time, and leave her in peace the rest. And he would not break her heart.

But.

How many times had Annalise contradicted her own reasoning with that slippery *but*? She hated this charade, but she came alive matching wits and words with Lord Gardiner. He was a rake and a rogue, but she ached to wipe the lines of worry from his face. He'd leave her soul in tatters, but she had to have one last day with him.

"Yes, I will ride with you to Richmond."

Chapter Twenty-three

Gard had no intention of letting matters rest until tomorrow. Miss Avery, Leesie—what the deuce kind of name was that?—might not be safe, no matter what the chawbacon in the park said. What if the stepfather came early? He could snatch her away and Gard might never know where she was. Nor did he have any intention of letting Miss Avery make up her own mind about fleeing or marrying the lobcock, despite his assurances to her. Seeing her in supposed peril had quite settled the question in his own mind, after the blood lust drained enough for him to think clearly. The woman was his. That's all there was to it, primitive male possessiveness toward his mate. He'd tell her tomorrow. Today he had to make sure she was protected.

While he was outside the park gates debating whether to go to the Clarendon and beat the towheaded fellow to a pulp, or go to Laurel Street and ascertain that Miss Avery was, indeed, staying there, a woman on a showy white mare winked at him. As a matter of course Gard noted that she had a good seat, nicely rounded. She had the magnolia skin and jet-black hair that some Spanish beauties possessed, set off by a black habit and shako-style hat with a red feather. An altogether fetching study in contrasts.

"Señor?" she queried.

His stallion Midnight neighed in greeting. "Me too," Gard seconded. "Si."

Considering that he expected to be a betrothed man in another day, and considering that he intended to do his damnedest to keep his vows, the earl felt entitled to one last fling. If Miss Avery did find out, she deserved the setdown for making a fool out of him at his own lodgings. She could take it for a lesson that he was not to be trifled with.

First he went to Bloomsbury, ostensibly to advise them of company that evening. No one was at home but the maid Lorna, polishing the banister, so he took the opportunity to look around the attics and cellars, searching for signs of occupancy. When Annie returned home, market basket full of fresh lavender for the linen closets and drawers, Lorna directed her upstairs, for " 'Is nibs is acting mighty strange."

Ross was reduced to tapping the wainscoting for hollow sounds, lifting the rugs for trapdoors, feeling like the most caper-witted cocklehead in nature, when he noticed Annie silently observing him from the doorway of the master bedchamber. "Looking for ghosts," he hurried to tell her. "Making sure nothing frightens away the lady I have coming tonight."

Annie left just as quietly. The glasses hid the tears that trickled down her cheeks, leaving paths through the yellowish powder. How sad, she thought, he was making a heartfelt assignation with one woman for tomorrow, yet he had to have another tonight. She was right to decide on Barny. Ross Montclaire couldn't go one evening without a female in his bed.

So let him go to hell in a harlot's handcart. Annalise no longer cared, and her bag of tricks was empty.

Until Maudine came back.

Gard repaired to the stables to see what he could discover from Tuthill. The man was as close-mouthed as a clam, except for the stream of tobacco spittle he managed to get on Gard's Hessians.

"Sorry, gov'nor. Didn't see you standin' there."

"You wouldn't know anything about any mysterious young ladies, would you?"

Tuthill scratched his head with the sharpening stone he was using on a wicked-looking knife. "You want one in a mask tonight? I doubt my Nan'd approve me goin' out lookin', gov'nor, but since that's all she lets me do, I'll try."

"Devil take it, you dolt. You know I meant a real lady, coming here."

"You bring a real lady here, my Nan and Annie'd have your hide for sure. You'd be eatin' stone soup and cinders for days. And they'd take the lady and wash her mouth out with soap and march her off to church or sommat."

The earl twitched his crop against his leg. The stableman was more like to tap his claret than tell the truth. "I am not happy with this situation, Tuthill."

"Not by half, I'll warrant." Tuthill tossed the knife to test its haft, accidentally slicing off one of the tassels on Gard's boots. "Sorry, gov. Needs more work."

Nobody answering Gard's description of the man who accosted Miss Avery was staying at the Clarendon. That is, they had no tavern-mannered, tub-of-lard jackanapes lout with straw-colored hair. There was a Mr. Barnaby Coombes staying there who was blond and stocky, but he was out for the day. No, my lord did not wish to leave a message. He *wished* to tear the man's heart out, but he said he'd return another time.

Angelita was whispering sweet nothings in Gard's ear on the way up the stairs. They were nothings indeed—the sultry wench didn't have a particle of sense, and not much English, either—but they felt good, until they entered the bedroom and she let out a piercing scream that was like to reverberate through his brain box for days. He turned as she began pummeling him with her reticule. "I did not do it!" he yelled, not knowing what he was denying, since he couldn't see beyond the beaded missile and he could not understand the Spanish curses she was raining on his head along with the blows.

Annie pushed past him, grabbed up the washstand pitcher, and tossed the contents at Angelita. "*Basta*, you ninnyhammer. Of course he didn't do it. How dare you think he did! Now, get out. *Vamos usted.*" Annie held the pitcher over her head, ready to throw that, too, if necessary. Angelita vamoosed.

Gard was already at the bedside before Angelita was out the door, screaming of *los locos*. He gently examined Maudine's blackened eye and split, bloody lip.

"I swear to you, whoever did this will be fortunate if he lives to see tomorrow's dawn."

"No, you must not, my lord. It was my man. He'd only beat me worse."

"Why did he do this to you, my dear?"

"Because I ran away from you yesterday and

192

brought no money home, only the lovely bonnet. He said I had to come back, so I did. Annie says you're not a brute after all, it was all a hum." Looking up at him through the one eye that opened, she confessed, "I don't understand the joke, but Annie says you'll fix things right."

Gard looked at Annie, so confident, so trusting. Oh, Lud, how could anything make this right?

Eventually he promised to find Maudine somewhere safe, perhaps with Mother Ignace. Zeus knew, not even Cholly's mother was *that* broadminded. He gave her the ring that had gone begging in his robe pocket all these nights, knowing how she liked pretty things, and the promise of whatever blunt she needed, until she was settled somewhere, somewhere her so-called protector could never trespass. He also vowed to teach the scum of a procurer what it felt like to be pummeled by a stronger force. Meantime Maudine should stay right where she was as long as she wished. Gard wouldn't be needing the bed; he'd never bring another woman here. The house was jinxed.

Later, when the girl was asleep with the help of a little laudanum, and Gard's fury was eased with a little cognac, he asked Annie to play for him, to calm his nerves.

While Annie sorted through the music, the earl reviewed the day's events. Mostly he pictured Maudine's battered face atop Miss Avery's vibrant body, under that damnable veil. The thought of his Lady in Green in the hands of a vicious, greedy man made his pulse pound louder than Annie's tentative practice chords. B'gad, he *had* to keep her safe!

"Annie, I know—"

"I know I should not have put the girl in your bed, my lord," she interrupted, turning on the stool so he could see himself reflected in her dark glasses.

193

"But she was so frightened. I had to prove to her there were no . . . ghosts there."

"No, I wanted to discuss—"

"I don't suppose you can find her a position as a lady's maid?"

"Not for any lady I know. And I do not think Maudine is suited for a life of service. That type of service. She likes fancy clothes and jewels too much. But what I wanted to ask you was about Miss—"

Annie hit a few wrong notes in succession, then stood up. "I am sorry, my lord, but this has been a distressing evening for me. I cannot concentrate on the music. Will you please excuse me? I must see about Miss Maudine at any rate. Good night, my lord."

"Wait, I need to know—blast!" She was gone. That woman and Tuthill obviously shared a family distaste for the truth. The only difference between them was that Annie didn't spit and Tuthill didn't have a mole on his cheek.

Aggravated beyond reason, Lord Gardiner went to one of the new gambling dens, hoping to lose himself in a game of cards. None of his acquaintances seemed eager for his company at their table, however.

"Sorry. We're just playing the last hand." Or "Too bad, we already have a fourth." Ivory-tuners were at the craps tables, and Kitty was presiding at the roulette wheel, which left only the hardened gamesters playing faro, never his choice, never among such unsavory company. He left and went to White's.

The Duke of Afton got up and left when Gard walked in, not even nodding to the younger man in passing. He'd cut the earl since the night at the theater, so Gard did not even blink, until other gentlemen turned their backs to him.

"What's going on, Cholly?" he asked his friend.

His complexion as red as his hair, Cholly got up from his comfortable seat in the quiet corner. "Sorry, old chap, promised m'mother to make an early night of it. Busy day tomorrow, don't you know."

The earl lifted a brow. "What, you too, Cholly? My best friend?"

Cholly sank back down. "Ain't it time for you to have a look-see at your Suffolk property?"

"I just did, not a fortnight ago."

"Then a cruise on your yacht? You ain't been out sailing in ages."

"There's been a war going on. I don't wish to be blown out of the water by any eager Revenuer, either." He looked around at the heads turned away, the eyes not meeting his. "Why?"

"You just looking peaked, is all."

"I meant, why am I being treated like a leper?"

"You know how it is, the rumor mill and all. I don't believe a bit of it m'self. Not about the boys, leastways. Or the whips and chains. I mean, it was hard enough believing Don Juan was in decline."

"Boys? Whips and chains?" he asked in a fading voice. *That* was how Annie discouraged his light-skirts? By all that was holy, and a few things that were not, Gard swore he'd see that woman burn in hell.

"It'll all blow over, don't you know. Always does. Some noble will run away with a coal-heaver's daughter or something and they'll forget about your little peccadilloes. Uh, supposed peccadilloes. You might consider a change of scenery, meantime."

Gard considered returning to Laurel Street and causing a furor that could be heard back in Berkeley Square. Instead, a weasel named Fred received the brunt of Lord Gardiner's fury. Fred would not

195

be bothering Maudine or anyone else any time soon. The minor altercation left the panderer waiting for the sawbones, and left Lord Gardiner winded and too muzzy-headed to confront Annie. Another day, he thought, wrapping a handkerchief around his torn and bloody knuckles. As for the rumors, Ross decided a change of scenery was indeed needful, starting with tomorrow's visit to Richmond.

Chapter Twenty-four

The road to Richmond was nearly empty at such an early dawning of the morning. The polite world made their jaunts to the nearby countryside at a more respectable hour, after their chocolate and sweet rolls. Only draymen and drovers were on the road, starting their daily treks into the City. They waved and nodded to the attractive couple and their grooms, on their way to the famous gardens. The working journeyers thought nothing of Miss Avery's veil, the roads being so dusty and all. Gard thought everything of that accursed scrap of netting, enough so he found the most secluded spot, among some trees, on a knoll where they could see anyone coming. While Clarence tethered the horses some distance away and Mick unpacked the blankets and pillows and hampers, Gard held his breath. Miss Avery seemed to be admiring the view from their grassy hill.

"It's much too early for nuncheon," he said finally, "but my cook packed us some hot cider.

Should you like some now, to take away the morning chill?"

"Please."

Gard pawed through the baskets, searching for the jar wrapped in towels, and two mugs. "Here, ma'am."

Annalise looked at the inviting steam rising from the cup, then at the mesh covering her face down to the chin. No one was near, and Lord Gardiner already knew her identity, this one at least, so where was the harm? If she only had this one last day to enjoy, let it be as herself. Annalise held her mug out to him; Gard held his breath. She started to remove the hatpins. Gard started to sweat. Then she removed the hat, veil, and all.

"By all the blessed saints." The earl took a hasty swallow of his cider, burning his mouth, tongue, and esophagus. "Heaven help me" was all he said when he could speak again. She was an angel with a silvery halo of tiny ringlets, the sweet, gentle smile of a madonna. She was a temptress, though, a siren with the sea-green eyes of a mermaid. Green eyes he expected, but not the dancing gold flecks that spoke of joy and laughter. She had fine bones and a perfect nose, not too sharp, not too tilted. There was a beauty mark—a real one, not a patch—beside her mouth that just invited kisses. "I'll be damned."

Gard's eyes were dry from not blinking. His mouth was dry from gasping. Everything else about him was damp from the two cups of cider he'd spilled as his brain caught a glimpse of paradise and forgot its job on earth. Her lips were twitching at his moonstruck attitude, so he gathered what wits he had left, poured two more mugs, offered one to Annalise, and promptly burned himself again.

"Why don't we take a stroll while the cider cools?" she suggested, amused and at the same time incredibly elated that she could have such an effect on this worldly man. No wonder he was a womanizer, if a comely face could so impress him.

They walked where there were few people, saying little, admiring the early spring blooms. Gard was thinking that the idea of marrying the girl for righteous reasons alone had gone begging, along with his mental faculties.

"Miss Avery, I know something of your difficulties," he began. "The prattleboxes have been busy, and I . . . I would deem it the greatest honor if you would permit me to safeguard your future."

Annalise hid her face in a cluster of daffodils, inhaling their scent, convincing her heart not to shatter. "I am sorry, my lord, I cannot accept. Thank you, but your solution will not wash. Sir Vernon is still my legal guardian and has the right to dispose of me and my money as he sees fit. I do not think he will see his way clear to letting me become any man's mistress."

"Do you think so little of yourself," he asked angrily, "and of me? I am asking for your hand in marriage, Miss Avery."

Marriage? Lord Gardiner was asking to marry her? Annalise may have dreamed such an event; never did she hope to hear it. Never would she have, either, if he knew how she had made such a fool of him by playing at his housekeeper. With deepest sorrow she had to refuse this offer, too. "But I am underage, my lord. Sir Vernon will never permit it; he will never release my dowry. I would be coming to you penniless and worse, with a background in trade, a scandalous family history, and a tattered reputation. I would only bring shame to your family."

"Somehow I do not think that matters these days," he said dryly. "I fear my own reputation, unsteady at best, has gone aground on gossip island."

"But you are an earl, time will erase the memories. I am a country nobody and I am ruined."

Now Annalise meant her reputation. Lord Gardiner thought she meant that clunch Barnaby Coombes. He swore to murder the dastard. Nor was he going to bother doing the thing up properly by issuing Coombes a challenge, no more than he had called out Maudine's pimp. Still, Miss Avery's giving her innocence to that boorish Barnaby was a definite facer. Coombes was a slowtop for letting this gossamer creature slip through his hands like fairy dust, but how could she not be enough for a man? Any man.

And was Gard going to let her fly away, too? He never minded a previously owned horse, but a wife? Good grief, he even brought his own sheets to strange inns. He never considered that when he eventually married he might have to worry about his heirs being of his flesh and blood, but a woman who was tempted before the vows was just as likely to be tempted after. He never thought Ross Montclaire would wear horns. Those fashionable arrangements where spouses went their own ways had never appealed to him, and less so now, thinking of sharing this divine body, that heavenly smile. Hell! He never used to be jealous. He never used to care.

Annalise understood his silence. He had offered for her out of kindness, but her difficulties were too much for even his broad shoulders to bear. His was an ancient title; he owed his ancestors a better bargain than a tarnished bride. But how could she simply walk away from him, the honorable thing or not? Honor be damned if it meant a lifetime of misery!

"My lord," she said into the quiet, "I have reconsidered. I should like to become your mistress if we can go away somewhere Sir Vernon cannot find us."

Another facer! "My dear, you cannot have considered. There has to be a better solution than that."

"Why? Marrying Barny would be selling myself anyway. I'd simply become a prostitute with a license. I am sorry. I can see I have shocked you, but that is how I would feel." She may have shocked Lord Gardiner, but she half surprised herself, too. On reflection, she realized she did not think so poorly of the women who traded their favors, not after knowing Mignon and Maudine. There were so few ways for a woman to be honorably independent.

Mostly, Annalise admitted, Mignon had been correct days ago. She did want Gard; she did hate seeing him with those other women. She was willing, even eager, to taste the forbidden fruit of his passion for herself. She wanted to be able to touch his firm strength, to feel the wiry curls on his chest, to caress his lowered brows, to know his kisses. The thought of kissing Barny made her gag. If love were the greatest deterrent to promiscuity, and if Gard grew to love her a little, maybe he could be faithful. He must care some already, to offer her his name.

While Annalise searched her heart and came up a wanton, Lord Gardiner also plumbed his soul. Incredibly, he found honor.

"No, I could not. You are gently born, a lady. It would be wrong."

"I never thought to hear Lord en Garde discourage a woman," Annalise said with a laugh. "What difference can my being a lady make to a rake like you?"

"I may have the name, but I swear I have not had a woman since I met you."

"I know. That is, I know how you must feel. I could not let another man touch me."

Ah, those were sweet words to Lord Gardiner's

ears. "I hold the lease on a place in Bloomsbury, by the bye," he offered tentatively. Of course she knew.

But Annalise answered noncommittally: "It is common knowledge that you rent my aunt's house. Sir Vernon will hear of my being there before the cat can lick her ear. I have to leave London, with you or without."

She'd leave London without him when cows sang the national anthem. "Very well, I'll make arrangements." He lifted her hand and pressed a kiss at the wrist, above her riding glove. Annalise was sure she'd made the right decision, if such a simple touch could make her toes tingle in her boots. It needn't be permanent anyway. When she reached her majority she'd be wealthy enough to live on the interest and her memories. Four years, unless he tired of her first.

"I think the cider should be cool enough to drink," he was saying, although he was thinking that he needed something cold instead, to chill the fever in his blood from her closeness. She smelled of roses and lavender and horse, all his favorite things. "And I am devilish sharp-set"—though not with hunger—"so perhaps we might open those hampers."

They ate cold chicken and Scotch eggs and sliced ham and fresh bread and cheese and tarts. Their hands touched and their eyes met and Annalise's cheeks grew flushed. They spoke of her parents, his childhood, books they had read, places he had traveled. They did not speak of tomorrow or the days to come.

When Annalise yawned after the meal, Lord Gardiner suggested she take a nap, for yesterday had been trying and they still had the maze ahead of them, then the long ride home. She demurred, not wanting to waste a moment of his company, but she did lean back on the pillows. Soon her eyes drifted closed and her breathing became even, albeit Gard tried not to notice the rhythmic rise and fall of her chest. He withdrew a small drawing pad and a pencil from one of the baskets. Although he thought he could stare at her forever, memorizing every detail, he wanted a record for that night, and any night they were apart, in case his brain ever doubted the existence of such perfection.

No, she was not perfect, he noted as he drew. Her chin was a trifle too pointed, reminding him of Annie and that harpy's stubborn streak. He quickly put all thoughts of his wretched employee from his mind. Not Annie on a day like today, he swore, getting back to his sketch.

Some might consider Miss Avery's beauty mark an imperfection, too, he considered, studying to get the placement of the mark exactly right, near her mouth. His hand stilled as he deliberated on her soft lips, slightly open as she slept. No man alive could find fault with those lips. Of course he'd have to feel them under his to make sure.

Her skin was too milky, even for one with such silver-blond hair. Of course every blush colored her pale cheeks delightfully, telling Gard that his touch affected her, too. She'd been sick and indoors or veiled, he reminded himself. Country sunshine should have her looking not so ethereal, not so fragile that he'd have to worry about holding her as close as he ached to. Disposing of her stepfather and that jackass Coombes should also eliminate the dark shadows of worried sleeplessness from under her eyes.

Too bad her eyes were shut. He wanted another look into those green depths, and he didn't even have his colored pencils. Too bad she had clothes on. Lud, he wanted her so badly, it hurt. How was he going to manage until he made her his?

And how soon could he manage the thing?

"Tomorrow," he told her when she woke up, her cheeks tinged with pink when she met his intent gaze. "I'll meet you tomorrow for our ride and discuss what I'll have planned. I have already asked Clarence and Mick to keep watch over you tonight, just in case. They can reach me at Grosvenor Square or my club, or at Laurel Street. I am sure you'll wish me to consult the staff there about our plans."

Sure, was he? Annalise did not want to consider the outcome if he mentioned making Miss Avery his mistress. Henny'd be like to poison him and Rob would have his guts for garters. And Annie? Annie was aghast at the moral depravity—and delighted. It should be an interesting conversation all around.

Chapter Twenty-five

When the world turns its back, a fellow can always count on his mother to stand by him. There she was, the dowager countess Gardiner, Lady Stephania, standing by her only son in the entry hall of Gardiner House amid mounds of luggage, waiting for her coach.

"I would not stay in this sinkhole of venery if your father's ghost danced naked on my bedpost. Especially if he danced naked on my bedpost. I am going home to Bath, and I pray God I get there before the gossip, so I can still hold my head up in church."

"Mother, I can explain. Please wait."

"Wait?" she screeched, punctuating her outrage with jabs of her cane's gold-studded tip to his midsection. "Why should I wait, you codshead, to see the last hope of the Gardiner family locked away in Newgate prison?"

"Come, Mother," he said, pushing aside the cane before his waistcoat had a permanent indentation, to say nothing of his stomach. "Things cannot be as bad as all that."

"Oh, no? Then why are two Bow Street Runners waiting for you in the library?"

"I have no idea, as hard as you may find that to believe. I suppose I shall have to speak to them to find out, my lady, so feel free to go about your business of washing your hands of the head of the household. Of course you'll miss meeting your new daughter-in-law, but we'll get to Bath sooner or later, I am sure."

The dowager didn't bother asking anything about the girl, for all the good it would do, with her son's back disappearing down the hall. Lady Stephania didn't care if the chit was respectable or not, as long as she was willing to marry Ross. At this point the countess was glad enough he was bringing home a female, any female. She gave the orders to have her bags unpacked.

Two men with red waistcoats were indeed waiting in the library, watched over by Foggarty the butler and a footman, just in case the minions of justice saw fit to take the law—and whatever else they found loose—into their own hands.

"Gentlemen?" Gard nodded dismissal to the servants, who left reluctantly.

"Yer worship," one of the Runners greeted him in return. "Would you mind comin' along wi' us to Bow Street? Seems 'is 'onor the magistrate 'as some questions to put to you."

Gard offered his humidor around, then lit a cheroot. "Do I have a choice?"

The Runner who was doing most of the talking scratched his balding pate. "Well, you does an' you doesn't. We could get a writ of arrest on suspicion, 'owsomever we don't 'appen to 'ave it right now. On t'other side of the coin, most nobs don't like 'avin' their names broadcast about as'd like to occur, iffen we process a warrant. Don't suppose it'd bother you much, what with the talk already goin' the rounds."

"And too late if it did." The earl tapped the ash off his cigarillo. "What's this all about anyway? What am I supposed to have done now? Let me guess. I had an illicit relationship with Princess Caroline? No? Then with Napoleon, or his horse, or his grandmother."

The Runner scratched his head again. "Gor'blimey, you been busy, ain't you."

The matter actually concerned a bracelet, a gaudy but expensive bauble of multicolored stones set in gold medallions which the magistrate's secretary dangled in front of Gard's eyes in the shabby office at Bow Street. It was stolen property, according to Lord Ffolke, the gentleman-turned-law-officer in charge of the investigation.

"Very interesting, my lord. But what does it have to do with me?" Gard wanted to know. "I do not recall ever seeing it before."

"There's a reward out for this and a list of other pieces taken from an estate in Worcester. A jeweler brought it in for the money. He says he bought it from an actress at Drury Lane. Does that refresh your memory any, Lord Gardiner?"

"With due apologies, Lord Ffolke, I know *many* actresses at Drury Lane."

Lord Ffolke slapped his pudgy knee and chuckled. "I'm sure you do, my boy. Anyways, this one, Bessie O'Neill, reports that she received the trinket from you, for services not rendered, so to speak."

Gard shook his head. "I have no idea to what you are referring, my lord."

"Well, here's the bite with no bark on it. Word is that you're not much between the sheets, that you'll try anything to stir up a little interest. Bessie didn't do the trick, but she got paid anyway."

Gard was wondering if it was too late to book passage on the next ship bound for the Orient. What with the long journey, exploration of hidden temple sites and vast unknown regions, he might be gone for ten or twelve years. Which was about how long it would be before he'd dare show his face again in London.

"My lord?"

"Oh, yes, sorry. Woolgathering. You say I gave Bessie this bracelet?"

"No, your housekeeper actually handed it to Bessie, she said. You aren't going to give us some folderol about your servants having expensive gewgaws to distribute to doxies without your approval, are you?"

His housekeeper, Miss Avery's servant, most likely had access to a king's ransom in jewels. The she-witch was using Annalise's wealth to buy off his paramours!

He picked up the bracelet from the cluttered desk and pretended to study it once more. "Oh, *that* bracelet. I left it with the housekeeper for safekeeping because I had no use for it, I thought. It's too vulgar for my usual birds of paradise. They prefer diamonds or rubies, it seems," he said with a wink. "I won it in a game of cards, don't you know. And I, ah, did not fail Bessie. I failed to keep the appointment. My staff must have felt she deserved recompense for her time—I always insist they be courteous and generous to my particulars—and this was the only thing of value around. You must not believe everything you hear, you know, especially a man in your position."

"Indeed, indeed." Lord Ffolke was nearly convinced. This story tallied much better with the handsome devil seated at ease in front of him than did the idle chitchat of a bunch of old windbags at White's. "Then you won't mind telling us from whom you won the bracelet?"

"Only if you'll tell me what this is all about."

So Lord Ffolke told him how Sir Vernon Thompson had put up rewards for information leading to the recovery of his stepdaughter, an escaped Bedlamite. She took the family jewels and raided the household account, not that Sir Vernon was looking to press robbery charges against the girl or anything. She was too addled to know right from wrong. Sir Vernon merely wanted her back, where the family could look after her. He was also willing to overlook any irregularities in the jewelry's arrival at Bow Street, in exchange for information.

"Is Sir Vernon in town, then? I don't seek the reward, of course, I just wish to see the unfortunate girl taken care of. I'll go talk to him myself, and give him what assistance I can."

"Kind of you, my lord. Sir Vernon arrived in the City today. I already had my secretary visit him at the Clarendon, where he keeps rooms. I wish we had more to report, to relieve his worries. Now, if you'll just give us the name of the gentleman you played cards with, we'll be on our way with the investigation. You did give your word, my lord."

"So I did. Unfortunately I am not positive who actually put the bit of frippery on the table in the first place. Too much to drink, don't you know. Of course you do, if you heard all the other rumors. In fact, just between us, that's how most of the tittle-tattle started." He leaned closer, so only the magistrate could hear. "I was entertaining a regular dasher, a lady of the ton, a widow, don't you know. But I had overindulged, and fell asleep before I could, ah, entertain her properly. In a fit of pique she gave out that I was, shall we say, as responsive as the warming brick she had to put in her bed."

The magistrate slapped his knee again and Gard sat back, satisfied he'd done the possible to scotch some of the rumors, the important ones. Let this doddery fool think he was drunk; Gard realized now he'd been drugged!

He went on with his testimony. The sooner he got this over, the sooner he could knock a few heads together. "I think I won it the night I sat in for a round with Repton and his crowd. Eccles, Hastings, Jelcoe, I believe. I don't usually gamble with those Captain Sharps, but there you have it. Drink makes a man do strange things."

Before going to the Clarendon, Lord Gardiner stopped off home to place one of his dueling pistols in his greatcoat pocket, to exchange his cane for a sword stick, and to slide a thin stiletto inside his topboot. And to accept a folded note from his silent valet.

"What's this, Ingraham? I'm in a hurry."

"My resignation, my lord."

Gard ripped the thing up unopened. "Balderdash. You cannot leave now. Who else can make sure I am bang up to the nines for my wedding in a day or two?"

Gard left as soon as Ingraham regained consciousness.

Sir Vernon and Barnaby Coombes were having dinner in one of the private parlors. Lord Gardiner invited himself to join them.

"I believe you have lost something of value," he commented as he selected a slice of beef.

Sir Vernon chewed his own meat slowly, gesturing the already red-faced Barnaby to remain in his seat. Thompson noted the earl had not removed his greatcoat, nor handed his cane to the footman. It paid to be observant about these things, he had learned in many years of gulling the pigeons, just as it paid to listen carefully to the blockhead oafs he'd sent in search of Annalise. One of the fools even managed to recall a description of Lord Gardiner's housekeeper. Tallish she was, with a pointy chin and a wart, and all her hair pulled under a cap. Oh, yes, the man had added under Sir Vernon's patient questioning, she'd been wearing green-tinted spectacles, the same spectacles his dear stepdaughter had worn when he last saw her. The baronet did not know about the woman in the park—Barny had kept his word to Annalise so far—but he knew all about Lord Gardiner's housekeeper. He just hadn't had time to get her away from the house yet. The earl was no greenhead flat, though, nor doltish footman.

"Did you come for the reward, my lord?" he asked, playing his cards as close to his chest as the earl. "Are you below hatches at Gardiner House, then? Odd, that's one rumor I haven't heard."

Gard helped himself to a scallop of veal. "Not at all. Just wanted to find out how the recovery of the heiress was going."

Barnaby sputtered until he recalled the earl's punishing right. He subsided, gulping down his ale. Sir Vernon sipped from his glass more slowly. "I believe I shall have happy tidings shortly."

"Yes, I believe you shall. I am henceforth taking over the search for Miss Avery, and responsibility for her welfare." The earl put down his fork and stood to his considerable height, the capes on his greatcoat making him loom even larger over the others seated at the table. He was no longer the amiable dinner companion; he was a bird of prey. "Understand this, both of you. You have nothing more to do with the lady. You"—he addressed Barny, who was eyeing the distance to the door—"shall not talk to her, threaten her, or make any effort to see her. If you are thinking you can kidnap her and elope to the border, think again. You'll be dead before you reach Gretna Green. Do you understand?"

Barny understood he hadn't a snowball's chance in hell of getting Leesie's dowry now, not with this handsome, well-heeled, and titled bastard sticking his aristocratic nose in. He finished his ale and nodded.

"And you, sirrah," the earl ground out, turning to Thompson, whose eyes were narrowed in anger, "will agree with my terms."

"What, give that innocent child into your keeping? No one would deny my right to keep her from such a dissolute libertine."

"I deny your right. You are no better than a pimp, selling her to this mawworm. And if you think to declare her insane so you can lock 'that innocent child' away forever, I'll make sure Parliament takes up the debate." When the other would have spoken, he went on, staring at Sir Vernon with deadly intent. "I have the means and I have the influence to get what I want. You'll have to meet me on the dueling field if you choose to get in my way. Miss Avery shall be free to live her own life if you hope to live yours."

Chapter Twenty-six

"I have decided to accept the earl's carte blanche," Annalise quietly announced to the Tuthills before dinner, in case Lord Gardiner arrived that night to discuss the arrangements with them. "I cannot keep hiding and running, feeling threatened all the time. Nor can I marry Barny, feeling as I do." She went upstairs to her room.

Without making a sound, Henny took the pot off the stove—lamb stew, Rob's favorite—and threw the entire contents out the back door to the hogs. The fact that the hogs were in the backyard of her cottage in Worcester made no never-mind.

A bit later Rob sat picking cold chicken from his teeth with his knife. "So Missy falls from grace and I go hungry," he complained to the replete and somnolent dog Clyde at his feet in the stable, to which he'd been banished. " 'Is nibs gives the chickie a slip on the shoulder and I get to sleep in the barn. Seems to me the gov'nor has a lot to answer for when he shows up."

* * *

Ross was at home, thinking about going to Laurel Street that evening. From what he knew of the baronet, Sir Vernon was not one to throw in his hand until all the cards had been played, including those dealt from the bottom. If Thompson was going to make a move, it would have to be soon, before Gard finalized his arrangements. This was contingent, of course, on Miss Avery's stepfather knowing her whereabouts.

Gard decided that Bloomsbury was his own best chance at finding the elusive female. Either she was on the premises or he could persuade Annie to divulge her location, after he convinced the housekeeper of the girl's danger. Annie owed him something, by Jupiter, after making micefeet of both his social life and his social standing.

In any case, he could not call on Miss Avery in all his dirt, stinking of horse and needing a shave, so he called for a bath. Trying not to fret, telling himself that Clarence was looking after her and so were the Tuthills and Annie, he paced the floor while waiting for the cans of hot water. Ingraham was humming contentedly in the dressing room as he laid out the attire he deemed appropriate for a visit to the future Lady Gardiner: black satin evening knee smalls, sparkling white linen, white brocaded waistcoat, and midnight-blue swallowtails that would take himself and a footman to fit over his lordship's broad shoulders.

The man's cheerful humming was grating on Gard's already sensitive nerves. Impatiently he picked up his sketch pad and thumbed through it to the end. Could she really be as beautiful as he remembered? If the picture from Richmond was accurate, she was even more so.

Idly he flipped back through the pages until his fingers paused at the drawing of Annie playing the

214

pianoforte. Nice hands. Then he turned the page to stare at the other likeness of the housekeeper, the one that depicted the ugly cap, the flat chest . . . and the pointy chin, the mole to the right of her mouth. He ripped the page out of the book and held it next to the last portrait, the one where he'd worked so hard to position Miss Avery's beauty mark correctly, to the right of her mouth.

Annalise. Annie Lee. An ass of an earl. His bellow of rage caused the footman to spill the two cans of hot water he carried.

Hot water be damned. Ross plunked himself down in the cold. Not even that cooled his blood. "The hell with clothes," he told the dismayed valet, pulling on his buckskins again, grabbing the frilled dress shirt from Ingraham's arms and buttoning it any which way. If not for the frail old man trembling in consternation, Gard would have dispensed with a neckcloth altogether. He snatched up a starched length of muslin and tied it in a rough knot. "À la Jack Ketch," he snarled at poor Ingraham as he stuffed the dueling pistol in his waistband and dragged on an old hunting jacket.

"Shall . . . shall I have your carriage brought round, my lord?"

"No, I'll walk. By the time I get there, maybe I'll be rational enough that they won't add *strangler* to my list of sins." And if Sir Vernon got to her first, Gard raged, the baronet would merely be saving him the effort.

Ingraham was searching in the trash for his letter of resignation.

Clarence was across the street, watching out for the Lady in Green. Of course he was. Any looby could have figured it out. Any looby but a moonstruck rakehell. How could he not have seen? All those inconsistencies, all those coincidences! He waved Clarence off, telling the man that he'd look after her. Ha! He hadn't looked after her when she was right under his nose! The earl wanted to bang his head against the lamppost for being such a noddy. Instead, he banged Tuthill against the stable door a few times for being a lying, cheating, scheming snake. He desisted when he felt the tip of Tuthill's knife pressed dangerously close to his inseam.

Tuthill spit to the side but did not move the blade. "I told her lack of sex'd make a man violent." He pressed the knife a little harder. "Lack of these might cure the problem. Works on horses all right."

Gard released his hold on the smaller man's shoulders, cautiously stepping back out of range. "Insolent bastard."

"Arrogant lecher."

They traded insults like boys in a schoolyard until Rob turned his head to spit, taking care to avoid Clyde. As he turned back, a pistol fired, the ball taking his knife right out of his hand. "Just an accident," he called out to the shouted queries, and "Damn good shot," to the earl. Then he went on. "Way I see it, my sticker's gone but your rattler's empty. What do you want to do now?"

"I want to go inside, and I am bigger, stronger, and younger."

Rob nodded. "You might get in, or you might not. Either way, you won't get out to see the dawn. I got so many crimes in my dish, killin' a nob won't make the noose any tighter."

"I'll bet you do, you old horse thief. Lucky for you I'm not a violent man."

"Too bad for you I am. And you might be bigger 'n all that, but I know more dirty tricks."

"I'll bet you do," Gard said again, losing patience with the stable hand, if that's what he was. "So are you going to try to stop me or not?"

216

"Depends on what you're lookin' for in there."
Ròb jerked his head toward the house.

"Revenge, mostly."

"Can't argue with that. Figure you've got a right.
What else, though?"

Gard snarled, angry at the thought of an earl
seeking permission to go courting from a thatchgallows horse groomer. "What are you, her father
or something, that I have to declare my inten-
tions?"

"Someone's got to, looks like."

"Oh, stubble it already. Enough. I am still a gentleman."

Tuthill was satisfied with that, enough to curl up
in his makeshift bed in an empty stall with Clyde
for company. He wished the earl luck.

Ross went around to the front door and knocked.
Annie opened the door and curtsied, then looked
beyond the earl for his companion.

"No, Annie, I have no lady friend with me tonight, but I am sure your diabolical mind had something planned for our entertainment. What was it
to be, poisoned toadstools? Leaking roof? Rocks in
the mattress?"

Drat, she wished she'd thought of half of those!
All she had were some overfed mice that wouldn't
scare a grasshopper. Then she realized he was
standing in the parlor, legs spread apart, arms
crossed across his chest, scowling fiercely from under lowered brows like some seafaring brigand.
"Are . . . are you very angry, my lord?"

"Angry? No, I wouldn't call it anger. Mind-
numbing blood rage is more like it, Annie. You
know, when all you can see is red in front of your
eyes and smoke starts pouring from your ears and
you—"

He had no hat or gloves for her to take, but he

did have a pistol tucked in his waistband. Annie started backing toward the door. Gard stepped that way, blocking her retreat.

"I have another idea for this evening, since you have frightened away all of my other interests." His voice was low, measured, implacable. "I thought you might provide the night's entertainment."

Annie glanced toward the pianoforte and licked her dry lips. "I don't think I could—"

"Oh, no, Annie, music wasn't at all what I had in mind." He took a step toward her, close enough for her to see the twitching of his jaw muscles. She backed up until her legs hit the sofa. When she couldn't go any farther without putting herself in an even more disadvantageous position, Annalise crossed her own arms over her own chest. She refused to be intimidated, she told herself, trying desperately to keep her knees from knocking together so loudly that he must hear them. She raised her chin defiantly. "I do not want to—"

"No. Tonight we do what I want. What I've been wanting to do since the day I met you." He put his strong hands on her shoulders, dislodging the shoulder pad that made her look deformed. Then he moved his fingers closer to her throat.

"My lord?" Her voice was at least an octave higher than normal.

"What, Annie, frightened? Just as those women were frightened by what they saw? Just as I was frightened, thinking I could never—"

"What . . . what are you going to do, my lord?"

"This," he declared, pulling the green-tinted spectacles off her nose and throwing them into the hearth, where they shattered with a tinkle of glass. The fear in her eyes sent a twinge of remorse through Gard, but only a twinge. This was ugly Annie, sharp-tongued Annie, Annie the trickster, who

218

had made his life hell. "And this." He grabbed that awful cap off her head, releasing the silver curls, but he did not stop there. While one hand stayed fastened to her shoulder in an iron grip, the other used the muslin fabric to scrub her face. He did not even try to be gentle as he rid her of the disfiguring mole and the yellowish powder. "And this," he moaned, pulling her into his arms at last. She was brave and beautiful Annie, clever Annie, Annalise, who was his. "Oh, God, I have waited so long to—" Holding her in his arms was not the unalloyed delight he was expecting. In fact, it felt somewhat like embracing a boy, he imagined. He jumped back as if scalded. "Damn and blast, whatever you've done to your body, undo it!"

Annalise blushed. Or was her face red from his scrubbing? "Here, my lord?"

"It's Gard, dash it. And I refuse to call you Miss Avery, not when you've led me such a dance. I'll try for Annalise if you wish, but I'm afraid you'll always be Annie to me."

"Annie sounds fine." Always sounded better. "I'll, ah, go fix my gown," she said with a shy smile.

"You'll get rid of that monstrosity altogether, my sweet, or I'll throw it in the fire along with your cap. And hurry. We have a great deal to discuss."

In a daze Annalise unbuttoned her gown and unwrapped the binding around her chest. She was alive and he still wanted her. Two miracles in one night! She grinned, standing there in her chemise, thinking that the night was still young. Then she took to wondering what to wear. Not another of her black gowns, for she had no desire to kindle Gard's rage, and definitely not her heavy riding habit. Her flannel nightrail? Never.

She slipped up the back stairway and surveyed the selection in the lady's dressing room off the master bed chamber. Not even for Ross Montclaire was Annalise Avery going to put on one of those filmy, transparent bits of harlotry. Not the ostrich-feathered robe, either. Finally she went to the other dressing room and put on his robe, wrapping the maroon velvet nearly twice around her and cuffing up the sleeves.

She started down the front stairs, being careful not to trip, and then she did not have to worry at all, for she was in his arms, being carried down.

"Oh, Lord," he breathed in her ear, "I have waited so long for this. I want you so badly."

"I know, Gard," she said from her place tucked against his chest on his lap on the sofa. "You've been so long without a—"

He shook her gently. "Little goosecap. Don't you know the difference between wanting a woman, any woman, and wanting one woman so badly, no other will ever do?" When she shook her head, tickling his chin with her soft curls, he told her, "I'll have to show you, then. Uh, just how much do you know about men anyway?"

"Only what I've learned from you this past few weeks."

"Then you and Barny didn't . . . ?"

"Of course not!" she proclaimed, which statement required another lengthy embrace, one that left her robe partly open and his shirt partially unbuttoned. Annalise had finally gotten to feel those dark curls on his chest.

Breathing heavily, Gard asked, "Will you come upstairs with me?" The sofa pillows were slipping around, and he could only picture that virgin bed upstairs, with his virgin bride lying beside him. She wasn't his bride yet, his conscience told him, but his baser self answered that she would be soon enough, and with her swollen lips and dreamy eyes, she'd follow him anywhere.

But what if she regretted it later? the inner debate went on. She deserved a little torment for his suffering, was the reply. Annie, his precious Annie? Gard sighed and compromised. Very well, he'd take her upstairs, where he could touch her, look at her, feel her warmth against his skin—and that was all. Perhaps he might sweeten his retaliation by bringing her to the brink of passion, then telling her he was too noble to continue. After all, he was no rutting beast, no adolescent. He could hold her soft, luscious body in his arms and still keep control of his own passion.

And for his next act he'd hold back the sun.

Chapter Twenty-seven

While Annalise and Lord Gardiner were so pleasurably involved, Sir Vernon, from his carriage parked across the street, was pleasurably watching the candles go out one by one. First his minion came around to report that the lights were out in the kitchen and the rooms below stairs. Stavely returned in an hour to report a candle to the rear of the ground floor, which was extinguished shortly thereafter. Finally the front parlor grew dark except for the fainter glow of a dying fire, and lights bloomed upstairs. Sir Vernon told his dark-clad assistant to wait half an hour, then get busy. The smarmy footman gathered his equipment and silently crept away, eager to exact retribution for being duped so badly, even more eager to earn Sir Vernon's gold.

The baronet was willing to pay whatever it took to get rid of his little problem—tonight. By tomorrow the interfering earl could present the girl to the ton, as the ordinary, well-behaved female she was, not a raving lunatic. Worse, he could marry the chit.

The haut monde—and the authorities—might conclude that the missing heiress was indeed the veiled horsewoman he finally heard about from Stavely, but they might never realize she was also a lowly servant. So if the housekeeper met an unfortunate end, one, moreover, that left her body unidentifiable, then to all intents and purposes Thompson's ward was still alive, just waiting to be returned to the bosom of her loving family. And he'd have at least four more years to milk her estate, especially if Lord Gardiner and those Hennipicker people also perished. Sir Vernon filed his nails while he waited.

It was a kiss to make every other kiss feel like an uncle's. It was the Marco Polo of kisses, going where no kiss had gone, opening worlds of wonder. It heated their bodies and clouded their minds, ringing bells in both their ears. And they hadn't gone past the bedroom door.

Bells? his lordship thought. Bells? It was a fine kiss indeed, but bells? Then he heard a dog barking and someone calling "Fire!"

"Blast it, Annie, if this is another of your tricks, I'll—"

"No, Gard, I swear!"

They both realized the room really was warm, not just their bodies overheating, and their minds were not fogged at all, they were full of smoke. Annie started to cough. Gard pulled a blanket from the mattress to beat at the flames if necessary, giving the still-chaste bed only one melancholy glance. Annie ran to the washstand and poured a pitcherful of water over them both before they dashed down the stairs. The earl had to steady her frequently, as she lost her footing in the trailing robe.

The front hall was engulfed in fire, so they made for the rear stairs and the back door.

"You go make sure Henny and Rob are out," Annie called, shoving him down the first few steps while she ran back to her own room to gather her jewels and her reticule and her riding habit.

"You fool," Gard shouted, wrenching the stuff from her and dragging her out. "As if I'd leave you!"

"But Henny and Robb?"

"Are already out. I heard them shouting. Now, come before they try to get back in to save you!"

But the kitchen door was also in flames; there was no exit that way. Annalise managed to grasp the mouse cage before Gard hauled her along after him upstairs again, where the fire was starting to travel along the hall carpet, licking up at the wood paneling and the wallpaper.

"Damnation!" Gard swore, not releasing his hold on Annie's wrist. He made for the smaller parlor before the flames could reach the draperies, and shoved Annie facedown onto the love seat. "Stay there!" he ordered while he searched around the room for a fireplace poker, a chair, a heavy stool to throw against the window.

"Why don't you just unlock it?" Annie demanded from his side, suiting action to word before Gard nudged her aside and threw the window open, then jumped down, holding his hands out for her. First she passed down the mouse cage while he swore. Then she retrieved her jewel box and reticule and riding habit from where he'd tossed them.

"For heaven's sake, woman, you are taking years off my life with every second's delay! Get yourself out here *now*!"

Annalise looked down at him, with soot on his face and his shirt open and untucked, appearing more like a buccaneer than ever. "I do not like it when you shout at me that way, my lord."

"My God, Annie, do not get on your high horse now. Please don't torture me this way!"

She read the anguish in his eyes and sighed contentedly as she jumped into his arms. "You really do care."

The fire brigade managed to save some of the house, but not from smoke and water damage, naturally. The Watch declared the fire suspicious. How could they not, when it arose in two separate locations at the same time? None of the neighbors saw anyone lurking about. In fact, no one saw or heard anything until the dog's barking awoke the neighborhood again after the pistol shot. Clyde was the hero of the hour and Henny the heroine for making Rob sleep in the stable, where he could hear the little terrier and alert everyone before they were overcome by the smoke. Annalise, Rob, and Henny were still hugging one another and Clyde when the fire engines rolled away. The earl came in for his fair share of exuberant affection, too, although Rob merely shook his hand.

They were alive. They were also damp, dirty, exhausted, and homeless. "Enough," Lord Gardiner declared. "Tuthill, harness up the carriage. It's time we got out of here. It's beyond foolish to survive a fire and perish of pneumonia. Besides, whoever set the deuced fire might still be about, getting up to who knows what other mischief." He stood closer to Annalise, shielding her with his larger body while his eyes tried to pierce the shadows.

Annalise agreed. "I am certain one of Rob's disreputable friends must own an inn or someplace with rooms to let. No respectable hotel would accept three such ragamuffins as we appear, nor Clyde, of course."

"Gammon. You are all coming to Gardiner House in Grosvenor Square."

"Now who is being a nodcock? You know you cannot take me to Grosvenor Square. I don't even have any shoes!"

"What the devil have shoes got to do with anything? You'll be safe there, that's all that matters," he insisted.

Annalise took his arm and pulled him away from Henny's hearing. "Gard, you cannot take me to your house," she hissed in his ear. "Your mother is there, isn't she?"

"Of course she is, or else I'd take you to Cholly's or Aunt Margaret's."

"Has all that smoke shriveled your brain, my lord?" Annie stomped her foot, then recalled she was barefoot and got even angrier that Gard was being so obtuse. "You cannot bring your mistress home to your mother, my lord earl."

"Stop throwing the title in my teeth, little shrew. You are not my lover at all, or did I miss something between 'Oh, Gard' and 'Fire'?" He put his finger to her lips when she would have protested that the intent was there, if not the deed. "I am not bringing my mistress. I am bringing my fiancée. Mother will be delighted."

"Gard, you cannot tell your mother such a Banbury tale!"

"No such thing, my pet. It's true, and always was. I have intended to make you my wife for ages now. That's the best way to protect you permanently from fortune hunters, be they relatives or suitors, and to restore your reputation. My mother is one of the highest sticklers. No one will dare criticize her daughter-in-law." And, he said to himself, she'll make damned sure there will be nothing to criticize while we are under her roof. He determined to get a special license as soon as possible.

"No, Gard, I cannot let you do this. We can simply go to an inn. My reputation be hanged!"

"That's very well for you to say, my dear, in your chameleon disguises, but what about me? A respectable wife is about the only thing that can salvage the micefeet you've made of my good name! We're going to Gardiner House, and that's all."

Ross was right: His mother was thrilled to welcome the prospective Lady Gardiner and her servants even though the hour was late. An emergency, he explained, a fire having destroyed Miss Avery's lodgings.

Miss Avery, the heiress? An earl could reach higher on the social ladder, but the gel was Arvenell's granddaughter, and that counted for nearly as much as the fortune. Lady Stephania was liking the match better and better, as long as the chit wasn't the moonling gossip was claiming. Gard was able to reassure her on that score, and that Miss Avery was respectably chaperoned by her old nanny.

The dowager floated down the stairs in a drift of chiffon, delighted with the news she could relate to her husband's spirit. Maybe now the old fool would let her sleep in peace. She smiled as she let Ross lead her to the Adams drawing room, where Miss Avery was waiting.

The smile died a painful death when Lady Gardiner finally confronted her promised replacement. Annalise stood by the fireplace, her boyishly short hair in damp tendrils, her skin as soot-darkened as a blackamoor's, her feet bare, and her body barely covered by a man's oversize robe. And she was clutching a cage of rodents.

"Mice!" the countess shrieked, throwing herself into the nearest pair of arms, which happened to belong to Ingraham. The ancient valet had come to see if he could assist his master after the harrowing events, and to get a good look at his lordship's intended. One look was enough to drain the blood from his head and send it to his feet. Being embraced by the countess was one shock too many. He collapsed onto the floor, taking the countess with him, where she remained screaming that the fifth earl was spinning in his grave, that, with a Bedlamite for a mother, the seventh earl was like to have two heads or think he was Nero, that if the rats were not destroyed immediately, she'd have the sixth earl drawn and quartered.

Gard was not sure which was worse, the fire or his mother's tantrum. He knew the latter left Annalise more shaken. For that reason, and others too base to consider, he did ask Henny to sleep on a pallet in the room assigned to Miss Avery.

"She'll feel better having someone familiar nearby in a strange house," he explained, "and there will be less bibble-babble about us arriving in the middle of the night if the servants know you slept with her."

Henny was a bit intimidated by the grandeur around her, and the earl in his own surroundings was not the handsome lad who ate in her kitchen. He was a peer of the realm, all right, aristocratic down to his bare toes. She curtsied. "Yes, my lord. As long as you think it's necessary."

The night had been hell except, of course, for the few moments of euphoria with Annalise in his arms. Gard reflected that sending that Tuthill scoundrel off to find a bunk in the stable was nearly as enjoyable.

"So you ain't above a few dirty tricks of your own, eh, gov'nor?" Rob muttered on his way to another hard, itchy, lonely bed in another cold, smelly stall.

"You better not think it's necessary for too long if you know what's good for you."

Lord Gardiner just grinned.

Chapter Twenty-eight

*A*nnalise couldn't stay. She couldn't sleep, either, so she lay in bed, listening to Henny's soft snores, counting all the reasons she had to leave Gardiner House and its owner, instead of counting sheep. The sheep would have looked back at her with their placid woolly faces as they marched across the landscape of her dreams. Instead, she saw Gard, with one dark, raised brow, an unruly curl hanging on his forehead, and that soft, one-sided smile.

She couldn't accept his offer of marriage. Except the infuriating man had not actually offered, he had ordered their engagement the same way he ordered dinner or ale or a hot bath, without a by-your-leave for Annie. He was too used to having his own way, was my lord Gardiner, too arrogant and domineering for her taste, Annalise tried to convince herself. He was also kind and noble, with a deep-seated sense of honor that often collided awkwardly with his rakish, raffish ways. Like now, when he was planning to marry a girl who had agreed to become his mistress.

Annalise knew he was intending to marry her to keep her safe and to keep her name from the gutter. Oh, he liked her, too, and desired her, she was well aware, but, heavens, the man was a rake. He liked a different woman every day. He was infatuated with her now, but how long before the bonds of matrimony became a noose? How soon before he resented being forced to do the honorable thing, resented her? How long before he strayed? She did not think she could bear it when his eyes no longer gleamed when she entered a room, or he started to find pressing business elsewhere. If only he loved her . . . but that was a sheep of a different color.

And she'd never be accepted in his world, no matter what he claimed. Annalise saw the way the dowager responded. If his own mother could not welcome with equanimity a scandal-ridden hoyden, the rest of society was sure to be even less accepting of coal-king Bradshaw's granddaughter. She'd be cut; he'd be ostracized from the life he enjoyed. Or else he would still be invited everywhere—without her.

All of that was assuming, of course, that they lived long enough to face the ton. Sir Vernon was not like to give up, not even if they married. He'd fight for the money, dragging the sordid case through public trials, or else he'd resort to more villainous efforts like the fire. Annalise had no doubt as to the blaze's instigator, nor that he'd try again. If the baronet was never to see a groat of her fortune, he'd want to get even. Annalise was already responsible for the destruction of her aunt's little house in Bloomsbury; jeopardizing this magnificent mansion was unthinkable. Besides, earls made large targets.

Gard could never be convinced to go into hiding,

she saw that now; the earl was just fool enough to challenge Sir Vernon, or do something equally as nonsensical. Sir Vernon was not constrained by the rules of honor, so she'd never have a moment's peace, worrying for Gard's very life. Her friends were already in danger, especially Rob, whose past could not afford scrutiny, and every minute they remained with her magnified their peril. She had to leave.

At dawn Annalise rose, washed, and donned her riding habit and a pair of boots that had been placed in the dressing room for her. The boots were too big, but she stuffed some handkerchiefs from a drawer into the toes. When Henny went off with Rob to see if any of their possessions could be salvaged from the fire, Annalise sat down and wrote a note. She was going to Northumberland, she penned, where she should have gone all along. The duke was bound to accept her rather than see her go into service in his own neighborhood. She had enough money for the coach ride, and she'd be long gone before Sir Vernon stirred from his bed, so they were not to worry or try to follow. She sealed the note and marked "Henny" on the front.

No words came to fill the blank sheet she intended for Lord Gardiner. Her hand could not possibly form the letters to spell good-bye, and her tears would have smudged the ink anyway.

Shutting the bedroom door firmly behind her, Annalise went down the marble stairwell and asked the venerable butler standing at attention there the way to the stables.

Foggarty bowed and gave her the direction. Miss Avery *looked* a proper lady, he judged, which just went to show how deceptive appearances can be. Everyone knew you didn't do anything to excite a madwoman to violence, though, so he did not comment that proper young ladies never left the door without an escort and they always waited for a horse to be brought around to them. She didn't ask about the mice; he didn't ask her destination. Having closed the door behind her, Foggarty wiped his brow. Ingraham was right: It was time they retired.

Annalise turned the corner for the Gardiner House stables and kept on going. She was familiar enough with London to know she could find a hackney stand at the next intersection; the jarvey was bound to know the coaching inns. She regretted having to leave Seraphina behind, but Rob was sure to take good care of the mare and Annalise would send for them all when it was safe. She regretted having to leave the earl even more. Who will take care of him? she wondered. Certainly not his high-strung mother or doddery retainers. Not a one of them was liable to tease him into laughter or make him lose that awesome dignity. Of course there was an entire continent full of women just waiting to smooth back his hair and erase the longing from his sky-blue eyes.

With tears in her green eyes, Annalise did not see the coach and four following her progress.

It wasn't much of a struggle. Sir Vernon threw a blanket over her head from behind, then Stavely carried her to the carriage. The baronet held an ether-soaked cloth over her face until she stopped thrashing about.

When she woke up, her mouth was dry, her insides were in an uproar, and Sir Vernon was across the coach from her, reading a newspaper. "Good afternoon, Annalise," he greeted her politely, setting down the paper and pouring her a glass of wine from a bottle by his side. "Here, have some of this. It will help settle your stomach. Unfortunate side effect of the stuff. Nasty, but effective. Oh, and thank you. That was very kind of you to keep to your early hours, especially after such an eventful evening."

She took the glass and drank most of it down, hoping the spirits would clear the muddle in her head, too. The baronet refilled her glass and leaned back, smiling. It was not a smile to warm an abducted heiress's heart.

"Where are you taking me?" Annalise demanded. "I won't marry Barny no matter what you do!"

"I'm afraid that is no longer an option, my dear. Nor is my plan to keep you under lock and key. Your noble protector promises to put a spoke in that wheel, also. Too bad. Those were the more pleasant choices. No, my dear, you've been a bit too much trouble already. I thought first we might simply dispense with your company somewhere along the road, but that's too chancy. So we are going to Dover right now, and then on to Vienna. My poor ailing stepdaughter needs a change of scenery, according to the doctors' recommendations. Where better than the gaiety of the Peace Congress, where all of Europe is convened?"

"You are taking me to Aunt Rosalind?" Annalise asked optimistically.

"That is who you wanted to visit, isn't it? Regrettably, somewhere between Calais and Vienna, my unfortunate, deluded ward, you shall run away with the footman Stavely, who is, incidentally, driving this carriage."

Annalise made an unladylike noise. "I wouldn't have Barny. What makes you think I'd wed that scum of a servant?"

"Oh, there needn't be any wedding, although I am afraid Stavely might insist on his conjugal rights. No, I'll go on to Vienna, mourning your loss but washing my hands of such a hopeless case. I won't have to give up your estate until you reach your majority, naturally, since you made such an unsuitable match and without my permission."

"And when I do reach twenty-five?"

"Oh, I am sorry, my dear, I thought you understood. You won't see twenty-two. Stavely will be able to settle handsomely in the colonies, and you?" He shrugged and picked up his newspaper again, holding it to the window for better light. "Whoever knows what finally happened to that demented Miss Avery?"

"And you think I'm just going to sit here all the way to Dover and not make a fuss at every toll and changing stop?"

He looked at her over the top of the paper. "Oh, I don't think you'll cause much of a problem. That wine you just drank was dosed with enough laudanum to put a horse to sleep."

By eleven o'clock Gard was in possession of a special license, thanks to his godfather the bishop; a ring, an emerald, naturally, surrounded by diamonds; and promises from three modistes to deliver within the afternoon everything a lady of fashion needed and dressmakers to make sure it all fit.

By twelve o'clock he was at the Clarendon, asking after Sir Vernon.

"I'm sorry, my lord. The baronet checked out early this morning."

"Did he happen to mention where he was going? I have some information for him."

A coin helped the clerk recall: "He didn't leave anyplace to send messages, if that's what you mean, but he did ask to see the shipping schedules from Dover."

Excellent. The cur was leaving the country and saving Lord Gardiner the effort of encouraging his departure.

Not so excellent. By one o'clock he realized Annie was gone. So did the rest of Grosvenor Square, when he was finished shouting. How could his butler have let her go out unaccompanied? How could Henny and Rob go off and leave her in a strange house? How could his mother sleep all morning on his wedding day? How the hell could he make up Thompson's lead?

Thompson had a cumbersome coach and four that had to stick to well-traveled highways. Lord Gardiner on Midnight and Tuthill on Seraphina had no such restrictions beyond resting the horses occasionally. These horses were bred for stamina besides, not like the tired nags Sir Vernon had to hire at the changes. At each posting inn where the earl or Rob inquired, they were closer to their quarry, close enough by late afternoon to stop for some bread and cheese and ale. One more hour of hard riding should put the coach in sight.

"There she is," Rob finally shouted, taking the pistol out of his waistband. The earl followed suit and would have ridden straight after the carriage, but Rob indicated they ride across a hill and come out ahead of the coach, face on. "And let me say it, gov'nor, please?"

Before Gard could ask what the deuce Tuthill wanted to say, they were coming down the slope. Rob fired his pistol, then he yelled in an awesomely authoritative, menacing voice: "Stand and deliver!" He ruined the effect for an astounded Gard by following his command with "Damn, that felt good."

Any coachman worth his salt would have known he could never outrun two mounted horsemen, armed and in front of him to boot, but Stavely wasn't a real coachman. What he was, was ready to face near death instead of the certain death he saw looming ahead in the person of Lord Gardiner.

He was already having trouble controlling the frightened cattle after the gunshot, but he lashed them with his whip anyway to get more speed.

The carriage horses bolted forward, sending Gard and Rob flying out of their way and then after them again.

"Pull up, man!" Gard ordered, brandishing his pistol at Stavely, but the footman couldn't have stopped those horses if his life depended on it, which it did. As chance would have it, there was a sudden bend in the road. Without a steadying hand at the ribbons, those wild horses were never going to make the turn. As the earl swore from one side of the leaders' heads and Rob cursed from the other, Stavely decided to save himself from the inevitable accident and the implacable earl. He jumped. If he'd waited a few more seconds, he'd have hit some bushes instead of the rocks.

By dint of incredible skill and a measure of luck, Rob and the earl were able to turn the horses after all. They couldn't stop them yet, but the frenzied beasts would be winded soon. Meantime Rob wiped his forehead as he rode alongside the left leader. "Just like old times," he said, grinning at the earl. "Damn, I forgot how much fun this is!"

Inside the coach, all the commotion and being tossed around had roused Annalise from her stupor. Her head ached and she was more nauseated than ever from the effects of the ether, the laudanum, and riding backward. She never had been a good traveler.

"Stop the coach," she cried weakly, and ridiculously, under the conditions. There was no one to hear her, however, for Sir Vernon was standing up across from her with his head and upper torso out the coach window, trying to get off a clear shot at the earl from the jolting coach.

If she were a man, with a man's strength, Annalise considered hazily as she absorbed the situation, she could lift Sir Vernon's legs and hoist him out the window. But she could barely lift her head, much less Sir Vernon. If she were less a lady, or perhaps less dizzy, she could take a page from Mrs. Throckmorton and kick him, but her booted feet seemed miles away, all four of them.

So she did what she could, since it appeared no one else was going to stop this hurtling vehicle before she cast up her accounts. She picked up the heavy bottle of drugged wine and swung it with every ounce of strength she could gather, slamming it against Sir Vernon's leg with a satisfying crack.

Luckily for Annalise, Thompson dropped the pistol when he smacked his head on the carriage roof, trying to get back inside to collapse on the seat, clutching his shattered leg. He would have killed her for sure right then if the gun remained in his hand.

Annalise stared in amazement at the still-intact bottle in her hand, then at the blood dripping down her stepfather's face and oozing between the fingers on his leg. She clamped her hands over her mouth just as the carriage stopped and the door was flung open.

"Annie, my darling! Are you—"

"Get out of my way, I'm going to be ill," she managed to say, running to the other side of the carriage.

So much for grateful maidens swooning into the arms of their gallant rescuers.

Chapter Twenty-nine

$\mathcal{T}$hey did not reach Dover that night at all, what with having to locate the magistrate, a surgeon for Sir Vernon, and an undertaker for Stavely. Squire Josiah Nutley, the magistrate, was a florid-faced, friendly man, delighted to invite nobility to accept his hospitality for the night. His wife gathered Miss Avery to her ample bosom, weeping over the sad story and vowing to make sure the poor girl had everything she needed, once Squire whispered into her ear that he'd actually seen the special license in his lordship's pocket.

Fanciful tales of abductions and evil stepfathers were all well and good for the Minerva Press; Mrs. Squire Nutley liked happy endings, which to her meant orange blossoms and church bells, not any young couple riding off into the night with naught but an unsigned scrap of paper to keep them respectable. No, she wouldn't hear of them traveling on to Dover, not when Miss Avery could share a bed with her oldest girl and the boys could bunk together so Lord Gardiner could have their room.

After the briefest of rests and a bite to eat in the kitchen, Rob Tuthill volunteered to ride back to London that night to reassure the earl's household and to fetch Henny with Miss Avery's new wardrobe. There was no way Rob was staying in a magistrate's stable. There was also no way Annie was going to return to London without Lord Gardiner, she insisted, and no way he was leaving without seeing Sir Vernon embark on a ship bound for anywhere far away. They'd all meet tomorrow in Dover, it was decided.

While Rob was riding by moonlight on a borrowed horse, just wishing he'd be set upon by one of his old friends, Annalise was upstairs, gritting her teeth, listening to girlish giggles and rapturous sighs over her handsome betrothed, who had already reminded her at least thrice that if she hadn't been such a peagoose as to run away in the first place, she would never have been abducted. His lordship, meanwhile, was drinking inferior brandy with the genial squire and settling Sir Vernon's fate.

The baronet was induced, by the simple expedient of withholding his laudanum, to sign a confession in the magistrate's presence. The crimes enumerated included the abduction, the fire, embezzlement of trust funds, attempted murder, and enough other legal-sounding terms to have him clapped in prison if he ever set foot—or crutch, as seemed likely—in England again. Gard was satisfied, or would be as soon as the dastard was carried aboard a ship, and the squire was almost satisfied that justice was being tempered with the right amount of mercy for such a blackguard as Sir Vernon. He was getting off easy, feared the squire.

"One thing puzzles me, my lord," Nutley complained when the baronet was securely locked up for the night. "If the young lady broke his leg with a bottle, and he broke his head on the carriage, how did his jaw get broke and his gun hand get a knife through it?"

"Oh, didn't I tell you? He tried to escape on the way here."

With a busted leg and a banged head? Now the magistrate was happy. Justice was served best with a firm hand, he always said.

Sir Vernon was deemed well enough to be transported to Dover the next morning, if one didn't have to listen to his moans. Squire and Mrs. Nutley lent a driver for the coach and a maid for Miss Avery, but the maid had the unhappy task of tending the baronet instead, for Miss Avery refused to share the coach with him. She much preferred to ride a well-rested Seraphina next to his lordship's Midnight.

Lord Gardiner installed Annalise in two rooms and a private parlor at the Three Sisters Inn before seeing Sir Vernon aboard the packet for France. He sent the Nutleys' servants home in a hired coach with a generous tip and a finer bottle of brandy than Squire was used to drinking. This one even had excise labels on it. He also sent a smoked ham from the inn's kitchen along to Mrs. Nutley, to thank her for the hospitality. Then he went in search of a vicar, but the nearest man in orders was at a deathbed vigil.

"Dash it, the wedding will have to wait for tomorrow after all," he announced to Annalise in the private parlor, going to warm his hands by the fire.

"There will be no wedding, my lord. I thought I made that clear."

The chill reached his toes. "You did not deny it to the Nutleys when I said we were engaged."

"I couldn't let those nice people think . . ."

"What everyone else is going to think," he completed. "And worse, if Tuthill and his wife do not get here soon. You widgeon, you *have* to marry me."

"No, *you* have to marry *me* because of your confounded honor, which you may now consider satisfied by the offer. Thank you, but I do not want an unwilling husband who has to be forced into marriage." Annalise was proud; her voice hardly quivered at all.

"But I am not unwilling." Gard insisted. He held out his arms. "Come, I'll show you how much I am looking forward to the wedding."

"That's lust," she said, keeping her distance. "You don't love me."

Gard blinked. "I don't? Then why have I gone around milling down everyone who looks at you sideways? Why have I moved heaven and earth to get the special license so I could have you next to me forever, without waiting another day?"

"You do? You really love me?" Tears started to well in her eyes.

The earl gathered her into his arms. This time she went eagerly. "Of course I do, you adorable ninny." He addressed the curls on the top of her head. "I loved you from the first day I saw you in the park. I thought you were royalty, you know, so proud and elegant."

"And then you discovered I was just a hobbledehoy coal-miner's granddaughter. You must have been disappointed."

"Never, I just found how right I was. You are the queen of my heart, Annie. Please say you care for me?"

She looked up, eyes shining, without leaving the warmth of his embrace. "I must have loved you forever, I was so jealous of those other women. You were calling me Miss Green and them 'sweetheart.' I was green with envy!"

"There will never be another, I swear," he declared, and sealed his vow with a kiss.

When Annalise could speak again, she smiled and said, "I know."

Gard raised an eyebrow. "You know what? That I'll never have another woman? Just what are you planning, Annie?" he asked suspiciously.

"Just this." She wrapped her arms more firmly around him and raised her lips for another kiss, telling him without words that she'd bind them together with love and passion enough for any man.

Some moments later Gard cupped her face in his hands and gently kissed the beauty mark to the side of her mouth. "Then it is all settled? The vicar can come in the morning and you won't have flown away before the ceremony?"

"Well, that depends. You haven't asked me."

Gard was confused. "Asked you what, my love?"

"You haven't asked me to marry you, my lord. You simply told me. You informed me that I had to marry you or you had to marry me. I believe those were statements, not requests. Either I have equal say in this marriage, which means my wishes are consulted, or I won't do it."

Gard tossed a cushion from the sofa onto the floor at her feet and kneeled on it. "Lud, what I don't do for you. And you wonder if I love you?" Then he took her hand and brought it to his lips. "Miss Avery, my dearest Annie, will you do me the greatest honor, make me the happiest man on earth, by accepting my heart and my hand in marriage?"

"Yes, my dearest Gard, I will," she said with a sigh, tugging on his hand.

He stayed on the ground, when she wished him up for another embrace. "Tomorrow?"

She pretended to consider. "That depends on one condition, my lord. Can we have our wedding night tonight?"

He laughed and pulled on her hand until she was in his arms, on the floor. "My endless delight, you can have whatever your heart desires, as long as it's me." He loosened his hold on her only long enough to unwrap the neckcloth borrowed from Nutley, which left a rash under his chin.

Annalise was very near to having her conditions met when a banshee's wail split the air. Even before turning to the doorway, Lord Gardiner cried out, "Lord have mercy, am I never going to get la—"

"Aunt Rosalind!" Annalise scrambled up and into the embrace of a tall, blond-haired woman in sable and rubies. "Oh, Aunt Ros, I am so glad you've come home, but everything is all right now. However did you find us? Oh, there's Rob, and Henny!" Annalise was so in alt over seeing her aunt again, she forgot the civilities for a moment, which gave Lord Gardiner time to button his shirt and run his fingers through his hair while Tuthill looked on, grinning.

"Aunt Ros, may I present my fiancé, Lord Gardiner? Gard, Lady Rosalind Avery."

"Not anymore, dear," her aunt informed them all, dragging forth a small, bespectacled man from behind her. "Elphy's wife finally expired—in her lover's arms, I might add, lest you think I'm being disrespectful of the dead—so it's Lady Elphinstone now."

After exclamations and congratulations and more embraces and handshakes, the new Lady Elphinstone went on: "Now that we're married, Papa has decided to forgive me, the old curmudgeon. He wrote me in Vienna, telling me to come home and bring Elphy for his blessing. He also charged me to see what Sir Vernon was nattering on about."

"He was dreadful! I am sorry about your house, Aunt Ros."

Lady Elphinstone waved one beringed hand in careless disregard. "Oh, Elphy has a grand place right in Mayfair. As soon as we all get back from visiting Papa, we'll hold your presentation ball there."

Gard spoke up for the first time. "*We* are returning to London tomorrow, after the wedding. My Lady Gardiner shall be presented from Grosvenor Square."

"What, after some hole-in-corner ceremony nobody will believe happened? Not on your life." Lady Elphinstone crossed her arms over her bosom and raised a familiar pointy chin in the air. "You haven't asked her grandfather's permission, either, I'll wager. Pray, do you want to complete the chit's ruin? We got here just in time as it is, I swear. No, you'll come along to Northumberland, meet Arvenell, and get his blessings. Then we'll call the banns and have a lovely wedding in the Arvenell chapel with half the shire present. That should do the trick."

"That should take months!" Annalise and the earl chorused.

Lady Ros patted her niece on the cheek. "Don't be so impatient, dearest. I waited all these years for my darling Elphy."

"Like hell you did," Lord Gardiner said with a growl before turning to his betrothed. "We can be remarried in Northumberland in a chapel or in a turnip patch, however many times you wish, Annie, but we are first getting married right here. By special license. Tomorrow morning," he firmly declared. Then he added, "Aren't we, Annie, please?"

She looked at him and smiled. "Whatever your heart desires, my lord, as long as it's me."

Romance at Its Best from Regency